BOHEMIAN LAW

MISTY WALKER

To my Ty-bot. Your reminder that, "the book won't write itself" kept me on task and focused. Turns out you were right, it didn't write itself.

PLAYLIST

"Good Vibrations" by The Beach Boys

"Just Exist" by Eliza & The Delusions

"Mother" by Charlie Puth

"Sweettalk my Heart" by Tove Lo

"hot girl bummer" by Blackbear

"Teeth" by 5 Seconds of Summer

"Goodbyes (feat. Young Thug)" by Post Malone

"Trampoline" by SHAED & ZAYN

"Time (Edit)" by NF

"Sunflower" by Post Malone & Swae Lee

"Such Great Heights" by The Postal Service

"If We Never Met" by John K

"damage ☹" by Naaz

"What Am I" by Why Don't We

"The District Sleeps Tonight" by The Postal Service

"In the End" by Annika Rose

"Boys Like You" by dodie

"Sun in Our Eyes" by MØ & Diplo

"Forgetting All About You" by Phoebe Ryan

"Lights Down Low (feat. gnash) by MAX

"Turn! Turn! Turn!" by The Byrds

"Blowin' In the Wind" by Bob Dylan

"Nothing Better" by The Postal Service

BOHEMIAN LAW

Victoria—

Let love rule!

XOXO—

CHAPTER 1

Theodora

"**P**ULL YOURSELF TOGETHER, THEA," I MURMUR to my reflection. I grab my lipstick and paint on a healthy coat of coral. Today is my engagement party, and I use the term loosely because no one has asked me to marry them. It's been arranged. For my family, an engagement party is really when the groom's family pays the bride price. Today, Wen's family is paying my family fifteen thousand dollars for the privilege of marrying me.

Cousins, aunts, uncles, friends, basically every Romani within a hundred-mile radius are outside waiting for me to descend the steps of my trailer. I take a final look at myself. I'm wearing a formal gown that matches my lip color almost perfectly. The off-the-shoulder puffy sleeves I would typically love look ridiculous. The sweetheart neckline swallows my small breasts, taking away my femininity. The see-through lace bodice is itchy and irritating. A gigantic bell skirt usually gives me the grand entrance I crave, but today it makes me look like I should enter a children's beauty pageant. Or it could be the two-foot-tall tiara on my head that makes me look pageant worthy. Yes, it's definitely the tiara. I don't look like an eighteen-year-old girl facing an arranged marriage. Or maybe that's exactly what I look like, at least to my family.

Normally, I would jump at the chance to dress up this way.

Normally, I think the more glam, the better.

Normally, I would rush out of this trailer to show off my brightly-colored dress. But normally, I'm not being sold off like yesterday's meat. Everything just feels so wrong.

I put on my too-tall gold heels that will no doubt sink into the field with every step and take a deep breath, blowing it out in an audible puff. I try to walk out of the trailer, I really do, but I just can't. Instead, I fall onto the narrow couch that sits along one side of the small space across from the kitchen. The thick plastic covering the cushions makes a crinkly noise and I sigh. The gold flowered fabric underneath looks brand-new because ever since the day Mom and Dad bought this trailer, they have covered it. Comfort be damned.

Scanning my surroundings, I see my childhood. I've lived all of my eighteen years in this twenty-three-foot trailer. My parents' bed on one end, my two sisters and me in the loft above, and my brothers crashing wherever they land. Sometimes the pull-out couch, sometimes outside, and sometimes the floor. They don't seem to care they've never had a real bed. We're a wild bunch by nature.

Boisterous ramblings outside bring me back to my reality. My engagement party. My fiancé. It's not that Wen is a bad guy. He's actually nice, but he's more like a brother to me than a future husband. Both of our families, along with five others, have been caravanning all over the U.S. together for as long as I can remember. He's handsome enough with wavy brown hair, light green eyes, and a stocky, muscular build. All good enough traits, but he looks like me, like my brothers and sisters and cousins. He looks like family, not a lover.

A knock startles me and I focus on the opening front door. Mom pokes her head in. "Get your ass out here, Thea, or there'll be a riot." Just as quickly as she appears, she's gone again, the door closing. I know she's right. Functions like these usually end in drunken fighting, but if Wen's dad thinks I'm being disrespectful, the fists might swing way too early in the night.

I get up from the couch, shake off the nerves, and step out. What lies before me is one hundred percent insanity. A large tent is outlined with all our trailers. Underneath the tent are long tables with coral linens, chairs covered in the same fabric, huge gaudy centerpieces featuring tall Lily of the Valley blooms being held up straight by bright yellow rocks in clear vases with massive yellow ribbons tied in bows around them. There's a seven-tiered cake on top of one of the tables. It's bright yellow, with edible pearls circling around each layer and a few Lily of the Valley blooms top the tallest tier.

One might wonder if Lily of the Valley is my favorite flower. It's not. They're just expensive and at these events, expensive is key even though no one here has real money. We live like peasant people in mostly broken-down trailers. We fill our water tanks with jugs at the car wash. All the women are handy with a needle, so we can sew and mend all of our clothes purchased at thrift stores. We forage most of our food from a grocery store or restaurant dumpsters. We're a Romani family. We don't live by laws. We roam until we find a place we like, stay there until we get evicted by the cops, and then roam more. We have short tempers and curse like sailors. We don't seek higher education, don't have birth certificates, and sure as shit don't make nice with gorgers. But because we spend most of our lives in squalor, we save for when there's a reason to celebrate, and when there is, we do it big. No expense spared.

I look at the people milling about. Everyone dressed in their absolute best. Most people would look around and see tacky. Men wearing suits from all the colors of the rainbow, women wearing dresses fit for prostitutes, and children decked out in miniature versions of what the adults have on, but to us, this is tradition. The more outrageous the better, everyone trying to outdo the other. I smile, knowing they're all doing this for me, even if marrying Wen makes me cringe.

"Don't you look fuckin' fantastic!" My twelve-year-old sister, Indiana, compliments. She herself is in a ball gown with ruffles shaped into giant roses on her skirt. I make a mental note to deconstruct her dress sometime so I can learn to make one just like it.

"Thanks, sis." We hug as close as we can get with so much fabric around our lower halves. A clearing of a throat breaks us up and I look at the source of the sound before wishing I hadn't. It's Wen. He's in a coral tuxedo that matches my dress to the very shade. His hair is greased back in his usual way and he's sweating profusely along his hairline. Guess I'm not the only nervous one. "Hey-a, Wen." I punch his arm lightly in a friendly gesture, hopefully communicating just how I feel about this arrangement.

"You look gorgeous," he says, putting an arm around my waist. I hear the clicking of camera shutters, so I allow the exchange and return it. Technically, we shouldn't have any contact until we're married, but our families are a little more relaxed. We're allowed side hugs and hand holding. Now we're engaged, so even a kiss on the cheek is acceptable.

"Looky here!" Mom shouts, followed by a chorus of "over here" and "smile for the camera" from all the bystanders. Wen and I do as we're told for a half hour before I call it quits and tell all the assholes to find something else to take pictures of.

We make our way to the table labeled *Future Groom and Bride*. He pulls my chair out for me, which creeps me out because not long ago we were giving each other wedgies and wet willies. When had everything changed?

Our dads stumble over to our table, each with forties in their hands. You can throw a five-thousand-dollar engagement party, but you can't account for class with this bunch. They stand in front of us, clapping each other on the back and grunting out congratulations. Wen and I sit awkwardly, wondering what our roles are in this manly exchange.

"Don't they make a goddamn good-lookin' couple?" Dad claps Braithe, Wen's dad, on the back.

"Fuckin' right they do!" Braithe claps Dad.

"This is what it's about. Bringin' two families together. Can't fuckin' wait for some grandbabies to pop out of my girl." Dad puffs his chest out proudly and I shake my head. Sometimes he's even too crass for me, and I once drew a dick on my sister's forehead. She was six months old, and I used a sharpie. It was like a gift that just kept on giving. Every time Mom would walk around the band with that baby on her hip, I would laugh myself stupid.

"Too bad she doesn't have those nice birthing hips just like Lavinia," Braithe says.

Dad's face instantly turns bright red in anger when Mom's "birthing hips" are mentioned. I roll my eyes. *Here we go.*

"What the fuck are you talkin' about *my* goddamn wife's hips for?" Dad gets in Braithe's face and Braithe throws his forty down, sending beer spraying all over. Normally, I would encourage this behavior because watching two overweight men fight is fuckin' hilarious, but it's my engagement party and everyone went through so much hassle for it, so I step around the table and get between them, resting a palm on each of their chests.

"Now, now, boys. It's too early for fighting. At least wait until after we have cake. Both of your wives put a lot of work into this, and you know what will happen if you ruin it." I try to reason with them. Both of them wince thinking about getting in trouble with their spouses. "That's what I thought. Now, Dad, go get Braithe another beer and then you two can go throw axes or something."

They both shrug and walk away. Crisis averted.

I walk back around the table and sit next to my betrothed.

"Thanks for that. Mom would have lost her shit if those two had come to blows." Wen leans in and kisses my cheek. I hear more cameras click.

"It's fine."

We eat our dinner and thank all the well-wishers for coming. Everyone is so excited, but I just can't get into it. I always knew they would marry me off young. I'm lucky they waited until I was eighteen, but now that it's a reality, my feet want to run.

"You two!" Mom sing-songs. "It's time to cut the cake!"

I look at Wen and shrug. He rises and holds his hand to help me. Unfortunately for him, I don't need a hand to help me up. He should know this. Even in six-inch heels, I can stand up perfectly fine on my own, thank you very much. I ignore his hand and get up, allowing my heels to sink into the lawn enough to ground me. He stares at his hand for a moment before shaking his head and going to the cake table without me. I'd feel bad, but just because I'm being forced to marry him doesn't mean I'm going to suddenly turn into a damsel in distress. It's better he accepts it now.

Everyone gathers around us, looking like a rainbow threw up. A sight that would usually make me giddy with excitement, but given the reason for this event, I feel like everyone is better suited wearing black.

It's not like they would stone me to death if I didn't go along with this arrangement. It's more like I'd be exiled. Tradition is huge around here. Occasionally, one of us will fall in love and marry a gorger, but when that happens, you're out.

You'll never be invited to family get-togethers, your kids will never get to play with all the other kids, and if you run into us on the streets, we will wish you well and move on. That's not what I want. I love my family. I love our way of life. If marrying Wen is the price I have to pay, then so be it. At least that's the lie I'm telling myself right now.

Everyone quiets around us and I know what will happen next. Wen drops to one knee with a small black box in his hand, and I panic. My feet get the overwhelming urge to run and I have to swallow back bile rising in my throat.

Mom, who took her place on my right, elbows me in the side, hard. "Knock it the fuck off," she whispers behind her smile, her lips not even moving. I look down at Wen, who stares up at me with dopey lovesick eyes as he opens the box. A teeny, tiny stone sits in the middle of a gold band.

"Theodora, will you marry me?" Seconds pass and no matter how many times I open my mouth, I can't say anything, I just stand there with a fake ass smile on my face. The one word I need to say just won't come out. Everyone looks around at each other with collective awkward looks on their faces. I can feel the heat of their stares on me and my panic rises. It's becoming hard to breathe as I look for a way out, but the crowd is gathered too tight. There is nowhere to go. I look down again as Wen's face morphs into irritation. The more time passes, the more difficult I'm finding it to spit out the one word everyone is expecting me to say. I open my mouth to speak, not sure of what will come out, but I'm cut off.

"She said yes!" Mom shouts and throws her hands in the air.

I did? I don't have even a second to think about it before everyone is crowding around even closer and celebrating. Someone is shaking a bottle of champagne over the crowd, dousing us all in alcohol. The little kids turn their faces to the sky and open their mouths, hoping to catch the liquid. The cake gets cut and served. Wen wraps his arms around me and plants a wet kiss on my cheek and me? I just watch it all happen. Watch my life end, watch my choices taken away, and watch my future go poof.

After I come back into myself, I make the wise choice to drink. It's the only way I'll live through this party. Grabbing a bottle of whatever is on the table, I chug, take a breath, then chug more.

"It's going to be one of those nights, huh?" Wen asks, already knowing the answer. Here's the thing. I like to party. I've been boozing it up since I was sixteen. I've even chased my booze with a cigarette occasionally. Our people may have a shorter life expectancy, but while we're here, we fucking live it up.

"It's a party, right?" I say, moving my hips to the music. I love to sing and dance. If I'm ever short on cash, one trip to any street corner and I can bring in enough money to buy a bike my little sister eyes, or a new car battery for Mr. Boswell's old Chevy, just by singing and playing my guitar.

"I was hoping we could steal away for a bit and talk?" His sweet puppy dog eyes pull at my heartstrings for all of three seconds before I want to smack him straight. I know he's happy about this arrangement. Ever since puberty, he's looked at me differently, but I'll never not see the pudgy boy with buck teeth, a slight lisp, and who was three inches shorter than me. He may have shot up in height, lost the baby weight, and grown into his teeth, but I can't see him any differently. I've tried for the sake of our union. I just can't.

"Maybe later? I love this song and my sisters want to dance with me." I point over to where Indiana and Charity are danc-ing, moving to the music like certified strippers even though they're twelve and seven. It's so fuckin' cute.

I make my way over to them, spinning and swaying in time. Charity, who's seven, is bent over on all fours with her legs straight, twerking her tiny little bum all over the place. Her long poofy skirt jumps and bounces with each move of her tush. I smack her ass a couple times, making her giggle.

My parents watch us and laugh, clapping to the music. Young married couples are making out in the shadows, teenagers are sneaking liquor and beer behind the trailers, older kids are tending to their baby siblings, men are throwing axes in the corner, nearly everyone having the best time, except Wen. I spot him at our table, angrily studying his beer. He's the only one not having fun. I guess it's time to go have a talk, because things have been stressed between us since our dads decided we should marry. We really have been friends our whole lives and I hate it when he's pissed off.

I leave the dance party and approach our table. "Wanna take that walk?" I ask, holding my hand out for him to grab. His face brightens, and he grabs hold.

"Yeah. Let's go." He leads me away from the craziness before dropping my hand.

"What's going on with you?" I ask, nudging his shoulder with mine.

"Nothing really. I just feel you pulling away from me the closer we get to the wedding. It should be the opposite. We should be getting closer." His eyes narrow in suspicion, but I don't know what he thinks I'm up to.

"Come on, Wen. It's no surprise I'm not excited to get married. It has nothing to do with you specifically, but we've talked about this since we were kids. Neither one of us wanted to marry at eighteen."

"You're wrong. The last time we talked about this, girls had cooties. Of course I didn't want to marry one. It's been ten years since then." He lets out an annoyed sound and throws his hands up in frustration.

"Okay, maybe it's been ten years since you agreed with me,

but it's not been ten years since I've told you how I felt. We're best friends, basically family. It's hard for me to make that switch in my head." I try to explain the best way I can without damaging his ego.

"What you aren't considering is this is gonna happen, whether or not you're on board. You've got to quit pushing me away. I won't stand for it." He stomps his foot, throwing a two-year-old tantrum right in front of me, and it turns me off even more.

"The wedding's not for six more months. Give me some time to come around to the idea." Just call me the queen of procrastination. I know I won't ever want to marry Wen, but I have six more months of freedom and damn it, I will make the best of it.

CHAPTER 2

Lawrence

A PLACE FOR EVERYTHING AND EVERYTHING IN ITS *place*. I organize my active files, stacking them neatly in the right far corner on my desk. I close my laptop and place it in my leather briefcase before flipping off the lights in my office and head out through the casino and into the parking garage. I spot my black Porsche 718, centered perfectly in my assigned stall, and press the auto start button on my fob.

Sitting down on the ridiculously comfortable leather, I pull my phone from my briefcase and check it for messages before driving to the restaurant. Nearly one in four car crashes are caused by distracted driving and I, for one, don't plan to be a statistic. Three text messages and four voicemails. Seeing the voicemails are work related, I ignore them until later tonight. Opening the texts, I see all of them are from Chloe.

> **Chloe: This just isn't working out for me.**
> **Chloe: I left your ring on the island in your kitchen.**
> **Chloe: I hope you have a wonderful life.**

I read them and reread them and then reread them again. She can't be serious. She's breaking off our engagement in a text? I can't believe it. I hit speed dial one on my phone. It rings twice before telling me they have disconnected the number. I check the phone number, and yes, it's right.

Chloe and I have been seeing each other for three years. I had only proposed to her last week. I search my memory for anything amiss, but nothing comes to mind. Just this morning we had coffee together and made plans for dinner at a rooftop restaurant in Tahoe. I think back and wonder if there were any signs.

"Good morning, Chloe." I approach my fiancée from behind as she makes coffee.

"Yeah, hi." She's never been a morning person, so I expect her clipped tone.

"Did you sleep well?" I wrap my arms around her, kissing her cheek. Before she can respond, I pull away and turn my head. "Haven't brushed yet?" I wrinkle my nose at her.

"No, I like to have coffee before I brush my teeth. You know that." Her blond hair is piled on her head and she's only wearing my button-down. I frown.

"Chloe?" I start. "Is that my Thom Browne oxford?"

She knows I hate it when she wears my most expensive shirts to do mundane tasks in. Like drinking coffee, which she's doing now.

"It was just for a minute. I needed caffeine and I know how you feel about nudity in the kitchen. It seemed like the lesser of two evils." She shrugs.

"I don't understand why the choice is to wear a four-hundred-and-fifty-dollar shirt or be naked. You have a drawer full of clothes in my room." Because really, there are at least twenty other options. She huffs at me and storms away.

I pour myself a cup of coffee and sit down to read the Wall Street Journal online. After catching up with the financial world, I rinse my cup and place it in the dishwasher. I gather my briefcase, keys, and cell phone and set out to find my fiancée. She's applying makeup and making a mess of it all over my bathroom counter. I go to the linen closet and pull out one of the black hand towels I purchased for this exact reason. She must have forgotten. Back in the bathroom, I pick up her cosmetics and lay them down on the towel, saving my marble countertops from staining. Chloe huffs at me again, but I know she must appreciate I take impeccable care of my things, so I chalk it up to her not finishing her coffee earlier.

"I'm heading out," I say, leaning down to kiss the top of her head. She doesn't respond and I don't wait. I have a schedule to keep. As I move to walk out the door to the garage, I notice Chloe's shoes from yesterday are thrown haphazardly by the door. I pick them up and place them on the shoe rack and make a mental note to shoot her an email later, explaining the importance of keeping my floors free from the germs shoes track in and without the scratches heels can leave. Sometimes she forgets, but I know she must admire my attention to detail and occasionally I have to remind her of how I accomplish that.

No, nothing comes to mind. It was a normal morning. Frowning, I place my phone in the phone holder and put my car into reverse. The drive home takes fifteen minutes, as always, and I pull into the garage. Entering the house, I'm struck by how cold it suddenly feels. Chloe may have not left her things lying about, but her lack of presence is still noticeable.

In the kitchen, the Harry Winston diamond engagement ring sits in the middle of the island. No note, no explanation, just the ring. I pick it up and walk to my bedroom closet where I put it in my safe, then sit down on my bed for a think.

I've always had my life planned out and now I find myself thirty-two years old, the CFO of the largest casino in Reno, Nevada, wealthy beyond what I had expected to be, and completely and utterly alone. I have no family left. Mom and Dad passed away within a year of each other when I was twenty-three. I'm an only child, as were both my parents. Their parents died when I was just a boy. I have no friends because I devoted all my time and attention to my career and more recently, Chloe.

I take my time undressing and then put on street clothes. I'm not normally one to wander, but I feel the need to take a walk to think, maybe try to figure out where I went wrong. It's summer and there isn't a more beautiful place to be than the beaches of Lake Tahoe, so I get back in my car and make the hour-long drive from Reno.

It's a Monday night and the beach I choose is deserted. I roll up the bottoms of my jeans and take my shoes off, choosing to feel the sand between my toes despite the pathogens lurking. I'll shower and scrub when I get home. I walk for nearly an hour, trying to make sense of the turn my life has taken and before I know it, it's almost dark outside. I turn around and start back toward where I parked.

A large group of people have congregated since I passed by this stretch of beach and they've started a bonfire. I know this is against the law, but I'm too caught up in my own goings on to call the local authorities. I sit down on a large rock to watch the rambunctious crowd for a bit. Their music is blaring, they have portable grills cooking their dinner, there are children splashing in the water, and a few men are passing around a cheap bottle of liquor, something that will surely give them a hangover in the morning.

A few women and girls are dancing around the bonfire. One particular woman catches my eye. A long, flowy skirt covers her legs. Stopping just above her ankles. On her chest is a cream, crocheted bikini, and if I'm not mistaken, her dark nipples are showing through the tiny holes between stitches. Her skin is a dark copper tone and glows in the fire. Her chestnut brown hair is down, slightly curly, and whipping wildly around her face while she dances. Around her flat belly and ankles are chains of tiny bells that tinkle with every movement she makes.

The way her hips circle hypnotizes me, the way her ass

sways makes my jaw hang open dumbly, the way her full lips move as she sings along with the song has a bit of drool spill down the corner of my mouth. I swiftly wipe it away and shake my head, breaking the trance. This isn't me. I don't obsess over women. I've only had a handful of girlfriends and each of those were more arrangements than relationships. They wanted a wealthy, handsome man on their arm and I wanted to get laid regularly and not be alone. Even with Chloe, she wanted to show off her rich, successful boyfriend, and in return she got naked each night. She was beautiful, but I didn't pine after her. I didn't think about her when we weren't together, and I certainly never hid in a corner just to watch her dance.

I continue to watch, trying to keep my wits about me, for nearly an hour. She ate a hamburger, the ketchup and mustard dripping down her chin, and instead of embarrassment, she laughed and wiped it away with one finger. The same finger she then put in her mouth to suck the condiments off of. Then I stared, slack jaw again, as she took a bottle of cheap liquor and poured it straight down her throat, laughing as a little dribbled down her long neck.

I don't think I've ever witnessed anyone so free, so enchanting, so mesmerizing. For over an hour, I spy on her like a creeper in the shadows, knowing she would never know I was there.

It was when she started making her way down the beach and toward me that I panicked. I don't want her to see me. Her appearance alone turns me into a drooling idiot, and I don't have the emotional resilience to be made a fool of tonight.

She picked up a shawl somewhere on her way away from the bonfire and it's wrapped snugly around her as she takes long, slow strides and stares out at the water, the small bells around her ankle and waist still jingling with every step. Instead of making myself known, I chance her being too distracted, but right as she's three feet away, I lose my balance on the rock and fall into the sand. I hop up quickly and quietly, but it was no use because when I look back in her direction, she's peering right at me, laughing.

"You all right, mister?" she asks between giggles; her voice is deep and raspy. So much different than I had expected, yet so perfect in contrast to her feminine appearance.

"Ah, yeah. Yes. Sorry. Just seem to have—" My words trail off when I see her smile. She's quite possibly the most magnificent creature I've ever seen. My breakup with Chloe and the realization of my lonely, miserable life vanish with just one smile from her.

"Good, glad to hear it. You have a nice night." She strolls away again. I can't let her get away. I need to talk to her. Preferably without me sounding like a bumbling disaster.

"Wait!" I call out and jog to catch up. "Would you mind if I walked with you?"

Her eyebrows rise in stunned surprise before she shrugs.

"I guess it would be okay." And just like that, she's off again. At first, I can't think of what to say. I know nothing about her, so I have no points of interest to discuss. I'm so out of my element it takes a good five minutes for me to gather my bearings and strike a conversation.

"I'm Lawrence, by the way." She just nods. "And you are..." I trail off.

"Oh, Thea. Well, Theodora. But everyone calls me Thea." She briefly makes eye contact with me before looking away again, but in those few seconds, with the light from the moon reflecting off the water and illuminating her face, I could see her eyes were an unusual color. The colors in a raw golden nugget. Darker, shadowed streaks around her pupil, but it fades to a bright gold before going back into the dark color around the rim of her iris. I've never seen eyes like hers before.

"Theodora," I mull over. "That's an unusual name. Why did your parents name you that?"

"It means, 'gift from God'," she explains. "I was my parents' first born, and they wanted to thank God for giving me to them."

"I like it," I compliment. "Do you live in Tahoe?"

She smiles at me, like I asked a funny question.

"No, I don't live in Tahoe. I don't really live anywhere, except I kind of live everywhere." Well, if that answer doesn't make me scratch my head. She sees the confused look on my face and expands. "My family, we're pretty nomadic. We pick somewhere to go and then only stay in that place for a little while before moving on."

"Military?" I ask and she laughs.

"No, definitely not military. We're Romani."

"I don't know if I've heard of Romani people before."

"You might be more familiar with gypsies. We get called that often, but prefer Romani when it comes from others." She leans in and whispers, "It's kind of derogatory." She looks at the sky and throws her arms out wide as if she's asking something from the stars. "Wanna have some fun?" She lowers her arms and her gaze meets mine, one eyebrow crooked in mischief. The look in her eyes makes me nervous. I've already stepped so far outside of my comfort zone tonight. I'm out of control.

"It depends. What do you have in mind?" I'm almost certain I won't take part, fun is not something I'm used to having, but I'm still interested to know what her idea of fun is.

"Let's skinny dip." Smirking, she unties her bikini top. Her eyes never leave mine and I swallow, hard. Her bikini top gets thrown to the ground, one arm draped over her breasts. Her skirt comes off next, leaving her only in her panties and those goddamn strings of tinkling bells.

"I, uh, well. I don't, I mean. Maybe I'll just stay here and watch." I'm not a stuttering man, but this girl unnerves me. So much so I don't even tell her about the potential threat of deadly bacteria in lakes. Knowing fish poop in them is enough I'll never swim in a lake. Ever.

"Suit yourself." She shrugs. Her arm falls to her side, showing me her breasts. They're small but perky, and the cool air makes her nipples point in my direction. My jeans are suddenly very uncomfortable in the groin region. She turns toward the water, showing me her magnificent, tight ass and I bite the side of my mouth until I taste blood. I watch her round globes bounce while she jogs to the lake with fixed attention. She steps in and bends forward, scooping and tossing water into the air while laughing. She looks over her shoulder at me before stepping in farther and farther until finally diving in, fully submerging herself.

Seconds pass, then more seconds, and even more until I'm completely convinced she has drowned herself. The same moment I decide to call for help, her top half bursts from the water and her hair flips over her head, sending beads of water through the air. She looks like a goddamn mermaid out there. I get another quick look at her pert tits before she's under the small waves up to her neck.

"You all right?" I call out to her.

"Come on in! The water is perfect," she calls back. I'm certain the water is not perfect. This lake's water supply is from snow runoff and snow is the opposite of the perfect temperature for swimming.

"Uh, I'm okay." I tell myself I need to get going. It's almost nine o'clock, which is almost my bedtime. If I don't get at least seven hours of sleep, I can't function properly the next day. But I look out at Thea, splashing around, doing flips and handstands in the water, and decide it's not safe to leave her in the water alone.

After fifteen minutes of her swimming and me creeping, she finally leaves the water. If it's possible, her nipples are even harder than before and seeing her wet all over makes things harder on my end too. I'll most definitely have to rub one out tonight, but I'll have the most beautiful inspiration.

Thea pulls the elastic band of her skirt over her wet legs and up to her waist, then she covers her breasts with the completely ineffective bikini top before showing me her back and pointing at the ties. I take her hint and pick the two strings up in my hands, tying them together at her back.

"Thanks," she says, using her shawl to twist her hair into a turban. Clever girl.

"You're welcome. Thank you for letting me walk with you." I nod in her direction. "I'm going to head home now. It's getting late."

"It can't be later than nine o'clock. That's early." A slack expression takes over her beautiful face.

"Not for me. I wake up at five a.m. every morning, so to ensure I get enough sleep, I go to bed at ten."

"Five a.m.! Are you joking?" She laughs out.

"No, I wake up at five and then work out for an hour and a half before showering and heading to work. I don't think it's particularly strange."

"Law, I'm going to call you Law, okay?" She starts. It isn't okay because it's not my name, but I don't stop her train of thought. "I don't even go to bed until five a.m. most nights. I'm such a night owl."

I'm shocked. I've never once stayed up late, not that I can remember at least.

"Well, I have to be at work by seven thirty. If I didn't go to bed until five, I would be exhausted the next day." I try to explain.

"Where do you work?"

"At The Grand Royals Casino in Reno," I say proudly, because it's the best casino outside of Vegas. Five-star restaurants, world-class entertainment, and our slots are twenty-five percent looser. She perks up in recognition.

"Oh, I think I've been there. Is the Silver Duck restaurant in your casino?"

"Yes, it is. Have you been there?" Maybe she'll come back and I can see her again.

"Well, sort of. We mostly just scoured through the dumpster for food, but the chef there must be highly trained in ordering what he or she needs and doesn't waste much food at all." She continues her pace while I remain standing. Did she just say she was a dumpster diver? I must have misunderstood.

When she notices I'm no longer next to her, she whirls around. The look on her face, not embarrassed or ashamed, floors me. "So, you're homeless?" I try to ask with as much tact as I can. A question like that is hard to word while also being sensitive, but she just laughs.

"No! We aren't homeless. We have a travel trailer. We just prefer not to waste money on things like food or clothes when there is so much wasted already."

I almost gag. Eating from a dumpster is one of the most disgusting things I've ever heard of and doing it by choice instead of necessity makes it so much more disturbing.

"You'll catch a disease. You shouldn't eat trash." I don't want to be rude, but clearly no one has told her about germs and food borne illness from eating spoiled items. Once again, she just laughs.

"I've eaten this way my whole life and I've never even had a stomach flu. Don't you worry, Richie Rich, I'll be fine." She settles herself on a piece of driftwood and since I can't seem to peel myself from this girl, I join her.

"Tell me more about your family." I'm genuinely intrigued and also moderately concerned for them.

"Why don't you tell me more about yourself instead? I think you've heard enough about me for tonight," she counters. I don't really want to talk about myself. I especially don't want to admit my failure of a relationship with Chloe. I haven't even considered her for the last hour.

"There's not much to tell. My parents died shortly after I graduated from UNLV. I applied for jobs all over the country, but The Grand Royals Casino offered me the most money and the best perks after graduation, so I accepted their offer. I've been in Reno ever since. Not much more to tell."

"What do you do for fun?" She tilts her head and I take her in. Skin that is flawless and smooth, not even the beginning of a wrinkle anywhere on her. At thirty-two, I have a few crow's feet in the corners of my eyes and indentations in my forehead from scowling. This woman must be younger than I am.

"How old are you?" Why hadn't I asked this until now? I've seen the majority of her naked body and I'm suddenly very concerned she might not even be legal.

"Don't worry, Richie Rich. I'm eighteen. You aren't a pedophile," she teases and immense relief falls over me for two seconds before I realize I'm almost twice her age. I have no business being here, yet I can't pull myself away.

"Right. Of course. Fun. Hmm... let me see. Well, I enjoy experimenting with the stock market and I love to discover new restaurants." I tap my pointer finger on my lower lip, trying to think of what else. "Really, I'm just a workaholic who likes to tidy."

She full on belly laughs now. The sound is so melodic I laugh too until I realize she's laughing at me, and then I frown.

"Oh, Law. What are we going to do with you?" She stands

up and walks back toward the bonfire. Unable to stop myself, I follow her. Again.

"What do you do for fun that's so much better?" I ask. She stops in the sand and averts her eyes to the small waves.

"Well, you already know I love to skinny dip." She steals a quick glance my way, showing me a flirtatious grin. "And I love to dance and sing. I also love to explore and see new areas and new things. I love my family. They're a trip. I have two brothers and two sisters, all younger than I am. Together, we get into all kinds of trouble. I'm certain our mom's gray hair comes from our antics alone." A shiver runs down her, so I reach over and rub her arms up and down. Her eyes scrunch up. She looks down at the movement and then up to me. I drop my hands, sensing her unease.

"Sorry. I was just warming you up," I say in explanation and a soft smile plays on her lips.

"It's okay. You did warm me up. Thanks." She tosses me a wink and my dick hardens once again. This girl is so sexy, yet I'm certain she's not even trying.

We get closer to the bonfire and I start to head up to my parked car. She looks at me in confusion. I point up the stairs. "My car. It's up here. I better go."

"Gotta get your beauty sleep," she throws out with a wink.

"I suppose." I pause, gathering the courage to say more. "Thea?" I call after her.

"Hmm?" She gives me her attention once again.

"Can I see you again?" I ask while I move up the stairs.

"Perhaps," she says cryptically.

"Can I have your number?" I want to kick my own ass for the begging tone in my voice.

"Don't have one." She shrugs. "But don't worry. If we're meant to see each other again, we will."

"You don't have a phone? That's incredibly dangerous. What if there was an emergency?" Does no one take care of this girl?

"I'd figure it out, Richie Rich. I always do." She resumes her walk to her family.

I finish climbing the last of the stairs and my feet reach asphalt. I pull the fob from my pants and unlock my car. The streetlights glint off my car and something catches my eye. Four somethings, actually. Or, let me rephrase. It's the *lack* of four somethings that has my attention. My tires are gone and my car sits on cement blocks. The emblem from the front of my Porsche is also missing. How the hell did my alarm not go off?

"Motherfucker!"

CHAPTER 3

Theodora

I SMILE TO MYSELF AS I WALK BACK TO THE BONFIRE. The man is hot. His deep brown eyes took in more than just the show I was putting on. He made me feel *seen*. His brown hair is longer on top and closely shaven on the sides, which tells me he must be a professional. It definitely isn't the haircut of a day laborer like the men in my life who look shaggy even after the haircuts Mom gives them. His muscles strained the arms of his shirt with every movement, and not in a bulky way. He had the long and lean muscles of someone who works out in a gym. Then there's his mouth. His lower lip is bigger than his upper, making him appear to be pouting, even when he wasn't.

I hadn't intended to skinny dip tonight, but after talking to Law for only a short time, I knew he needed his world shaken up. I'm sure other girls would feel disloyal by getting naked in front of another man when they're engaged, but in my family, women are allowed to show skin and be flirty. It's when actual touching happens, we're scorned. It's why we can dress like we do with bare midriffs, low cut tops, and skirts barely long enough to cover the goods. We can *be* sexy, we just can't *get* sexy. Which is why I was so startled when Law rubbed my arms to warm me up. I'm not used to the touch of a man and his touch especially sent shock waves through my body.

I hear someone yell, "Motherfucker!" as I near where my family has set up for the cookout tonight. It has to be Lawrence. No one else is here.

I turn to my two brothers, instinctively knowing those two assholes had something to do with it. "What'd you do?" They both look guilty as hell. I huff and stomp to the parking lot.

"Thea! Wait!" Leander, my seventeen-year-old brother, yells, catching up to me. "You aren't going to tell him what we did, are you?"

Freedom, my fifteen-year-old brother, nods in agreement. "Those wheels are worth two thousand dollars!"

"You two are out of control! He is a nice man. That's so not cool." I rant and continue to the stairs.

"Oh, that's rich coming from you," Leander spouts off. I flip around and get in his face.

"What's that supposed to mean?" I place my hands on my hips.

"It means, you're the one who taught us how to disable high-end car alarms. You're the one who taught us how to quickly remove wheels. You, dear sister, are the one who told us we have to be on the lookout for opportunities everywhere we go." Leander folds his arms together with a stupid smug look on his face I want to slap off.

"I'm sorry if I assumed you had enough common sense to know you shouldn't steal from someone when *you* are the only person around to blame! There's a neon fuckin' sign above our heads right now that says 'we did it' because we, dear brother," I mock, "are the only fuckin' ones around for miles!" My face grows hot and my temper has spiked to all-time high. I can't help it when I give him a shove so hard, he falls on his ass into the sand. I flip around again and this time, no one stops me.

I get to the parking lot and Lawrence is sitting on the curb next to his car. His car that has no wheels. His phone is in his hand and he's mashing buttons as if the harder he pushes, the more effective he'll be. I sit down next to him and put my hand over his. "You won't have cell service, no matter how hard you jam your fingers into the call button."

He looks from his phone to me and I wish he hadn't. He has a vein protruding from his forehead and his face is pinched up tight in anger.

"I'm not sure what else to do. It's a five-mile walk to the main road and it's nine thirty at night. My wheels are missing from my most prized possession. Not to mention, my girl-friend, no, my *fiancée* broke up with me today, and the girl I met tonight, who I considered really cool, was only distracting me so her fucked up family could steal from me." He takes a couple labored breaths. "Any of that sound okay to you?"

I flinch from the fury in his voice.

"I'm so sorry, Law. My delinquent brothers thought it would be funny to play a joke on you. I'll go get them and have them put the wheels back on." I jump from the curb to go find those little twerps, but Lawrence's voice stops me.

"If it were a joke, my alarm would have gone off long before they removed my wheels. Jokesters don't know how to disable car alarms," he mumbles. His head lulls forward on his shoulders and he doesn't look mad anymore. He looks hurt, and it kills me. I say nothing.

When I get to the top of the stairs, I yell, "Hey, jockstraps. Come fix the mess you've made." I hear a lot of groaning and whining from the pair of them, but they come up. They open up the back of our van and each pull out a set of wheels. My brothers may be younger than me, but they're both bigger than me. We come from big stock, so it's not a surprise at all they're both well over six feet already, and sturdy.

Lawrence backs away from the car and watches as my idiot brothers lie down the tires, go back for tools, and then set to repairing his car. I keep my distance, guessing Lawrence doesn't want to talk to me anymore. When they finish and back away from the car, I look at them with my hands on my hips and say, "The emblem?" Leander is the one to pull it from his pocket and hand it to Lawrence. It cannot be repaired by dumb and dumber and I'm hit with a fresh wave of guilt.

Before Lawrence can close the door to his car, I approach him. "I really am sorry about all of this."

"Yeah, whatever." He shuts the door, but rolls down the window. "I need to go. It's been a shit day."

"Sure." I back away from the car, wrapping my arms around myself. He pulls out of the lot and I watch as his tail lights get smaller and smaller.

Leander and Freedom cautiously approach me. "Sorry, Thea," they mutter in unison. We walk back to where the family is and I find Mom. I recant the whole story to her, hoping she'll be a parent for once, but she just laughs. When she sees I'm not joining in, she turns to my brothers, her tone changing to mock irritation.

"You boys should be ashamed of yourselves." She points a finger at them. Her attempt at discipline makes the boys laugh and I can't help but join in. Neither of my parents is good at the whole punishment thing, and her even trying is hilarious.

My mood lifts after that and we all go back to having a good time. My big crazy family, singing, dancing, drinking, and laughing. They may drive me up the wall sometimes, but I wouldn't trade them for anything.

CHAPTER 4

Lawrence

L AST NIGHT WHEN I GOT HOME, I WAS IRRITATED. Mostly because I still don't know whether Thea really wanted to spend time with me, or if she was just keeping me busy while her brothers maimed my car. Then I remembered the skinny dipping and my cock grew impossibly hard. I had to angrily stroke out a release just so I could fall asleep, and I still tossed and turned most of the night, waking from dreams of a gypsy girl dancing by firelight.

Now it's morning. The sun is shining and the birds are singing, but despite the cheery disposition nature is portraying, I'm in a foul mood. Although Chloe didn't live with me, she stayed over most nights and without her here, it's lonely. I tried to stay at her small apartment once, but there was laundry all over the floor, dishes in her sink, and there was carpet. Wall-to-wall carpet. This may not sound like an issue, but do you know there can be up to two hundred thousand bacteria per square inch of carpet? I won't even start on pollen, dust, dirt, and skin flakes.

I didn't even make it through a night at her place before I was heading back to my sanitized marble tiles and clean fixtures. I don't know how anyone can relax while surrounded by filth. But today, I would almost welcome that because today,

I'm waking up alone. I don't enjoy solitude. Before Chloe, I was alone quite often. People say I'm not an easy man to get along with and I would argue against that point, but judging by the fact my relationships always end the same way and I've never had lasting friends, there may be some validity to their views.

I get out of bed and promptly strip the sheets and place them in the washing machine. I grab a fresh set from the linen closet and make my bed. I don't think I need to even discuss the amount of skin cells you shed while you're sleeping. I refuse to get into a bed if there are not fresh sheets on it.

I slept in after my long night, so I can't even go for a run, only increasing my agitation. I make a cup of coffee and take a shower. By the time I'm dressed and ready to head to work, my mood has not improved. Between Chloe and Thea, I've had enough uproar to last a long while.

Fifteen minutes later, I'm pulling into The Royal Casino's parking lot and making my way to my office. I'm always on the lookout for ways to cut operating costs, so as I walk through the casino, I'm eyeing every employee, every slot machine, and every table, to make sure everything and everyone we employ is valuable.

I enter my office, open all the freshly dusted blinds, and take a seat at my laptop. I have a busy day ahead of me with meetings to go to and reports to type up. Other people might feel daunted at my workload, but I thrive in it. Keeping my mind busy helps to calm my frayed nerves.

I've only been at it for three hours before my assistant, Monica, is popping her head through my door.

"Sir, I have a woman out here for you. She says it's urgent," she says hesitantly, knowing I don't enjoy being interrupted.

"Who is it?" I bite out, my eyes not leaving my screen. No one is on my calendar until later today.

"She said her name is Theodora."

I instantly sit up straighter and my eyes shift across the room to find something to fix, to straighten, anything to make perfect when the world around me isn't.

"Sir? Should I send her in?"

I jump from my chair and put my suit jacket on, buttoning it up and smoothing the fabric. Today I'm wearing a seven-thousand-dollar, navy Brioni suit. It's my favorite, and I wore it today to give me a boost from my downtrodden mood.

"Uh, yes, Monica. Th-thank you. S-send her in," I stutter out. I never stutter. This girl unnerves me to my core.

I stand facing the door with a hip resting on my desk and my arms folding in front of me. Only moments later, a vision of crazy curls in an outfit I can't figure out fills my doorway. She has on a layering of mixed pattern skirts and a thin white peasant blouse with a leather bustier that sits directly under her tits, propping them up. Her feet are adorned with flat leather sandals and she has a leather crossbody bag on with a long fringe that sways with her movements. She has more jewelry on than I can make sense of, probably five or six hoop earrings going up one ear alone. Long gold chains, along with a leather choker with a medallion, sits at the hollow of her neck. I don't know where to look first; she's too busy to take in all at once.

One thing I can see clearly are her nipples that are poking through her sheer blouse. She's not wearing a bra and if I strain my eyes just right, I can see the color of those dusky nipples and my mind goes back to how delicious they looked last night, wet and dripping with lake water. I almost would have ignored the potential of a staph infection, just for a taste. My pants become too tight once again and I have to close my eyes and recall all the operating costs of a new pool we're installing from my meeting earlier just to get some room in my boxers.

"Hi, Law. I'm sorry to barge in on you. I was hoping we could talk for a minute."

My eyes snap open and she's still here. She doesn't look at me, just starts roaming the office, regarding my artwork and bookshelf. It's alarming how such a small person can fill an entire room with her presence.

"Thea," I start. "I didn't expect to see you here. Actually, how am I seeing you here? I didn't tell you which department I was in."

"Oh, right. Sorry. It's amazing what you can find on the Internet these days." When our eyes finally meet, warmth takes over my belly. Those bright golden eyes bewitch me.

Uneasy about her wandering around my office, I pull out a chair that sits in front of my desk. "Would you care to take a seat?"

"Nah, I'm good. But thanks." She pulls out a book and flips through it. The book is *The 80/20 Principle* by Richard Koch. Definitely not light reading material. I approach her and take it from her hands, closing it and putting it back in place.

"I insist." I place a hand on the small of her back, at which time my cock twitches. It was a simple touch, but enough to send a spark south. I don't understand what it is about her. Thankfully, she stops roaming my office and does as I ask, sitting in the proffered chair. I then go around my desk and sit in my ergonomically correct executive chair. "Now, what can I do for you?"

"I've been thinking about last night and I feel so bad. I had no idea my brothers would dismantle your car," she says as she pulls her hair through her fingers. The girl who comes across as confident has a nervous habit.

"You've already apologized, and they put them back on. I'm not sure what else can be done." I rest my elbows on my desk and lean in slightly.

"I was kind of hoping I could make it up to you. Maybe take you to lunch?" she asks with eyebrows scrunched together in apprehension.

"I'm not sure I can today. I'm a very busy man." I may feel sparks between us, but I'm also out of control when she's around, and it's not an emotion I enjoy.

"Come on. It's lunch. You have to eat, right?" She smiles at me and I know I've lost the battle already. She's just so beautiful.

I sigh and check my schedule. I don't have a lunch meeting today. "I suppose we can go to lunch, but I only have an hour, so it will have to be quick."

Thea jumps from her chair. "No problem, let's go!" Her excitement is a tad bit infectious and I'm off my chair and tidying my desk.

"What are you doing?" she asks as she watches me put papers into their files, stack them nicely, place my pen and pencil back in their tray, close all my open windows on my laptop, and power it down.

"What do you mean?" I peek up and she's standing in the same spot with her head tilted, watching me. "I'm getting ready to go to lunch. You said we should go now." I have no clue what it is she's getting at.

"Yeah, but in an hour, you'll come right back to this spot where you will just have to get all of those things back out again." Her raspy voice makes even the most annoying comments sound pleasant.

"Yes, but for that hour, I would like to relax. And I can't relax knowing my desk is in disarray."

"You won't be here to see it," she says, but her tone adds a "*duh*" to the end.

"It has no effect on you one way or the other, so if it bothers you, you can wait in the lobby for me." She isn't the first person to be annoyed with my habits, but they're just that. *My* habits. I don't force anyone else to live by my standards, so they can all bug off. *Except Chloe, she had to adapt all the time*, a voice in my head says. However, that was different. Chloe was sharing my space and therefore should adapt to my rules.

"Geez, sorry." Thea inches her way back toward the door. "I was just sayin.'"

"Well, don't say." I finish tucking away my laptop and stand straight. "There. Finished. Ready?"

She rolls her eyes at me and opens the office door.

"Let's boogie." She gestures for me to go ahead of her, but I'm a gentleman, so I hold the door above her head and guide her in front of me. "Oh, okay. You do the whole chivalry thing. It's not necessary." She ducks under my arm and stands behind me, pushing me through the doorway.

Now through the doorway, I turn to the side and place a hand on the open door and once again, gesture for her pass. "I insist," I grit out.

"Law, I'm perfectly capable of holding the door open. It's not a sign of weakened masculinity for me to open it for you. I swear your balls won't shrivel." Her snide comment makes Monica gasp because no one speaks to me this way. I don't think anyone has my whole life. Thea cringes when she realizes the entire bustling lobby of coworkers and assistants have heard her comments.

"I understand, Thea, but you're going to lunch with me and when you're with me, I open the doors. Now please, stop causing a scene and just walk out the door so I can lock up." Properly chastised, she finally does as I ask and after locking my office, we begin our walk to the parking garage, side by side. I stare straight ahead with purpose, but I notice Thea is stealing glances at me through my periphery. I think I might unnerve her as much as she does me, and the corners of my lips crook up at this. "May I drive, or would that be a crime against your independence?"

"You may." She agrees. "But only because I don't have a car and I took a bus here."

I try to hide my shock. The summers in Reno are very warm and the winters are frigid. How does one get around without a car?

"What about the van from last night?" That heap of metal was nothing to look at, but it was theirs. Wasn't it? I hope they didn't steal it.

"Oh, that's my parents'. My dad does some labor jobs here and there and right now he's doing some housing construction. So, no car. Plus, there's the whole no license thing," she says nonchalantly.

"No license, how do you—" But I stop myself and respond with a simple, "I see." I know better than to be rude, despite her trying my patience at least once a minute.

We arrive at my car and I unlock it with the fob. I try to not walk over to her side first and open the door, but it's no use. Dad taught me how to be a proper gentleman and it's so deeply engraved into my psyche. I couldn't stop if I wanted to. Despite the tension in her jaw, she bites out, "Thank you" as she sits in the passenger seat. I get a whiff of incense as she passes, and it's intoxicating. Before I allow myself to bend down and sniff her like a dog, I close her door and round the car.

"Where would you like to go?" I ask while buckling my seat belt and starting the car.

"How about The Green Olive? It's just around the corner." She suggests.

"I've been there. It's good." I've actually been there numerous times because Chloe loved Mediterranean cuisine. I push that thought aside. So far, I have mostly compartmentalized the breakup and it will sit in that little cubby of my mind until I have the emotional capacity to deal with it.

"Great." Her hands go to her hair and she pulls it through her fingers again. We start the drive in relative silence, but after only a few minutes, Thea presses buttons on my touch screen control panel.

"What are you—" I try to swipe her hands away, fearful she'll accidentally call emergency services, but what she does is worse. She clicks the button for a pop station on the satellite radio. Music blares through the speakers at a volume this car has not used. I attempt to turn it down while also staying on the road, but she smacks my hand away. I huff in irritation before returning my hands to ten and two. She just smiles while singing and moving to the music.

Trying to pay attention to the road and her is difficult, but I manage. Her hands are in the air, moving fluidly to the beat, but that's not what captivates the most. It's her voice that has my mouth hanging open. She has perfect pitch and tone. The song is annoying and the lyrics, ridiculous, but when Thea sings it, I can't help but enjoy myself.

The restaurant is only five minutes away, and when I park, I'm regretful the drive is over and her singing has stopped. Of course she jumps out of the car before I can open the door for her. I had no misgivings she would allow me to.

There's a host standing at the entrance to the restaurant and he holds the door for both of us. She doesn't argue or cause a scene, just smiles and thanks him. This makes me stew.

"Why is it okay for him to hold the door and not me?" I whisper as they lead us to a booth near the window.

"It's his job. He wasn't being chivalrous."

"Regardless, when someone opens the door for you, you just say thank you and move on. It doesn't have to be a thing every time."

"Is this okay?" the host asks, gesturing to the booth.

"Yes, it's fi—" I begin, but Thea cuts me off.

"Actually, can we get a table near the door?"

I nudge her, both for being rude and not accepting the table and also because, why does it matter?

"Sure," he says through tight lips. People stare at us as we weave between their tables again just to go back where we came from. I scratch the back of my neck in irritation. "This okay?"

"This is perfect, thank you." Thea smiles, satisfied finally. We both sit down and place our napkins in our laps.

"What was wrong with the booth?" I ask, genuinely curious how her mind works.

"I just like being near an exit." She shrugs and places her elbows on the table, her chin cradled in her hands. Her cat-like eyes seem to know way too much about me. It makes me uncomfortable.

I open my menu and search for my favorite meal here, the lamb saffron kebab. "Do you know what you would like?" I peer around my menu at Thea, but she's still staring ahead, elbows on the table.

"I'll let you order for me."

I sit the menu down and look at her in shock. "Explain how that is not chivalrous."

"It's not chivalrous at all, it's actually barbaric. But if you must know, I'm not a very good reader." For someone admitting they're uneducated, Thea doesn't even bat an eye. I don't think she even understands the implications of adult illiteracy.

"Did you not learn in school?" I ask, flabbergasted.

"I would have, if I had gone to school." Her tone implies she's saying something benign when she's really dropping a bomb. "I can tell by the look on your face you're shocked. Let's order some lunch and I'll lay it all down for you and get it out of the way."

I nod curtly and luckily, we don't have to wait long to place our order because our waiter comes by not two minutes later. I order a hummus plate for starters and two lamb kebab plates. I add two mint lemonades and hand our menus to the waiter.

Thea sighs when she sees the expectant look on my face. "You already know my family are Romani," she starts, and I nod. "My great, great grandparents emigrated here from England. They were unfairly discriminated against, so they came to America.

"Every family is different. Some live in stick built homes and some travel, like us. We go to where there's seasonal work and then we move on."

"So, you've never lived in a house? Or gone to school?" I ask incredulously.

"Uh, no," she answers timidly. "I've lived in the same travel trailer my whole life. My parents got it when they were married and we traveled too much to go to school regularly." She shrugs. "But even if we were settled in one place, my family doesn't encourage girls to go to school."

My eyes go wide. "Why on earth would they not encourage girls to get an education?"

"They're more... traditional. You know, men work and women are the homemakers type of thing."

"And you're okay with it?" I blurt out.

"It's not that I'm okay with it, it's more like, that's just how it is. It's how I was raised, it's how my mom was raised." Her fingers twirl her hair.

Our waiter delivers our appetizer and we take a break from the heavy discussion. Thea takes a piece of warm pita bread and scoops a heaping amount of hummus and cucumber onto it. I watch transfixed as her beautiful lips part. The sound she makes when the food hits her taste buds is orgasmic and I'm suddenly jealous of the food.

I clear my throat to break the spell she cast on me while she made love to her food. "Isn't it against the law to not go to school?"

"Well, that's the thing. I don't really exist. At least not to the government." She takes a sip of her mint lemonade, her lips wrapping around the straw and making me wish for things I can't have. "This is so good." She's driving me wild, which is making me mad because I do not do this. I do not have this strong of a reaction to women, especially women who are polar opposites of me. She wipes her hands on her napkin and continues, "Anyway, I was born on my parents' bed. My four siblings were too. My parents didn't want to chain us to the government, so they never asked for birth certificates."

"What about a social security number?" I ask slowly, while watching her take another bite.

"Nope. Don't have one of those either." Our entrees come and things are quiet while we eat. My mind is reeling and I have a million questions, but don't want her to feel interrogated, so I shelf them. I won't likely see Thea again. We have no excuse after this.

"Do you like the kebabs?" I'm certain she does because the groans that have been coming from her mouth as she eats are the most erotic sound I've ever heard. I would love to know the sounds she makes when... no, can't think about that.

"Oh my God, they're so good. I don't get to eat out often and my mom makes the same things over and over, so I have a limited palette," she gushes.

"I'm glad." I place my napkin on my plate. I managed a

few bites, but my time is better spent watching Thea eat. She devours the entire plate, and when she runs a finger along the leftover sauce and brings it to her mouth, I want to equally cringe for the poor table manners, and also ask her to do it again, only to let me suck it off this time. I'm going insane. I need to get out of here before I do something stupid like lay her down on the table, spread the sauce all over her body, and lick it off. Slowly.

The waiter comes by, removes our plates, and leaves the check. I go to grab it, but Thea gets there first and holds it to her chest so I can't steal it away.

"Nuh-uh. It's my treat." She shakes a finger in front of my face.

"Thea. I don't mind. Please let me pay the bill." I've never once had a woman pay for my meal and the idea short-circuits my brain. Part of being a man, to me, is always taking care of the check.

"Nope. This is my apology lunch and I'm paying for it." She digs in her purse for a moment and then looks up at me. "You should go get the car. I'll take care of this and meet you out there." She's obviously not going to give in, and if she has to pay in quarters or something, I'm sure she doesn't need an audience to embarrass her, so I do as she asks.

I move the car to directly in front of the restaurant where I wait a few minutes for Thea to come out. She jogs out, the biggest smile I've ever seen on her face. Her eyes sparkle with what I think might be mischief, and as she nears the car, she looks over her shoulder. I follow her line of sight. Our waiter and the host run out of the restaurant, waiving their hands in the air and yelling something I can't make out.

"Go!" Thea shouts. I stall, trying to put the pieces together. "Law! Drive! Go!" Everything is happening so fast, I have no time to compute the situation, so I put my foot on the gas and bolt out of the parking lot. Thea just laughs. A deep, rich bellow makes me grin, even if I feel left out of the joke. "You did it!" she exclaims.

"What did I do?" I'm still smiling at her as I drive back toward work.

"You drove a getaway car!" She claps her hands and my face falls. I hang a right into a grocery store parking lot and stop.

"What do you mean I drove a getaway car?" Anxiety swims in my chest.

"We just dine and dashed!" Again, full of excitement.

"No. You said you were taking care of the bill." That's what she said, right? I quickly replay the conversation in my mind and I clearly remember her saying that.

"I did take care of it. In a way. I took care not to pay it. Do you know those mint lemonades were seven dollars each? I could grow a lemon tree and mint for maybe seventy-five cents. Then I could make an endless amount of mint lemonade and save myself the extra." Whatever she sees on my face makes her smile drop. She sets a hand on my shoulder. "Law? You all right? You look a little green."

I push her hand away and jump out of the car before pacing back and forth. I just committed a crime. "I've gone thirty-two years without knowingly committing a crime and now I just committed at least a misdemeanor. Or is it a felony? Oh God, am I going to prison? Did the waiter get my license plate number? Did they recognize me from the many times I had been there? This can't be happening." My breaths are short and shallow, my vision narrowing.

"Law, come sit down. You don't look so good." Thea places one hand on my back and the other clutches my arm as she guides me to sit on the curb. "Take some deep breaths for me. Come on. In." She sucks in a deep breath through her nose.

"And out." She expels the breath through her mouth. "Do it again." I mimic her breaths and after a few more times, I come back into myself. "Feel better?" she asks, still eyeing me closely.

"Yeah, I think I'm okay now." Until I remember what I've just done. I jump from the curb again and point a finger at her. "You!" I accuse. "I can't believe you made me an accomplice to your crime. I need to get away from you."

"Law, wait. You're just so uptight and I thought I could loosen you up. Show you some fun," Thea pleads.

"*That* is your idea of fun? That was not fun, that was a crime spree!"

"A spree would indicate there was more than one crime," she says under her breath, but I hear it.

"You think this is funny? Did you stop to think I could lose my job over this? What casino wants a thief working for them?" I'm shouting now.

"Come on, Law. You're blowing this way out of proportion!" She throws her hands in the air as if I were the frustrating one right now.

"Out of proportion? You don't even have a job. There's no way you could understand. I just need you and your family of criminals to stay away from me. I've known you for two days and both days have taken years off my life." I stomp over to my car and get in, slamming the door. I normally wouldn't leave a woman in a parking lot, but this woman rides the bus and there is a bus stop right on the fucking corner. She'll be fine.

CHAPTER 5

Theodora

I'VE NEVER MET ANYONE AS UPTIGHT AS THAT MAN. HE should thank me for trying to dislodge the pole rammed up his ass.

I walk the few steps to the bus stop, swinging my purse back and forth the whole way. I look at the posted bus schedule and realize I have a half hour to wait for the bus that will take me home. Plopping down on the curb, I recount my afternoon. I really thought he would get a thrill from the minor crime and the adrenaline would get his heart pumping. Something tells me that doesn't happen often with him. But instead, he's pissed off and I'm stewing in the desert heat, waiting for a bus.

As justified as I feel my actions were, I do also feel bad. Our lunch was going so well and I was having such a good time. Law is the hottest man I've ever seen. Him in a three-piece suit is a mood I have never felt before. Strong, capable, and sexy as fuck. When his eyes turned dark and intense as he watched me suck my finger, my body turned warm and liquid. I pictured placing my finger in his mouth and carnal need took over my body. I bang my head on my knees a few times to rid myself of those memories. He'll never want to see me again after this and honestly, I shouldn't see him again, anyway. I have less than six months until I'm married and I have absolutely no business getting involved with any man, let alone a gorger.

An hour and a half later, I walk up to where the seven families in our band are located. We're set up in an abandoned field that was going to be a housing development, but the owner didn't raise enough funds, so it just sits here. We've been here for a couple weeks, but in Reno for almost a year. It's the longest we have ever stayed anywhere. The older the parents get, the less they want to relocate and Reno has been good to us.

Gamblers have given me a jackpot of easy scams and the housing boom has given the men steady day labor work. The winters are a little cold, but all in all, I've enjoyed this area. I'll be sad to go when the time comes.

I trudge up the steps to our home. Mom welcomes me. "Hey there." She's sitting on the couch, folding laundry. I forgot it was laundromat day. I should have been here instead of trying to get Lawrence to forgive me. Honestly, what did it matter anyway? Just because I'm attracted to the guy, it doesn't change the fact I'm engaged.

"Hi, Mom, I'm sorry I wasn't here to help with laundry."

"It's okay. I had your sisters." She grabs a stack of folded pants and puts them into one of the many plastic tubs we own. There isn't a lot of storage in these RVs and we've had to learn to get creative with our space. "Where were you anyway?"

"Oh, I went to pawn a few things I picked up at the casino." I hate lying, but there's no way she'd understand why I did what I did today. My parents don't like us girls to go out into the world alone. They're lenient with me, but being alone with a man who is not our husband is strictly forbidden.

"Did you get some good prices?" she asks.

"Prices?" I tilt my head at her.

"For the things you lifted?" She quirks an eyebrow. I need to stop thinking about Law.

"Oh, my usual pawn shop was getting suspicious, so I scouted new ones today." Mostly, the men make money the legal way, well, legal for us since they use falsified IDs. I don't want to take Dad's or my brother's money, so I get my money running cons. Most of the women we travel with stick with the traditional rules, bearing and raising children, doing the housework, and cooking. But some of us prefer to take a more active role in our finances and are allowed to do so. We're lucky because a lot of Romani we have run into along the way don't even allow the women to leave camp, let alone run cons.

"You don't sound like yourself. Anything happen today?" Mom sits down next to me.

"I'm just tired. Maybe I better lie down for a bit." Today was a failure of epic proportions, and I just want to sleep it off. I stand up and move to climb the ladder to the loft I share with my sisters when Mom's voice stops me.

"Wen said he's coming around for you tonight. Indiana will chaperone." I lower my head in disappointment. Going out on dates for women of marrying age or engaged means chaperones. It's such an archaic tradition. A man can take a roll in the hay with anyone before marriage, but a woman's virtue is all she has, so it better stay protected. Yet another reason no one can know how I spent my day.

"Okay, I'll just lie down for a bit and then I'll get ready." I climb up the ladder and thankfully find the large bed empty. Crawling into the corner, I curl up into the fetal position. Ever since the engagement party, my mind has been so mixed up. My whole life I knew I'd have to marry within our culture, but now that it's happening, I'm getting anxious. Like time is running out for me to be me. Soon I'll be a wife and then a mother and it will all be over. I'll never have a chance to just be me again.

Now I've met Law, and despite how uptight he is, I'm attracted to him. An attraction I haven't had with anyone before. The way he watches me, the lust in his eyes. No one has ever looked at me like that. But it's more than that. Law challenges me and wants more for me.

Wen is a good guy, but he'll never allow me to be me. He wants a meek and oppressed wife. Someone who will make him the center of their world. I want passion and arguments and make-ups, not someone who wants to control me and expects me to be seen, not heard. I want a man who will try to take charge and then after a raucous fight and riotous make-up sex, he can give in and let me have my way. Something tells me Law would be just that man.

After letting my mind wander down paths it shouldn't for a while, I give up on a nap and climb down to get ready for my date. I know this date will probably include a walk somewhere and then ice cream, like every date we've gone on. I wish we could go back to doing the things we did when we were kids. Finding cows to tip, stealing tractors and cutting obscene images into their crops, loitering in stores and tuning the display TVs to porn before running away. That's the fun I want Wen and I to have again. Maybe then I could try to turn my feelings into romantic ones. But instead, he brings me flowers and chocolates, takes me for moonlit walks and ice cream. None of the things I want to be doing.

I go to the bathroom and put my hair in a messy bun on top of my head. It's hot and there are no electric hookups in this abandoned field, therefore no air conditioning. My skin is dewy with a sheen of sweat, so I don't bother with makeup, knowing it will just slide off my face.

I brush my teeth and change into an olive-green tank

dress. I leave all my jewelry. The more gold and bling, the better. Stepping outside, I notice Wen and Dad talking. I walk over and their conversation ends, leaving me to believe they were talking about me.

"Thea, you look nice," Wen compliments and looks at Dad before briefly brushing a kiss on my cheek. I give them both a tight smile.

"So, what are you talking about?" I demand, more than question. If you've got a reason to talk about someone, you've got a reason to say it to their face.

"Just discussing plans for after you're married, love," Dad says.

"You think the other half of the marriage party should know about her plans?" I know I'm being bitchy, but it's not the first time people have tried to make plans for me and I hate how it makes me feel like a child who doesn't know enough about the world to take an active role in their own lives.

"I'll leave you to it," Dad grunts out and walks away.

"Why do you keep talkin' to my dad about our plans?" I throw my verbal dagger at Wen.

"I have to talk about it to someone." Wen storms off toward his family's trailer, but I'm not having it. I know we haven't made definitive decisions about after we're married, but we just barely got engaged. We have time.

Before he can get to the steps, I get in front of him. "What we do after we get married is up to us, not my dad. Even if I'm not ready to talk about it, you have no right to talk to him before me."

"That's what you aren't understanding, Thea," he spits out. "It's up to me. Not you. You will be my wife and the mother of my kids, not my equal. You want to gallivant all over the city and steal a few things here and there so you can feel you are contributing? I'll allow it. At least until we have kids. Then it's up to me to make money for our family." He steps around me and opens the door, but before going in he says, "You're my wife, it's just how it is." Then he closes the door behind him, leaving me dumbfounded.

My eyes well with tears and I decide I can't be here right now. Fuck our date. I walk toward the main road, telling no one where I'm going. If they're all going to treat me like a child, then I'll act like one. I jump on the bus to the city, flopping down onto a bench. I need to think and to do that, I need space from all of them.

I watch out the window while my mind spins. Wen has never been blunt like this before. He's always included me in plans, or at least tried to before I changed the subject. It always felt like we had tons of time to make decisions. Last year when our parents told us we would marry, I wasn't shocked. We're in the same band, near the same age, and get along with each other. Back then, we had a whole year before we were even to be engaged, so every time Wen brought up our future, it seemed too early to talk about.

I get off on a random stop, not really caring where I go. Evening turned to night, and without conscious thought, I enter The Grand Royals Casino. It really is a nice place. Grand water fountains, real trees, and planter boxes filled with plants and flowers decorate the inside and huge skylights let in sun or like right now, moonlight. It makes you feel you're still outside. If it weren't for the sounds of the slot machines and the stale cigarette smoke smell, you might be able to trick yourself to believe you're in a garden.

I'm sure Law has already gone home for the day, so I have no reason to go to his office again. Even if he were here, he wouldn't want to see me, so I keep wandering. I didn't bring my purse and I only had a couple dollars tucked into my bra, which I used for the bus, so I have no money to sit and eat.

It's then I see a very intoxicated man tripping his way down the rows of slot machines. Occasionally he picks one to sit in front of and throws a twenty in. When he loses, he moves on. Every step he takes is unsteady, and he sloshes an amber liquid all down the side of the glass and onto the marble tiles. He would make the perfect target. I might get some dinner money after all.

The man is tall and thin. He has a large nose, a long forehead, and almost no chin to speak of. He might welcome the attention of a young pretty girl. I follow him around until he picks a *Wheel of Fortune* slot machine. He sits down and I sit on the stool next to him. He's having a hard time lining the cash up with the slot, so I reach across him and put my hand on top of his.

"Here, let me help." I flash him a flirty smile and put the twenty-dollar bill in.

"Thanks, loung yady," he slurs and I fake coy and look away, still smiling.

"I'm not that young," I say.

"Prolly too young ffffor me." His head sways as he presses the max bet button. He wins double his money. I jump off the stool and cheer for him. He eyes my small chest as I bounce and I know at that moment, I have him.

"Yay! Look! You won!" I cheer, way too enthusiastically.

"You're my lood guck charm," he says, putting his arm around my waist. Being this close, I smell the stench of liquor seeping from his pores.

"Maybe you need me to stick close for a while." I throw him a wink.

"I thhhink you're right." He grabs my hand and pulls me onto his lap. I fight the cringe and pretend to screech in delight.

"What's your name?" I bat my eyes and lean in close.

"Stanley." His voice is lust filled and I think this might be my easiest target yet. I slip off his lap and grab his hand, pushing the cash out button on the machine.

"Let's play more!" I jump up and down, allowing what little tits I have to bounce again.

"Yeah, okay," Stanley slurs.

For the next half an hour, Stanley loses close to two hundred dollars, which was all his cash. I talk him into going to the cash machine and pulling out five hundred more. The machine spits it out and I grab it, confusing Stanley. But then I tuck it into my bra, watching his eyes follow the money down. I grab his hand and pull him back onto the casino floor. Like a good boy, he follows.

When he's settled at a machine, I pull out a hundred and put it in the slot. He presses max bet and starts losing, again. This guy has got to be the unluckiest gambler ever. He looks around for a waitress, but there are none. I realize this is my out. Kissing him on the cheek, I whisper, "I'm gonna go find a waitress. You look thirsty." I let my lips linger near his mouth a minute before pulling away.

"Okay, order me a whiskey." He's sobering a bit, so the timing is perfect.

"Sure, sugar. Be right back." I wave and blow him a kiss. I can feel his eyes following my swaying hips as I walk away. When I'm certain I'm out of his sight, I bolt to the other side of the casino and take a seat at the café. Pulling the cash from my bra, I count the four hundred dollars still left and order myself a strawberry Italian soda. I deserve a little treat after tolerating that man for so long.

I should be nervous to sit here and people watch for a bit, but I'm not. This casino is at least one hundred thousand square feet and with hundreds of people milling about, Stanley couldn't find me if he tried.

I stand and leave a couple bucks for the tip and walk in the exit's direction. That's when I hear a commotion behind me. I turn to look and motherfucker! There's Stanley, surprisingly sober, with two security guards flanking him.

"That's her! That's the girl who took my money!" He's pointing at me, which makes everyone in the crowd look in my direction. I turn to run, but there is a security guard coming at me from behind too. With nowhere to run, I slump my shoulders and look at the ground, wondering how the hell I will get out of this one.

CHAPTER 6

Lawrence

I'M SCRUBBING THE KITCHEN SINK WITH BLEACH WHEN
my phone rings. Rinsing off my hands and then drying them
on a paper towel, I pull my phone from my pocket. It's the
casino. Being a finance guy, I don't receive after hours calls. Ever.

"This is Lawrence." I've often been told a friendly "hello"
is a more polite way to answer the phone, but I think keeping
things formal and impersonal is professional.

"Mr. Packwood, this is Chris Stevens, head of security."
His voice is clipped and my mind spins. Why would security
be calling me?

"Yes, Mr. Stevens. I know who you are. What can I do for
you?"

"Well, we had a bit of a situation this evening. We had a
woman steal some money from one of our guests. She has no
ID and refuses to give us her name. We would just call the cops
and let them deal with her, but she insists she's a good friend
of yours and asked us to call you." He doesn't even have to tell
me her name. I know who it is and the anger I felt toward her
from earlier resurfaces.

"Let me guess, wavy brown hair, gold eyes, tiny frame?" I
need not confirm my suspicions. I'm already pocketing my wallet
and keys, heading to the garage.

"Uh, her hair is in a bun, but it is brown and she has really unusual golden eyes." The security guy covers the receiver and I can hear his muffled question asking if her hair is wavy.

"Chris? It's fine. I know who she is. I'll be down there in fifteen." I pull out of my driveway as my Bluetooth connects and I suddenly hear a string of curses, followed by, "get your fucking hands off me!" Then there's a loud *oof* sound.

"Ma'am, ma'am! Calm down, we just have to check you for weapons before we can take the cuffs off." Chris sounds stressed, a reaction I'm well acquainted with.

"Chris?" I call out, loud enough he can hear me over the disorder in the background.

"Leave her in the cuffs." A smile forms on my face at the image of a spitting mad Theodora, hands chained behind her back.

"Sir?" Confusion fills Chris' voice.

"The cuffs, Chris. Don't take them off. I'm not sure what she's capable of." I lie, because I know she wouldn't hurt anyone, at least not physically.

"Uh, okay. We will just let her stew then." I can hear the smirk in his tone.

"Be there soon." I end the call and refocus on the road. I'm confused at how close I am to the casino when it's only been minutes. My speedometer shows I'm going twenty miles an hour over the limit. I never speed. I know the statistics of high speed crashes and therefore I follow all posted speed limit signs. I slow down and look around me for any sign of flashing lights to give me a ticket. There are none, so my racing heart slows.

What is it about this girl? She's done nothing but bring chaos to my life. I should have told Chris to call the cops, but she has no identification. She doesn't exist. I don't know what kind of trouble she can get in because of that, but I don't want her to find out this way. It's better she finds a way to get documented herself. If she wants that.

I park in my assigned spot and speed walk into the security entrance. My access card allows me into whatever room I want to be in. It's a perk of being one of the big bosses.

"Where is she?" The security guard at the desk is typing away, not even bothering to address me. He points to the hallway quickly and goes back to typing. I walk down the short hallway and hear screams. Found her.

"Get these fucking things off me now! I didn't even do anything! That bastard gave me the money! I earned it too, keeping him entertained all night."

I listen from just outside the door. Theodora is hissing and spitting all the excuses in the world. I briefly wonder how she entertained the man she stole from, but when I feel a touch of jealousy, I shake it off. She's nothing to me. Entering the room, I see Thea on a metal chair, hands behind her back. Hair has fallen from her bun, framing her face in loose curls. She's wearing a thin dress that shows every line of her feminine shape. The low-cut neckline shows the swell of those breasts I haven't been able to forget. I swallow and refocus on why I'm here in the first place.

"Thank God you're here." Chris drags a hand through his hair in obvious frustration. "She's all yours." He walks out the door to the room, leaving us alone.

"What have you gotten yourself into this time, Trouble?" It's an apt nickname and I decide to keep it. I sit down in the chair next to her. She doesn't acknowledge me, doesn't even look at me, so I gently pinch her chin between my thumb and forefinger, forcing her to see me.

When our eyes meet, my stomach drops. She has tears welling in her eyes and if I know anything about this girl, it's she doesn't break easily. This whole situation must have been more than she's equipped to bear. I drop my hand from her chin and stand up. Opening the door, I call out to Chris, "Can I get the keys to the cuffs?"

Chris rises from the chair he was perched in next to the first security guy and pulls the keys from his pocket, handing them to me.

"Release her at your own risk," he mutters under his breath. I want to stand up for her and make him understand why she is the way she is, but it's not my place. Theodora and I aren't even friends. I close the door to the room and hold up the key. She stands up and turns around. The second the cuffs click open, her arms wrap tightly around my neck. The cuffs fall to the floor and I just stand there awkwardly, hands by my sides.

Her body shakes slightly. She's dejected, and my heart breaks just a bit for this girl. I wrap my arms around her waist, noticing how nicely we fit together. She's the perfect height, so I don't have to slouch down like I did with a much shorter Chloe. No, I can wrap my arms around her at my full height and I love the way she feels crushed against me.

I bury my face in her neck and take a deep breath, inhaling her incense scent. It's woody and smoky and the most perfect scent for such a wild thing.

We hold each other like this for a long while. When I feel her body settle and relax, I pull away to look her in her eyes.

"You okay?" Red-rimmed and glassy, her eyes are half-lidded and I know she's exhausted. She nods and drags her palm over her runny nose before wiping it on her dress. I cringe and grab a tissue from the bookcase in the corner, handing it to her. "Let's go find out if I can get you out of this." She nods again and rubs the tissue on her nose. That's better.

She grabs my hand. Her snot germs seep into my skin, but I hold on right back. I have hand sanitizer in the car. It'll be fine. She needs me right now more than I need to be clean.

We walk out the door and approach the desk. The

security officers' gazes lock in on our joined hands before standing up and meeting my eyes.

"So, what happens now?" I ask.

"Well, the gentleman she stole from isn't pressing charges. He's allowed casino security to handle any consequences. We assured him she'll be criminally trespassed, so if she steps foot in the casino again we can arrest her, but she doesn't have an ID and she won't give us a name. Without that, it will be hard to add her to our list." He turns the computer monitor around so I can see the list of trespassed individuals, complete with pictures of each person.

"I can assure you she won't be a problem again."

"I can appreciate that, but we still need to add her to the list. It's protocol."

I steal a glance at the criminal and nod. I hope with my assurances, she can feel safe leaving her name and then this can all be over.

"Theodora," she squeaks out.

"Last name?"

"Uh, Vanslow." I don't know if it's really her last name. The way she hesitated makes me believe she was nervous to give it up, or she was making something up quickly.

"Okay, we just need to take a quick photo." Before either of us knows what's happening, Chris has pulled his phone from his pocket and snapped a pic of Theodora.

I give Chris a tight smile and we walk out the door. Once outside, I drop her hand.

"We need to talk," I say.

"Okay." She turns to face me. Her eyes are still sad and tired and her posture slouched and withdrawn.

"Do you want to come to my house for a bit? No one will interrupt us and I'll feel safe knowing I won't be an accomplice to a crime."

She winces, but agrees.

I drive us both to my house and park in the garage. She puts her hand on the door handle, but I grab her other hand, stopping her retreat.

"I would prefer if you didn't steal any of my stuff." I see the sadness pass at my mild accusation, but she nods. I want to feel bad for saying that, but I don't. She has been nothing but trouble since I met her and we obviously need some ground rules.

We walk into the house and the strong scent of bleach hits my nostrils, almost knocking me back a step. Earlier, after I had left her at the bus stop, I returned to work. But after two hours of trying to get something done, I called it quits. Distraction and annoyance clawed at me, so I went home where I scrubbed every surface I could get my hands on. I must have gone overboard because my house doesn't smell clean, it smells like a hospital, sterile and cold.

I ask her to remove her shoes and ignore the side eye she gives me. I then lead her to my sofa and motion for her to sit. When she sits without argument, I'm shocked. She's never once done as I asked without a fight.

"Would you like something to drink? Maybe some tea?" I could use something stronger, but she's underage and as much as I don't want to be a parent to her, she needs someone to help her make better choices.

"That would be perfect." Her small smile and acceptance of allowing me to make her tea shows she's trying. It's more than I could ever expect from this rowdy one, so I take it and go to the kitchen. Putting the kettle on the stove and twisting the dial to high, I peek over the kitchen island and to the living room where I left Thea. She's not on the sofa. I step around the island, searching for her beautiful brown mop of hair.

I find her inspecting the photos on my mantle. There are

a few of my parents and me from when I was younger, there's a picture of me in my cap and gown at my college graduation, and the last one is of Chloe and me, standing in front of a fountain at the casino on one of our mandatory date nights. If it had been up to me, we wouldn't have gone on dates after we agreed to a committed relationship. Once I knew she was my girlfriend, I had assumed we could give up the charade of going into public and finding new things to do together. I was wrong and since I had become an excuse giver every time Chloe tried to get me out, she implemented the date night rule. Twice a week I was required to take Chloe out. She agreed to let me choose the day, which I was grateful for, but that was the only concession she made.

It's that picture, the one of Chloe and me, Thea holds in her hands. She's staring at it intently and I have the urge to rip it from her grasp and throw it away. It means nothing to me and if I had another picture to put in the frame, I would have done so the day she left me. But I couldn't find one I liked and I couldn't remove the frame because it balanced the mantle out, so there the picture has stayed, taunting me with my failures.

I let her be and go back to the kitchen where the kettle is about to go off. Grabbing two mugs from the cupboard, I make our tea and place it on a tray with some milk and honey. I go back to the living room where Thea has moved on from the photos and is back to sitting on the couch, her fingers going to her hair, pulling it in between each one repetitively. I set the tray on the coffee table and sit next to her.

"You want to tell me what happened?" I start, breaking the silence. She looks up at me like she forgot where she was, before dropping her eyes again.

"I went home after our lunch and I just got overwhelmed. I ran away and walked around downtown before I ended up at the casino. I didn't bring my purse with me, so I made a quick buck. He was so drunk, I don't understand how he found me." She reaches for her mug, splashes in some milk, and drizzles some honey. She's so lovely, even when she's upset and distraught.

"I think you're missing the point. I don't understand why you think you can take from people and have no conse- quences. If you had been in any other casino, you would be in police custody right now. They would know you have no identification and I honestly don't know what would have happened to you."

She peers up at me from atop her mug as she takes a sip. I don't know whether to yell at her or kiss the fuck out of her. Which one would make her understand how reckless she's being?

"I don't expect you to understand, Richie Rich." She places her mug back on the tray and focuses her attention on me. "With your important job and your college degree, you can't possibly comprehend. I have no education or job skills. The only thing I've ever been taught is if you want something, all you have to do is figure out a way to get it." She furrows her brows and I can tell she really believes her way is the only answer.

I set my tea down and reach over, gently brushing a strand of hair that has crossed her cheek, she reaches up and places her hand over mine, cuddling her cheek into my palm for a brief moment before letting me go. The small contact endears me to her and I wish, more than anything, our circumstances were different. Wishing gets no one anywhere, so I straighten my spine, mind made up.

"I know that's what you think, and I know it's your reality. It's also none of my business how you live, but I'm begging you, please stop interfering in my life. This is the second time today you could have cost me my job, then I would be coming to your trailer to ask you to teach me a thief's life. I'm not cut out for it, so let's just go our separate ways." I give her a weak smile, but she doesn't return it. Her eyes are glassy once again and she's slouched over, caved in on herself. My resolve weakens once again before I take a deep breath and stand up. We have absolutely no business being in each other's lives. "Where can I take you?"

"You don't need to take me anywhere. I can catch a bus." She stands up and heads toward the shoe rack.

"Don't be ridiculous. It's half past eleven and I live far from any bus route. Just let me drive you." I put my shoes on as well and pocket my phone and wallet, keeping my fob in hand. Her eyes dart back and forth and I can almost see her brain trying to come up with a lie. "Trouble. Let me drive you. I'll never sleep unless I know you are home safe."

She nods and walks into the garage before climbing into the passenger seat. Sighing, I follow suit and get into the driver's side.

"Where are we going?" I ask again.

"I, uh, actually live pretty close." My eyebrows shoot up. How could she possibly live in my neighborhood? There are strict HOA rules against a caravan of travel trailers. I'm sure of it.

She directs me to the next housing development over and down a dead end where the pavement meets dirt. "I live just beyond there. I'll walk from here." She points down the dirt road and I look into the distance, seeing faint lights coming from the empty space.

"I see. Well, it was nice meeting you, Theodora." I hold out my hand for her to shake, even though we're so much closer than acquaintances. She sighs before reaching for my hand, shaking it briefly.

Climbing out of the car, I get a momentary glance of her perfect ass I've seen naked. The image makes me regret writing her out of my life before having the chance to explore it more closely. I watch as Thea walks until I can't see her through the darkness any longer. I'm grateful tomorrow is Saturday. I need the weekend to recover from her.

CHAPTER 7

Theodora

"**W**HAT DO YOU THINK OF THIS ONE?" Mom shows me a pattern for a dress that's more sheer than not, only embroidered flowers cover the model's nipples and coochie. Just days ago, I would've salivated over this dress. Now I can't bring myself to care.

"Sounds good." I go back to staring out the window of our trailer. Houses, real houses, surround our makeshift camp and I wonder what the lives are like for the people who live in them. Are they happy to have a mortgage and two point five kids? Is the mom a frigid bitch who blames her husband for losing herself after children? Maybe there are happy families, where the mom and dad spend every weekend taking their kids on adventures. Showing them the world and not just their small slice of space. I picture a straitlaced man, who uses coasters and washes his whites separately, but he married an uncivilized woman who shows him how much fun spontaneity can be and together they raise their family, living the best of both worlds.

I slam my head down onto the dinette table and moan loudly, completely forgetting both Mom and Wen's mom, Nuri, are over discussing wedding plans. Mom pats my back a couple times before giving me a good shove out of my chair where I land on my ass.

"What was that for?" I ask, jumping up and rubbing my now bruised tailbone.

"You need to get your head out of your ass and help with the planning. The wedding is just over five months away and you've done jack shit to help," Mom scolds. No pussy footing or tender moments with her. Only reality checks and harsh truths. She's always told it to me straight and I love her for it.

"I know it can be overwhelmin', Thea, but decisions need to be made." Nuri is much gentler. She has five girls and one boy, Wen. They're a more soft-spoken family, save for Braithe and Wen. Braithe is abrasive and most times, outright rude. I think the six females of the family have spent so much time traipsing on eggshells around Braithe, they eventually just retreated into themselves. Then there's Wen. He was a rough and tumble boy, the same way I was a rough and tumble girl, but he wasn't ever cruel. Now that he's grown, he's becoming his dad.

"Yeah, okay. Can I make a choice on the dress today, but decide everything else another day?" I beg with my eyes. When I get a disappointed look from my mom, I bring my hands up in the prayer pose and whisper, "Please?"

"Fine. Whatever. What dress do you want?" Mom spreads the patterns out across the table and I sit back down in my chair, glowering at each one. The general population would consider them scandalous, but they're normal for us. I pull one out that's absolutely gorgeous. A deep V neckline dips to the model's belly button, but that's the only shocking part about it because it has long, romantic lace sleeves and a lace skirt that just barely trails the ground in the back. The whole dress is lined in silk, so the only skin you can see is what's shown in the V. This is modest in my world.

"I think this is the one." I hold it up for Mom to see. She snort laughs, grabs the pattern, and throws it in the trash.

"I must have accidentally grabbed that one from the pile. That dress isn't you. You'd look better in this one." She holds out a pattern for an off the shoulder dress with two neon pink molded cups that cover the woman's boobs. There's an empire waist with a long black skirt and two slits that start at the waist and go down to the floor. The only thing stopping people from seeing her vagina is the middle panel of fabric. It's okay, but I'm still imagining myself in the first gown. It was classy and sophisticated. I can't help but imagine it's a dress even Law would approve of.

"All right, this one is pretty too." There's no point in arguing. I don't think I've ever been to a wedding where the bride wore white. I wouldn't want to embarrass Mom or Dad, so I agree. I'll fit in better wearing the second dress. "Am I free now?"

"Whatever. Go. Be young." Mom waves me away. I kiss both her and Wen's mom on the cheek and practically run out the door before one of them forces me to talk more wedding.

I take off on a walk, but when I see my seventeen-year-old brother, Leander, lying in the field on a blanket, I head over and plop down next to him. "What's up, bro-tard?" I don't miss the book he tucks under the blanket before giving me his attention.

"Not a fucking thing." He turns on his side, nonchalantly blocking my view of the book.

"Why aren't you working today?" I've been hearing rumors about Leander ducking out of work frequently lately. He and I aren't especially close, but he's my brother and if he's going through shit, I want to be there to go through it with him.

"I just took a day off. Is that okay?" He jolts upright and crosses his arms in front of him.

"I don't fuckin' care if you go to work or not. I was just asking." The tightness around his eyes eases some.

"What about you? Where were you so late last night?" His eyebrow quirks in challenge. And this is where our conversation will end. Apparently, we both have secrets we're protecting.

"Just out at the casino trying to score." All of us kids, at least the older ones, have used the casino to get some quick cash, and it's not a lie. Not really.

"Who drove you back?" I'm a little thrown off he knew I was driven back home. I'm not sure if he just saw the headlights of Law's car or if he had been hanging out in the field. I lie first to see how much he really knows.

"An Uber." I stand up to leave. This conversation is getting uncomfortable and I don't want to lie anymore. Our family will lie to any gorger's face without even a second thought, but we don't lie to each other. We're the only ones we can be honest with. Unless the truth includes making friends and possibly developing a crush on a gorger. That shit you take to the grave. "I'm gonna head out."

"Sure. Whatever."

I feel him watch me walk away, but I don't look back until I'm almost out of sight. But when I do, I see Leander has his book out again. I wonder what he's up to. Leaner and Freedom both know how to read proficiently. They were in school until eighth grade. Sure, we skipped around a lot throughout that time, but my parents enrolled them in school each place we went. Boys will eventually be men and need to provide for their families, so it's important for them to at least have a basic education. But it doesn't explain the book. It was a large hardback, so it couldn't be some dumb fiction he had picked up. I tuck this info away for another day and head off.

I have no destination in mind. I just want to get away. It's

Saturday, so there are many people milling about. Taking their dogs for walks, riding bikes, and dining at the neighborhood cafés. I keep going until I recognize certain houses, or a certain house, I guess, because when I look up, I realize I've taken myself to Law's house. I take it in more closely now that I'm seeing it in the daylight. There's no movement outside and a stealthy peek into his windows tells me he's not home.

I step back to the sidewalk and look at his yard. His lawn is mowed with straight lines going horizontally across the yard. He has well-pruned bushes lining the walkway and a planter box underneath his living room window. Curiously, the box is empty. No plants or flowers, just dirt.

It's that moment I know what I can do for Lawrence to apologize. I hustle around the neighborhood, collecting all the things I'll need for the surprise. He will love it.

CHAPTER 8

Lawrence

I PULL INTO MY DRIVEWAY AFTER GOING TO THE MARKET so I can meal prep for the week. I hit the button for the garage, but before I drive in to park the car, something catches my eye. It's flowers. Lots and lots of mismatched flowers in my planter box. I might keep my grass green and my bushes tamed, but that's the extent of my green thumb. No matter what I plant in that box, it dies, so I just leave it empty.

I put my car in park instead of pulling into the driveway and get out to inspect. Sure enough, there are flowers packed tightly into the four by six, cedar lined box. I don't know what all the flowers are called, since I can't grow them. I've never researched them. I do know there are a wild mix of blues, yellows, purples, and reds. Some tall and some short. To a trained eye, it might look scattered and messy, but since I don't know any better, it looks primitive and gorgeous to me.

When those descriptors pass through my mind, I bow my head and shake it. I think I know who did this. After taking a moment to compose myself, I look back up and all around, trying to spot the culprit. I see a slight movement behind Mrs. Gutterman's white alder, just a flash of a bright-patterned skirt.

I cross the street and can clearly see someone trying to hide behind the smaller trunk of the tree. "Trouble?" I call out to the girl who obviously never won at hide and seek when she was young. She still doesn't come out from behind the tree, but I can see one gilded eye peeking at me. I walk onto Mrs. Gutterman's lawn and stand in front of the tree. "You aren't good at this hiding thing."

She huffs. "How did you know it was me?" Coming out from her hiding space, she folds her arms across her chest like a child throwing a tantrum. Her breasts push even higher than their natural perky height and I can't help but take a beat to appreciate them. Then I mentally kick myself and snap back into the moment.

"I don't know anyone who would plant me flowers except one particularly large pain in my ass." She looks slightly hurt, and I feel bad for saying it. "Let's get out of Mrs. Gutterman's yard before she sics her Doberman on us." I hold my hand out for her and a small smile forms on her perfect Cupid's bow lips as she takes it.

We cross the street and I lead her onto my porch, where two rocking chairs sit. I don't use them often. Okay, ever. I don't enjoy giving neighbors the opportunity to come over and chat with me. I just want to enjoy my house without having to fake niceties. But I like the way the chairs make my house look, so they stay.

"I know you didn't want to see me again, but I still felt so bad. I wanted to do something nice for you and when I saw the empty planter box, the idea seemed perfect. I meant to finish before you came home." She looks almost childlike, begging for approval, and I can't turn her down. Each time we're together, it gets harder and harder to resist this attraction. I know she must feel it too or she wouldn't make so many attempts to see me.

"Well, I have to admit they're pretty," I say, admiring the big blooms. I sigh. "Thank you."

Her smile goes from small and hopeful, to huge and glowing. "Does this mean we can be, you know, friends, or whatever?" She's offering an olive branch and I feel sufficiently worn down, so I take it.

"Sure. Friends or whatever." We sit and rock in quiet for a moment, before I decide I want to ask more questions about her life. Friends do that. They get to know each other. "So you've lived all over, huh?"

"Yeah, mostly the western side of the U.S. In California, the men all did a lot of roadwork. We stayed close to L.A. once. They're always doing road construction there. In Oregon, they worked the timber lines. In Washington, they picked apples in the orchards, and in Colorado, they worked on a cattle drive. Here in Reno, they've been doing construction because of the huge housing boom." She pushes off the ground and the chair swings big and long. "Basically, they go wherever they can find work that'll pay them under the table or accept their fake IDs with little questions."

"And none of you go to school?" I'm stuck on this, because it seems cruel of her parents to chain their kids to the life they've lived.

"Leander and Freedom both completed school through grade eight before they dropped out and started working with Dad." That surprises me.

"What do you do with your time if you don't go to school or work?" My rocking is gentle and soothing compared to her wayward and fast. It feels like a metaphor for us.

"I help my mom a lot. There's so much to do at the band—"

"What's a band?" I ask.

"We call our group a band. Our band only has seven families in it, including us."

How have I never known these people still exist in modern society?

"Anyway, the sites we stay at are primitive. No running water, no electricity, so the women in our band have a lot of work to do every day just to have basic necessities like food."

I'm listening intently, so I miss my next-door neighbor advancing up the path to my house. Craig Seymour is a nice enough guy. Him and his wife just moved in and have been good neighbors, but I'm not in the mood for casual conversation. When he calls out a hello, I just give him a slight nod. He looks Thea up and down and it triggers something I've only experienced with this woman. Protectiveness and possession.

"Can I help you with something?" I stand up tall so I can look down on his shorter stature.

"Um, I don't know how to ask this." He rubs a hand on the back of his neck and looks uncomfortable. "We have one of those doorbell cameras." He looks at Thea again and I get the urge to pummel him.

"And?" My clipped tone gets his attention. "Most everyone does. What does that have to do with me?"

"It has nothing to do with you, exactly. It's just we came home and a few... *things* were missing from our yard, so we brought up the footage. It showed a young woman... uh, digging up some of our flowers." Craig looks back at Thea and the pieces come together. I sigh and sit back down on the rocker, surveying my little thief.

"You have a camera? In your doorbell?" she asks incredulously, always latching onto exactly the wrong parts of accusations.

"I'm sorry. This is uncomfortable, but my wife just planted them and she threatened to make me stay home tonight and plant her all new flowers if I didn't come over and talk to you. It's my monthly poker night and since Lars, the best player in our group, can't make it tonight, I stand a good chance at winning."

"No, it's fine. I'm sorry about this. I'll have landscapers come to your house on Monday and she can have them plant whatever she wants, on me." I see Theodora in my periphery. She's still stuck on the video cameras. I sigh for the hundredth time since meeting her and shake Craig's outstretched hand.

"Really? That would be great. Thank you so much." Craig turns to go, but he looks over his shoulder one more time at Theodora. Between him staring at her and the situation, my anger boils over briefly.

"Don't let your wife catch you staring," I blurt out. Thea smacks my arm and Craig looks embarrassed. He snaps his gaze away and promptly goes back into his yard.

"Tell me where you got all those flowers." I dig my fingers into my eye sockets in frustration.

Thea shrinks into herself like I've seen her do every time she's been caught. "Well, everyone has so many flowers. I didn't think anyone would miss them if I dug up one or two from each yard. I was smart and only pulled from two streets over, but then I saw your neighbor has those cute little flowers you can squeeze the sides together and they open and close to look like they're talking." She mimes squeezing the bud of the flower.

"They had Snapdragons?"

"Yes! Snapdragons. They're so pretty and fun." I rub at my temples for a moment, attempting to rid myself of the small headache forming.

"Trouble. You can't just take flowers from my neighbors!" I stand up and pace along the short cement pad of my porch. "I have to live here. Those people might walk by and notice they're missing a certain flower and oh look! I suddenly have the same one. It wouldn't take a genius to put it together."

She just throws a dismissive wave. "No one can prove your flower is the one they're missing."

"Except Craig and probably more than half my neighborhood who have security cameras!" This woman exhausts me.

"I don't live here. They won't know it's their flower because they won't see me." She grabs her bag and throws it over her shoulder and walks down the driveway.

"Where are you going? We aren't done talking about this!" I follow her to the sidewalk and step into her space. Our bodies are inches apart and the electricity I feel whenever we're this close zaps me.

"Yes, we are. I did something nice and you don't appreciate it. It's becoming a trend, so I'll leave and you'll let me!" She's talking through gritted teeth and her words are forceful, but she makes no move to actually leave. I take a step closer. She still doesn't move. I take one more step and I can feel her exhalations against the skin of my chin. I breathe in her incense scent. Intoxicating.

"Weren't you leaving?" I ask in a breathy voice. We lock gazes and I can't even bring myself to blink, but neither can she.

"I am," she whispers, her face coming even closer to mine. One more inch and we'll be touching. I reach out and place a hand on her hip.

"So, go." My other hand rests on the small of her back, pulling her body flush to mine. Her small breasts rub against my thin T-shirt and her rock-hard nipples poke through the fabric.

"I will." Her hands go to my shoulders and she tilts her chin, preparing for the inevitable. I eat up the distance left between us and crush my lips to hers. She tastes delicious, like fresh-picked strawberries. Her lips part, giving my tongue entry. We duel, each trying to gain the upper hand. Her hand snakes through the longer hair on top of my head and she tugs it roughly. I reach one hand down and grab her butt cheek, squeezing it harshly. It's not sweet and gentle. It's the buildup of days' worth of sexual frustration, all of it exploding into one kiss.

I don't know how long we stay there, but when a car honks as it drives past and a couple teenagers yell for us to get a room out their windows, we pull apart abruptly. She breathes just as heavily as I do, but her gaze is cast down to her feet rather than making eye contact like I'm attempting to do.

"I should go." She attempts to dart past me, but I grab her hips, halting her escape.

"Why do you have to go?" My cock could hammer nails right now and the last thing I want is for this annoying girl to leave.

"I need to get home." Thea still won't look at me and it's driving me crazy, so I tilt her chin up, forcing her to see me. When I see her expression, I drop my hands from where they're touching her. She looks more than upset, she looks disappointed.

"What's wrong?" I don't understand what happened. Just thirty seconds ago, we were devouring each other.

"Nothing, I just… I really need to go."

CHAPTER 9

Theodora

MY FIRST KISS. I JUST HAD MY FIRST REAL KISS. And it wasn't with my future husband. I'm such a fucked up mix of emotions. I look behind me and Law's still standing there, watching me. I touch my fingers to my lips to keep the sensation there. Tingly and warm, but with every step that takes me farther from him, the less I feel his lips. I drop my hand. It's no use.

I can't think of the implications right now. If Wen were to find out, or fuck, if Dad were to find out, I don't even know what would happen. I don't know if Wen has had experience, he probably has, innocence isn't expected of him, but it's more than expected from me, it's demanded. If a woman has even so much as touched her own self, she's considered dirty and impure. After that, no man will take her.

I walk out of his neighborhood and into mine. Well, my borrowed neighborhood. I don't belong anywhere. I've always loved that about our lifestyle, always seeing new places, having new experiences, but things are changing. Changing in my mind and in my heart because when I think of leaving Reno, when I think of marrying Wen, a crushing pain sears through my chest.

I see our compound in the distance. Indiana and Charity

chase each other along with Wen's younger sisters. Mom and Nuri chop vegetables for dinner and laugh at the kids who run around them. I smile as Charity runs past the cutting board and steals a carrot. Growing up like this was always so fun. Sure, there were chores, but mostly we just played, explored, and had fun. I don't think there is a better way to grow up. Everything we learned was taught through experience and will be helpful in the life we will live. No learning math we'd never use or doing science experiments that wouldn't help us survive in real life.

Mom sees me first and waves me over. I approach the prep area where dinner is on the agenda and give Mom a kiss on the cheek.

"Hey there, daughter, where you been?" It's not an unusual question, but considering where I've been, I instantly go on the defense.

"What? I can't leave? You want me to stay here all day and help you? I'm not married yet. I still have a few freedoms." Not only does my response shock Mom, but I shock myself. I hadn't intended to lash out. I need to get control of my emotions before everyone sees what I've been hiding.

"Of course not. I was just curious. I've never asked you to do any more than your fair share." Mom turns back to chopping, and guilt hits me hard. She didn't deserve that.

"Sorry. I guess I'm just having a bad day." I decide lying down in the trailer is a good idea so I can sort through everything before I lash out again. Before I can stomp off, Mom stops me with a hand to my arm.

"Nuri, would you mind if I took a little walk with my daughter?"

"It's fine, go. I've got this covered." Nuri takes the knife from Mom and shoos her away. I guess I'm going on a walk. I hang my bag up on one of the dead trees littered through our camp and catch up to Mom, who is out by the drainage ditch that runs through the property. Wild horses still roam this land and there is a herd of them taking an early evening drink. We don't get too close because they're skittish, but we walk along the opposite edge of the ditch in silence. Mom is the first to speak.

"What's going on with you?" she asks, straight to the point.

"I don't know. Maybe just wedding jitters." I steal a look at Mom and her face is hard, lips in a flat line and eyes trained on the ground. Mom is the most beautiful woman I know. While I have her wild and curly brown hair and gold eyes, she's voluptuous where I'm slight and flat-chested. She has all the exaggerated feminine curves I wish I had, but recently she has been tired. Lines are appearing around her eyes, lips, and on her forehead. Years of being in the sun have given her skin a thicker appearance.

"Maybe. But I know you, daughter. I think it's more."

I give her a partial truth. "Have you ever wanted to grow roots? Not move around. Find somewhere that belongs to you?"

She softens and she reaches over to grab my hand.

"It's crossed my mind, but I'll tell you what my mother told me. Roots don't always have to grow into the ground. Sometimes they grow between people. That can be what grounds you. Your family, your husband, your kids, they're what ties you to this world. You need not own the land beneath you to belong." She gives my hand a squeeze. "You aren't the first one to wonder if this life is for them and you won't be the last. What you need to think about is what you are willing to give up if you leave. Is it worth not seeing your family again?"

"Nothing is worth having my family disown me." If I

know one thing, it's this. She's right, my family is what makes me belong to this world. Mom stops our forward motion and holds me by my shoulders.

"I know accepting a husband your heart hasn't chosen is… difficult, but it's the only way. Your father and I wouldn't lead you astray. We know this is a good match. Wen's and your hearts will find their way to each other. You just have to give it a chance. The more you fight this, the more difficult it will be." I know she's right. Before I met Law, I wasn't happy to be marrying my friend, but I wouldn't fight it. Now I have felt the connection to Law and marrying Wen seems impossible.

The answer suddenly becomes so clear. I need to cleanse myself of Law. No more friendly meetups. No more forcing myself onto him. I need to focus on what is and not what I wish to happen. Besides, Lawrence will probably be happy to not have to deal with my particular brand of crazy anymore.

Mom and I walk back to camp and I help her finish preparing dinner. When I bring out large serving bowls of pasta and salad, I take in the sight before me with a new appreciation. Seven families, fifty-two people, are all here. Talking, laughing, arguing, being a family. I can't walk away from this on a hunch Law and I could make a go of it. I've known him for like two minutes. I've known these people my whole life. They've grown and multiplied, but so has their love.

I smile and set down the bowls. I take a seat next to Wen. He looks surprised, but smiles anyway and nudges my shoulder with his. This life may not be my dream, but I'm choosing it anyway. And there's power in that.

"I chose my dress this morning." I swirl a large forkful of noodles on my plate and shove them in my mouth. He laughs at me and takes his own bite.

"Is it white?" He barely gets out before we both start laughing.

"You'll just have to show up to find out." I attempt to flirt.

"Oh, I'll be there. I can't wait." His expression is hungry and I quickly avert my gaze.

"Eew, you two are gross." One of the other girls in our band, Kezia, is sitting across from us and I hadn't realized she was listening in.

"You're just jealous you aren't marrying me," Wen says with a puffed chest. I smack him in his overblown torso and he deflates, laughing. Kezia blushes.

"Kez, you'll be eighteen soon, right?" I ask. I haven't heard about any potential grooms for her. Usually rumors circulate when the girl turns seventeen.

"Yeah, next month." She lights up with excitement. Girls around here are usually excited to get matched. Most of the time it's with a group from a different area. Wen and I are not commonplace.

"Have your parents discussed who you'll marry?" I ask. Kez is more sheltered than I am. She rarely leaves the site and her parents have been stricter with her, not allowing her to even play with boys. The only time she's around the male species is at meal times. She has four older brothers and they guard her like everyone with a dick wants to bed her.

"They said they have a few ideas, but won't make any choices until my birthday." Her cheeks turn red and she looks down to her untouched dinner. "I'm sure it will be someone from another band since there are no single men of age in ours. Except Wen, and he's engaged, so..." She trails off. The blush spreads down her chest. This girl. Some guy will have a hard nut to crack if she can't even talk about getting married without turning into a tomato.

"Well, he's a lucky guy. Whoever he is," Wen compliments and stands up, grabbing his plate, stacking it with mine, and then holding his other hand out to help me up from the picnic table. I look at it for a long moment. "It's just a hand, Thea."

I grab it and we head over to the dishwash tub.

"Meet me by the ditch after dishes?" Wen points out to where a couple horses are grazing.

"Or you could help me with dishes and then I'd be done much sooner," I suggest.

"I've been working all day. Plus, that's a woman's work. You know how it is." He places our plates and utensils in the dirty dish tub and walks away. I roll my eyes. Woman's work, my ass. I'll bet Law would do the dishes with me. Scratch that, I'll bet he wouldn't allow me to do the dishes. He'd be too worried I wouldn't sterilize them properly. I smile. I'm sure I would get out of all the household chores with Law around.

I'd thank him in other ways. Ways that would reward both of us. I think back to our kiss and the warmth low in my belly returns. When our tongues met for the first time, I thought I was going to spontaneously combust. I wanted to melt but also shoot off like a rocket. I've never felt anything like that before. But as soon as the kiss ended, the guilt seeped in. I wonder what it will be like with Wen. Will we have chemistry too? I seriously doubt it.

Kezia, a few of the other older girls, and I work as a team to get the dishes done. The men sit around the fire, drinking and telling stories. Braithe is standing up and going on about something that happened when he was nineteen. "I went to take a piss in a truck stop bathroom. There weren't any urinals, so I went into a stall. I started hearing all kinds of noises from the stall next to me. Slurping and moaning. I realize, these dudes are fuckin' in the bathroom! I look down and see both their pants on the ground. I snatched up both their pants. I feel for wallets and they're both still in there! I hurry to zip up and take off out the bathroom door. Next thing I know, I have two dudes, naked as the day they were born, running after me. Both of 'em holding their junk and yelling some version of"— Braithe grabs hold of his manhood and starts running around the fire yelling—"come back with my wallet! My condoms are in there!"

The men all hoot and holler, laughing.

The women sit around a picnic table playing cards, using coins to bet on hands. Mom is a card shark. She may not have a formal education, but she can count cards with the best of 'em. Nuri must be getting her ass handed to her because she yells out, "You cheating bitch!"

I would worry about a fight, but I can hear the laughter in her voice. Mom reaches out over the table and sweeps all the coins into her pile.

The kids run around, playing hide and seek. Seven-year-old Charity finds another little boy and before he can run back to home, making himself safe, she throws a foot out to trip him. He goes skidding across the dirt, no doubt skinning his knees. Charity just laughs and skips off to find the next kid.

Watching all of this, I'm reminded for the hundredth time why I can't leave. Not having all this loud ruckus and chaos around me would be so sad. I just wish I could have this and get to know the man who has taken residence in my heart.

I walk out to the ditch where I agreed to meet Wen. I see him sitting on the water's edge and I take a seat next to him. The quiet settles in between us. It's not a comfortable silence, it's heavy and awkward. When we were kids, we never ran out of things to say. We were always plotting pranks or talking about what place we'd like to go next. This forced marriage has built a wall between us, solid and impenetrable. I hate it. I want my best friend back.

"Remember when we lived in Washington?" I smile at the memories of that place. "It was the only time we've ever lived in stick-built houses because the farmers had those tiny shacks for all the laborers."

"Yeah, I remember." Wen smiles too, picking at dead grass and throwing it into the water.

"Remember, as all the men would pick fresh ones off the trees, we would throw the rotten ones on the ground at them? They would assume apples were falling on their heads from the trees." We both chuckle at the memory. "You nailed Mr. Boswell in the head so hard he fell from his ladder. All we heard when we were running away was"—I clear my throat before using my best old man's voice to mimic Mr. Boswell—"'these fucking apples are possessed. They're the devil's fruit!'" We both laugh.

"Yeah, and no one would've known it was us if you hadn't felt so guilty about Mr. Boswell getting laid up with a sprained back that you told your mom." Wen looks at me and smiles. "Always have had a tough guy exterior but a squishy middle inside."

"I do not!" I defend, because the worst thing someone could call me is weak.

"You do so!" Wen shoves me with his shoulder, but I catch myself before I fall onto my side. "Remember? You made Mr. Boswell an apple pie and apologized. None of the rest of us kids would have done that."

"That's just being nice. Nice is not weak." I huff in irritation.

"It's a little weak." He smirks. "But that's what I like best about you. You're all brave and fierce in the moment, but afterward, when you've had time to think it through, you always do the right thing." The air grows thick between us and I can't help but feel like this conversation has drifted away from Mr. Boswell.

"Yeah, I guess you're right. I always do the right thing in the end." I agree.

"Whatever you're going through, it's okay. I see how tough you're being about marrying me. Pushing me away, not doing all the planning you should be. It's okay, Thea. I know you and, in the end, you'll do the right thing." Wen stands up. "Whatever you need to do for the next five months, do it. Whatever you have to do before you can settle down and be a wife, do it. Just remember who you are and what commitments you've made. If you do that, I know you'll be there on our wedding day, finally ready to be my wife." He holds a hand out to help me up, but now I'm annoyed at his assessment, so I stand up on my own.

"What are you talking about?" I know he can't be telling me I can be with other men. It would go against everything we have both been taught.

"I'm saying if you need to get into some trouble, run a couple cons, do it." He puts his hands on my shoulders and holds me there so we're eye to eye.

"And what are you going to be doing until we get married?" Now's as good a time as any to ask what I've been dying to know. Our gazes meet and it's the night sky or the question that makes his green eyes darken. His hands drop from my shoulders and he turns away from me, frustrated.

"You know women are held to a different set of rules and besides that, you don't get to question me like this. I'm not some pansy gorger who will let you walk all over me." He points a long finger right at me. "I've already been lenient with you. Even being engaged gives me authority over what you do and don't do. I'm telling you if you need to be irresponsible for this last bit, go ahead because after we're married, you'll be too busy raising kids and setting up a household of your own for all this nonsense you get yourself into." He drops his finger.

"You've been *lenient* with me? Did you really just say that?" Who the fuck does he think he is?

He crosses his arms. "You know the score, Thea."

"You're such an asshole. I hate you so much right now." My eyes narrow to pinpoints as I glare at him.

"Feeling's mutual, babe." He storms off, kicking up dirt and rocks along the way.

How did my best childhood friend turn out to be such a dick in adulthood? He thinks he can tame me? He thinks I'll calm down and be his little woman, popping out a herd of kids? That's not me.

I plop myself back down on the ground, not ready to face the crowd back at home. I hear clomps onto the soft dirt ground next to me and assuming it was Wen or someone else who wants to talk sense into me, I ask them to leave me alone. But when I look to my side, it's a beautiful horse. Just one, which is unusual because they always travel in groups. This horse is a light brown. A brief glance tells me she's a girl. She stumbles down the soft hillside until she reaches the slight stream. It's summer, so there isn't a lot of water to speak of, but enough for her to get a drink.

I watch her for a bit, jealous of her independence. Here is this wild and beautiful creature, no fences, no chains, just the freedom to roam and no one to hold her back. Then here I am, a wild creature also, but with invisible shackles around my ankles, making me a prisoner to my family, to tradition.

I climb down next to her, careful to not get too close or startle her. Her mouth moves along the water, drinking as much as she can, but her eye is trained on me. No doubt making sure there's no threat. I slowly reach a hand out. She doesn't jerk away or snarl at me, so I keep going until I meet her soft coat. All the wild horses out here are smaller than what I've seen at stables and a lot of them have ringworm, leaving scabby, hairless patches on their skin. I stay clear of the ones on her back in case they're painful.

I expect her to walk away once she's quenched her thirst, but she just stays there, her one eye still watching me closely. "What do you think, beast? You think it's okay to marry someone you don't want to?" Her hoof stomps on the ground and I take a small step back. "Yeah, I don't think so either. I'm officially out of options." Her hoof stomps again. "Oh, Lawrence?" I ask, as if I'm having a conversation with my best friend. "Yeah, he's great. Our kiss was epic. I want another one." Beast knickers and stomps her hoof again. "I think it's over, unfortunately. I don't want to string him along when nothing can come of it. Besides, he thinks I'm batshit crazy." I reach out my hand again and give her a rub. "And I guess I might be because I'm out here having a conversation with a freaking horse." I look over at her and feel bad for demeaning our time together, so I throw in, "No offense." She snorts in acceptance. "I'm exhausted. I'm going to head to bed. You all right here on your own?" Beast neighs and I walk away from her and straight to the trailer and to bed.

CHAPTER 10

Lawrence

I
T'S BEEN DAYS SINCE THEODORA WALKED AWAY, LEAVING me with tons of questions and a hard-on. That kiss was overwhelmingly intense. I've never lost myself like that before. Standing in front of my house, making out like a teenager. It's just not me. *But maybe you want it to be you*, a voice in my head says. I shake it off. If I don't have control over myself, I can't keep control over anything else in my life, and that can't happen.

So, just like every weekday, I wake up early and go for a run. It's the only time the heat isn't suffocating during the summer months. Back at home, I head to my weight room and put in an hour. I strip my clothes, place them in the washing machine, and head to the shower. As the hot water beats down on my back and I scrub every inch of my body, I try to release the tension of having Thea walk out of my life just as quickly, and outrageously, as she walked in.

I make it to work on time and get through my day by focusing on the numbers. The numbers that equal dollars. The dollars that come in and the dollars that go out. Holding onto the dollars we have, while also spending money that will bring in more profit. This work calms my frantic mind. It soothes any chaos that lurks from within. Some might call me a control freak, but really, it's just self-preservation.

"Sir, your three o'clock is here," Monica chirps over the telephone intercom.

I press the button to speak back. "Send him in."

Moments later, the person who would most be considered my friend, the COO of the casino, Mark, comes in.

"Heeeeeyyyyyy, sexy." He spreads the word out as he walks in the door, a huge smile on his face. "I've got a bone to pick with you." He sits in the chair on the other side of my desk and shakes a pointed finger at me.

"What are you wearing?" I try to take in his suit. Mark has an outlandish personality, and it comes out in his wardrobe. Today his shirt is a Victorian floral print with a maroon and black checkered tie, paired with maroon slacks.

"Just a little this and a little that." Mark brushes each side of his brow with a finger and a sway of his head. "Now, about that bone." He pauses to look down at where my crotch would be if the desk wasn't hiding it. "Not *that* bone. A proverbial bone."

"Yeah, I caught that." I'm sure he breaks the company's code of conduct daily just to get me to relax. Hasn't worked yet. I'll never admit it to him, but I enjoy his antics.

"A little bird told me you saved a spicy little thief from getting picked up by the police the other night." He crosses one long, thin leg over the other.

"A friend used my status with the company to get out of trouble, yes"—I clench my jaw—"and I don't want to talk about it."

"Okay, okay, no need to get your panties in a bunch. But like, if you did want to talk about it…" He trails off.

"Is there a reason you scheduled a meeting with me? Or did you just want to gossip like a teenage girl?" This is exhausting and I'm already drained from the aforementioned *spicy little thief.*

"Okay, yes. There is a real reason. I got your report about cutting a few positions. Since our fight about this last month was so much fun, I wanted to come and have a repeat performance." He's right. I did propose this last month, and we did have a fight over it. He won that round, but I plan to win this round, because I've seen too many of his supposed essential personnel meandering around the hotel like bored zombies.

Mark and I argue back and forth for an hour. Me showing him the numbers and video evidence to prove a few employees are not needed while he argued one slow day doesn't mean layoffs. Eventually we met in the middle and cut half of what I proposed, which is the number I was hoping for, but knew he would fight me. I'm getting what I want and he doesn't even know it.

"Don't take this concession to mean I'm happy, Mr. Grumpy," Mark says with another shake of his finger. As he walks toward my door, he stops and turns back to me. "Let's get drinks after work." Before I can even say no, he throws out, "Eight o'clock at the Sky Bar. See you there." My office door slams shut. As much as I want to text him to cancel before the echo of the slamming door stops, I don't. Maybe I need to change some things.

At eight o'clock on the dot, I'm at the trendy bar and searching for my flamboyant coworker. I spot him sitting at a small, round, bar height table, chatting with the waitress. As I approach, Mark jumps up and claps.

"Here he is! This is the one I was telling you about. Successful, handsome, and best of all, single!" He turns into Vanna White, displaying the prize to be won, and I roll my eyes, remembering why I don't go out with Mark. The waitress smiles and laughs a little, but she thankfully ignores the awkward situation Mark has put us in.

"What can I get you?" she asks, pulling out her notepad as I take a seat across from Mark.

"Vodka and soda. Top shelf, please. No twist." The waitress scribbles down my order and walks away.

"Booooring." Mark sing-songs and I just shrug. "So, now I've finally got you out of the office, spill the beans on the girl."

I should have known this is why he asked me to have drinks.

"There's nothing to tell. She was a friend. She's not anymore. That's it." I fold my arms and rest them on the table.

"Fine, I guess I'll have to get you drunk and ask again." He huffs like a petulant child.

"That'll be hard to do since I have a two-drink maximum when I go out." Not only is binge drinking unhealthy, it's also irresponsible on a work night. I'll already be out past my usual bedtime. No need to also contend with a hangover tomorrow.

"You're no fun and let me tell you, you are someone who needs some fun," he scolds. It's something Thea would say. If she were here, she'd be doing shots with Mark and then dancing all night. My mind drifts to the first time I saw Thea dance by the bonfire. I shake my head. She's gone and there's nothing I can do about it.

"Yeah, well. I'm not known for fun. You should know that by now." The waitress brings me my boring drink. It looks and tastes like a representation of my life. Bland and stable.

"That doesn't always have to be you. You can let go once in a while." Mark tries to reason with me.

"Yeah, maybe." I wonder if it's why Thea disappeared. Was I too boring? Too reserved?

"Maybe? Definitely!" Mark takes my drink out of my hand and in its place, he hands me some kind of electric blue concoction. "First things first, we call this drink an A.M.F." He quirks an eyebrow as I take a sip. At first it just tastes fruity, but when the alcohol hits my chest, I exhale audibly, sure if a match was lit, I would breathe fire.

"What does A.M.F. stand for?" I choke out, thumping a fist into my chest.

"Adios Motherfucker." Mark pushes the drink back up to my mouth and I take another sip. It goes down much easier this time.

Three A.M.F.s and a couple hours later, Mark has gotten the whole Thea story out of me. I'm not proud I caved so easily, but I have no one to blame but myself. And the A.M.F.s. Definitely blaming the A.M.F.s.

"I think you should go see her." Mark encourages.

"No, definitely not. Right?" Fuck me. When did asking Mark for advice start sounding like a good idea?

"You definitely should go see her." Mark snaps toward the waitress to get her attention. Over the course of the evening, I've somehow told the waitress, Crissy, about Thea as well. I'll be so ashamed tomorrow.

"Yeah, babe?" she calls out loudly over the music.

"We need the check. Lawrence over here is going to go get his girl." He smiles mischievously.

"Yay! Please come back and tell me what happens." She places her hands in a prayer pose, begging me.

"I'm not, I mean, no. I'm not gonna go there. I can't, right?" I slur out. Why do I keep asking for advice on this?

"You have to! She's obviously into you and just feels like you were judging her." Crissy tries to reason with me, and maybe she's right. There's a common thread in all the tragedies of my love life, and that's me.

"Okay." I slam my hands down on the table and stand up. "I'll do it." Mark and Crissy clap enthusiastically. I'm sloshed, but I manage to stumble out the door, leaving Mark with the check. I'll have to reimburse him tomorrow.

I may be drunk, but I'm not stupid, so I take an Uber to the dead end before the dirt road leading to Theodora's place. I'm still hyped up on all the encouragement from Mark and Crissy, so this still feels like a good idea.

I turn on my cell's flashlight to prevent falling on my face, but with the way the world is spinning, that might happen anyway. I stumble down the dirt road, noticing lights still lit on most of the trailers. A large rock trips me, probably on purpose, to warn me about what a terrible idea this is, but I regain my balance and shuffle on.

That's when I think I see her, or maybe there's two of her. I pause long enough to lose my double vision. She's sitting at a wooden picnic bench with two young girls, maybe her sisters? There's a row of candles down the table and the illumination is enough I can make out her face. Her hair is being held back by a scarf, the ends of it going over her shoulder along with her long hair. She's smiling hugely while throwing cards down on the table. The two girls are laughing at something Thea has said, and while I can't make out what it was, just hearing her raspy voice makes me smile.

I flip my flashlight off as I get even closer, but still under the cover of night so she doesn't know I'm here. Near enough to hear their conversation, though. I've never been a creeper, but it seems to happen frequently with this girl.

"You're fucking cheating!" The smallest one accuses Thea. She can't be more than ten. A potty mouth must run in the family.

"Did not! You just suck at poker." Thea gathers all the cards and starts shuffling.

"When you get married, will you still play cards with us every night?" the third girl asks. It takes a second for the question to register, but I definitely heard the word *married*. If Thea's going to marry anyone, it will be me. *What the fuck am I thinking? She and I aren't anywhere near marriage.* I shake my head and try to make sense of what's going on.

Thea smacks the girl on the back of the head hard, judging by the echo the smack made. "Of course, cuntster. Get it, cunt and sister. Cuntster."

Thea laughs are her own joke, but her two sisters cup their hands around their mouths and yell, "Boo!"

I can't keep up between the crass language from kids and the talk of marriage, it's just too much. This was a mistake, a huge fucking mistake. I turn around to leave, but before I can make my escape, another rock comes out of nowhere and trips me. This time I'm unable to catch myself. My phone and I go crashing to the ground, loudly.

"Shit. Shit. Shit," I curse under my breath. I crawl on all fours, searching for where my phone ended. Fuck it, I'll just get a new one. I stumble to my feet, but before I can get too far, I hear the voice I can't get out of my head.

"Law? Is that you?"

I slowly turn around, praying for this to not be happening, but it is. Thea is standing there, flashlight aimed directly at me with two smaller versions of herself on either side of her. Fuck, she's gorgeous. She has on short jean shorts and some kind of lacy cream tank top that ends before her shorts begin, giving me a peek at her flat midriff.

"Oh, hey. Uh, Thea. Weird to run into you like this." I attempt to come up with a believable story, but my liquored up brain can't think quickly enough. "I was just, uh, taking a walk," I say, scratching the back of my neck, and I'm pretty sure I'm swaying. Either that or the earth is moving. Wait, the earth is always moving. That must be it.

Thea smirks knowingly. "Oh, really? At midnight? On a Thursday?"

"I couldn't sleep?" I try.

Thea looks at each sister. "Indiana, Charity, give me a minute."

"No fucking way, we're not leaving you here with this *gorger*," the smallest one says. Quite the little sailor, that one.

"I'll be fine. Now get lost." Thea points back toward the trailers and the two girls march away, both cursing and kicking dirt. When they're out of earshot, Thea turns back to me.

"Wanna try that again?" She places a hand on each hip and tilts her head. Her lips are pursed and I just want to be kissing them again. I blow out a breath and decide the truth is all my drunken mind is capable of right now.

"I had a bit to drink tonight"—I hold up my thumb and forefinger, spacing them apart an inch to prove it was only a little—"and somewhere between sobriety and this"—I motion up and down my body—"I decided it was a good idea to confront you."

"Confront me?" Her brows furrow in confusion.

"I kissed you and you disappeared, like vanished. Into thin air. I mean not literally, because no one can really vanish, but—"

"Law! Focus!" She cuts me off. "How much did you drink? You smell like a distillery." Her nose wrinkles up.

"It doesn't matter. I just came to find out why, but then I find you here, talking about getting married. Why are you goin' to get married, Thea? You could marry me. Don't marry anyone else." I stumble forward a little and Thea grabs hold of my arm to steady me.

"You really are drunk, huh? And for the record, that wasn't how I wanted you to find out." Thea releases my arm and looks at the ground.

"So, you are getting married? And not to me?" I'm an idiot. This whole night has been a mistake. I need to get away, but my stomach decides this is a good time to revolt against all the alcohol I drank. I get a few steps in before I bend over and spew the entire contents of my stomach.

As the last of the retching hits me, a hand is on my back and another is on my arm. I try to shake free. I don't want her hands on me. She has utterly turned my life upside down and there is nothing I want more in this moment than to go back to before Thea.

"Law, you need help. You're too drunk. Let me get you home." She doesn't touch me again, but she stays with her arms out, I'm assuming in case I trip again.

"I don't need your help. I need the opposite of your help." It comes out as one long, slurred word. My body feels heavy and my head is foggy. I need my bed. I spit out the last of the vomit and look around. Trying to decipher the direction I need to go to get home.

I must have chosen poorly, because Thea calls out, "You're going the wrong way."

"Yeah, well, I'll find it on my own." I'm acting like a child. Apparently, that's what I've been reduced to tonight. I look around and pick a different direction and try going that way. I only make it a few shaky steps before Thea ducks under my arm and forces it over her shoulders.

"Let me get you home. After that, I'll leave and I won't come back." Her arm is around me and she has a hand on my chest. I'm too tired and worn out to keep fighting, so I nod in acceptance.

Thea turns me in the correct direction, only stopping for her to crouch down and pick up my phone. She alerts me to rocks I need avoid and when I drag my feet, she reminds me to keep moving. I know she can't be having an easy time holding some of my body weight, because she grunts and groans and curses a few times before I recognize my street.

We struggle through the last bit of the walk and up at my front door. "Where's your keys?" Thea breaks her hold on me and I lean my body against the doorjamb.

"Pocket." A one-word answer is all I'm capable of.

She reaches in and when her hand gets close to my dick, I jump and yank her hand out.

"I'll get the key." I pull the key free and attempt to un-lock my door, but the damn thing won't fit in the hole. Thea reaches for the key. "I've got it." I shove her hand away, but the fucker just won't fit. Maybe it's the wrong one, or the wrong house? I look the house up and down. Looks familiar.

Thea takes advantage of my momentary distraction and snags the key. "Just let me do it." She shoves my shoulder slightly with her own and I barely catch myself before I fall. "Sorry," she squeaks out when I've righted myself.

She must have chosen the right key because the door opens up with no problems. She reaches over and forces me to lean into her again as she gets me inside. The room is dark, so I flip a light on as we pass the switch. The clean lines and modern furniture of my living room and open concept kitchen come into view. She tries to walk farther into the room, but I stop her.

"Shoes." I kick my own off and point down to hers. Her nose pinches, but she removes her shoes.

She helps me to the couch and deposits me there. I lie down and throw an arm over my eyes. The lights are just too bright and I have a massive headache already brewing behind my eyes. I vaguely hear her opening and closing cabinets, turn-ing water on and off, and then I feel her sit next to where my body is lying prone on the couch.

"Law, sit up for just a second to take some painkillers and drink some water." I open my eyes a sliver and can see her holding the water and a closed fist around the pills.

I pull myself to sitting just long enough to swallow the medicine and guzzle the entire glass of water before I lie back down and pull a pillow over my face. I fall asleep to the sound of Thea humming a song I don't recognize. Her husky voice lulls me deeper and deeper until I'm gone.

I wake with a jolt, sitting up quickly only to be struck with a massive, sharp, shooting pain in my head. I lie back down and moan. After the blinding ache subsides enough for me to try again, I sit up. Slowly this time. Noting I'm on the couch and not in my bed. I scan my surroundings and try to get my bearings. What the fuck happened last night?

I remember going for drinks with Mark. I ended up drinking his disgusting, blue—my stomach lurches. I jump from the couch and run to my bathroom. Bile and saliva are all that's left to come up while my stomach twists and squeezes. A hand on my back startles me and I sit up.

"Theodora?" I take one look at her and the memories of last night flood back into my mind. I moan and lean back over the toilet. The clusterfuck of events turns my stomach even more.

"Do you need anything? Can I bring you some water?" Her hand gently pats my back.

"Just go. Please," I say into the toilet, making my words echo. Her hand leaves my back and the bathroom door clicks shut. It's only then I feel safe to pull my head out of the bowl and flush. I shakily stand up and spend a long while showering and brushing my teeth.

Half human again, I leave the en suite with a towel tied around my waist and come face to face with the girl I can't escape.

"I told you to leave." I don't give her a chance to respond before I'm inside my walk-in closet. I grab a pair of gray sweatpants and a T-shirt. Letting my towel drop, I quickly dress. Back in my room, I find Thea fucking sitting on my bed. "Why are you still here?" I know I'm being gruff, but especially after last night, we have nothing left to say to each other.

"I wanted to make sure you were okay. You were such a mess last night, and I was worried you'd get sick again in your sleep." Her head is down, her fingers are in her hair, and her body droops.

"Well, thank you, but as you can see, I'm just fine." I walk out of my bedroom and into the living area. A quick look around tells me she must have slept in the very uncomfortable chair next to the couch because a blanket from my closet has been tossed on the floor next to it. I feel like an ass to treat her this way when she went out of her way to get me home and make sure I was okay.

I sigh and go into my kitchen. I make a pot of coffee and while it's brewing, I take more painkillers and down a glass of water. I hear a stool scrape along the tile. Why won't she leave? She made it very clear last night nothing could come of us because she's getting fucking married.

"I was hoping I could talk to you." Her voice is so small and un-Thea-like.

"I think you said enough last night." I reach for a coffee mug and hold it up to her, my eyebrows raised in question. She nods, almost imperceptibly. I remove a second mug and pour two steaming cups of coffee. The aroma sharpens my hazy mind. I set one mug in front of her and prop my hip against the counter, the other mug in my hand.

"I need to explain a few things to you. About me. About my family." She wraps her hands around the mug and takes a sip. She smacks her lips together and mock gags, her normal dramatic self returning and despite my efforts, I smile slightly. "I'm sorry. I thought I could be a grown up and drink this black, but I can't. Where's your sugar? And do you have cream?"

I point in the direction of the sugar bowl and open the fridge, pulling out a quart of milk. "Milk will have to do. I don't have cream."

"Anything will do, thanks." She dumps at least two tablespoons into her cup and then enough milk to make the coffee a light tan shade before bringing it to her lips and taking another sip. She puts away the milk and sugar and goes back to the stool, sitting down.

"Better?" I question before sipping more of my black coffee.

"So much better. I don't know how you drink that." She wrinkles up her cute little nose and points at my cup. "Anyway, like I was saying. I need to explain." She sighs and takes a deep breath, letting it in through her nose and out through her mouth. "My family has certain customs that are outdated, and one of those customs is arranged marriage."

I shake my head. Of all the excuses, an arranged marriage was never one I considered.

"Are you serious?" I put my mug down and place my hands flat on the counter. Needing the stability to hold me up.

"Very." She cringes. "Very serious. I realize it's strange to outsiders, but to us? It's just normal. Most of the time, girls are even married before they're eighteen, so I'm actually lucky they let me and Wen wait."

"Wen? That's the name of the guy you're marrying?"

"Yes. Wen and I, we grew up together. He's part of our band. Our families believe they're doing us a favor by matching us so I can stay with them." She shrugs her shoulders.

"Do you want to marry this Wen guy?" I still can't believe

arranged marriage exists these days in America. I assumed it was reserved for places like India.

"No." Her voice is brittle and I think she might cry, but she takes a steadying breath instead. "Wen is a friend, my best friend actually. Or he was. Before the whole marriage thing. Now, I can't even bring myself to look at him."

"You're eighteen, Trouble. Why don't you just tell them no and do your own thing? You're young, but you're an adult. No one can make you do something you don't want to do." I walk around the island she's sitting at and take the stool next to her, spinning her stool to face mine. I tip her chin up to look at me.

"You don't understand." A single teardrop falls down her cheek, leaving a dark streak behind. "If you denounce your marriage, they kick you out. I have no choice. They would shun me. I wouldn't be able to see my sisters and brothers anymore, let alone my mom and dad. My family, they're everything to me."

I cup her cheeks in my hands and wipe away the tear streak with my thumbs. "I could help you. If you wanted to leave, I would help."

"You couldn't give me my family back," she whispers, pulling my hands off her face and standing up. "I need to go. I'm probably in a lot of trouble for last night."

"Do you want me to come with you?" I stand up too and follow her to the door. "I could explain what happened."

A small smile appears on her sad but beautiful face. "No. Nothing you could say would make it better. You're a gorger to them and not to be trusted."

She steps into her shoes and then wraps her arms around my neck. I return her hug and squeeze her tightly to me from around her waist. I pull back slightly.

"I want to kiss you. Just one more time." I feel her warm

breath on my skin. She nods her agreement and then my lips are on hers. My hangover disappears as endorphins flood my body. We're so close, I can feel her heart beating from her chest through mine. Our lips nip and suck at each other until her tentative tongue peeks out. I accept it greedily into my mouth before it swirls with my own. I can taste her sugary coffee and it makes me smile against her lips. Only for a split second, though, because I need more.

More of her and me together.

More of this lie.

More of everything she gives me.

I gently bite down on her lower lip and give it a slight tug before placing my forehead against hers so we can catch our breaths. This only lasts for a moment before we devour each other again. Thea gets brave and sucks my tongue into her mouth, making me moan. She wraps a leg around my hip and I catch it with my hand, holding her in place. She grinds into me and I can feel the heat of her pussy through the fabric of our clothes. It makes me wish for all the things I can never have with her.

One of my hands goes into her hair, tangling the strands between my fingers as our lips and tongues move together. Her own hands move up and down my back, her fingernails dragging with each movement. I regret having a shirt on. I want to feel those fingernails digging into my skin. I want her to write her desire into my flesh so I have something to remember her by.

All too soon, she removes her thigh from my hip and pushes herself out of my arms. My head falls down, my arms drop to my sides, and my eyes close. Thea and I are a paradox. There isn't a world in which we make sense.

I don't look up as I hear the door open.

I don't breathe as she walks out the door.

I don't move as the door clicks shut.

I just hold onto every sensation of her being mine, even if it was all a sham.

You know the craziest part of this whole thing? I don't think she brushed her teeth this morning, and I don't care in the least.

CHAPTER 11

Theodora

I T'S ONLY A TEN-MINUTE WALK FROM LAW'S HOUSE TO our camp when I cut through the neighborhoods. I spend that time trying to come up with an excuse for last night. I don't give myself a chance to think about Law and our goodbye kiss. If I do, I'll just cry and I can't show back up at home with red, swollen eyes.

The only thing that will save me is if Indiana and Charity kept their traps shut about me leaving with a man. A gorger. Chances are about fifty/fifty. If they stayed out of trouble while I was gone, then I doubt they said anything. However, if they did something naughty and are trying to get out of punishment, then they most definitely threw me under the bus.

The morning is hot and suffocating. Sweat drips down my back and saturates my shirt. When I finally see our group of trailers, I'm drenched and parched. No one is milling about, but it's only 8:00 a.m. The men heading to work are the only ones awake at this hour.

I open the door to our trailer as quietly as I can, sticking my head in first to see if anyone is awake. The curtain is still drawn around my parents' bed, their only semblance of privacy. I see two small lumps in the loft I share with my sisters. I don't see my brothers anywhere, but that's not abnormal. I tiptoe inside and shut the door silently. I slowly climb the ladder to the loft, knowing exactly which rungs are squeaky, and I avoid them. I've just gotten to the top when the curtain opens and Dad hauls himself off his bed.

Dad is a burly man. He's a good amount overweight, but it's all settled in his belly. Romani men tend to be hairy and Dad fits the bill. He has hair growing out of his ears, a thick fur on his back, chest, and shoulders, even his toes have a layer of dark growing around them.

Dad is in his underwear and as he stands up, he scratches himself and farts. He hasn't noticed me and I'm trying not to gag as I take the final step up to my bed. I cover myself up and watch as he makes a batch of instant coffee to put into his thermos. Mom adores Dad, everything about him. She even likes the body hair. I once overheard her telling Nuri about how it makes him feel manlier. So fuckin' gross.

I try to imagine Wen when he's older. I can only guess he'll start growing a forest of fur at some point. Just because he doesn't have it now doesn't mean it won't happen someday. Maybe it already has and he manscapes. A shudder runs down my back.

Dad pours the coffee into his thermos and gets dressed in his work uniform. Old, worn-in jeans and a T-shirt with pit stains. He pulls a clean pair of socks from the bin under their bed and sits on the plastic-covered couch to put them on, along with his shoes.

"You just going to watch me get ready for work, or are you going to do some talking?" His deep voice is trying to stay quiet, but it still rumbles through the air. Dad's eyes meet mine and I know I'm busted. I huff and climb down the stairs. Dad jerks his head toward the door and I follow him out. We sit down on two plastic lawn chairs by our door.

"Wanna tell me where you were last night?" He has an

eyebrow raised up high as he leans down, resting his arms on his thighs.

"Did Indie and Char say anything?" I need to know what kind of lie to tell.

"Nope. I was in bed before them." Okay, good. That gives me a good direction to go.

"I met someone a few days ago, and she needed some help last night. I crashed at her place when we finished." I keep my voice steady so I don't expose myself.

"That right?" Dad stands up, thermos and keys in hand. "Well, don't get too comfortable hanging out with a gorger. I don't like it."

"I won't, Daddy. It was just this one time." I peer up at him, searching his face for any kind of suspicion, but there's none.

"I'll see you later." Dad gets in the van and moments later Braithe and Wen stumble out of their trailer, both bleary-eyed and not awake yet. Braithe hauls himself into the passenger seat and Wen opens the door to the back, but before he gets in, he looks at me. I offer a small smile and wave. Wen just stares before shaking his head and getting into the vehicle.

What was that about? Maybe he knows I was out all night. Maybe Indie and Char got to him. I'll have to interrogate them when they wake up.

The van drives away after a few more men load up. I go back in the trailer, then climb into the loft and under the covers. My tiniest sister curls into me and I lay an arm over her, kissing the top of her head and breathing in the smell of youth and freedom.

I finally allow the emotion of leaving Law to flood my mind. Every time I think I have flushed him from my life, we find our own crazy way back to each other. Like magnets drawn together. I'm the South Pole, and he's the North.

Completely opposite in every way, but an inexplicable attraction neither of us can explain.

I think that's over now. We have hit the end of our path together now that he knows my whole truth. I allow the tears to fall. I pull my sister even closer and let her comfort to ease my mind. I'm doing this for them. It's not just me who would suffer the consequences of my actions. Being exiled would leave all four of them heartbroken. So I let it all out, and when the exhaustion becomes too hard to fight, I fall asleep.

Later that day, Indiana and Charity confirm Wen saw them walk home alone last night. He asked who I was talking to, and they told him the truth. The little shitheads. Luckily, they don't know Law's name or anything about him. They could only tell him he was a gorger. There are hundreds of thousands of male outsiders around here, so Law will remain a mystery.

"Who the fuck was he?" Wen asks me for the millionth time. I'm furiously scrubbing dishes after he gave me the third degree throughout dinner.

"I don't have to answer to you. He was just a friend. He needed help, so I helped him. That's it, now stop asking." I, not accidentally, spill a bowl full of dirty, soapy water down the front of him. "Oops, better go clean yourself up."

"Thea, this isn't over. You're about to be my wife. You can't just go around with other men." He storms off to his trailer and slams the door.

"Good riddance," I huff, rolling my eyes. I lose myself in the work of washing the dishes, ignoring everyone and everything around me. My fingers prune as I scrub and when I finish, I turn my bin over to dry and toss the apron I had on.

I look around to see what everyone is doing. I see Freedom chasing Indie, Char and a few other girls around with a dead squirrel. They're squealing in horror while Free just laughs and keeps chasing them. I look for Leander, not spotting him in the chaos all around the compound.

Curious about his whereabouts, I walk out into the field I had found him in days ago. It's still light outside, and it doesn't take me long to spot him. He has the same blanket outstretched. He's on his stomach facing away from me. If I didn't know what I was looking for, I would think he was napping. But I know there's a book under his arms and he's reading intently. He hears my approach and quickly covers the contraband.

"Want to tell me what you're hiding under the blanket?" I sit down next to him, outstretching my legs and leaning back into my hands behind me. Leander is a cute young man. His dark hair is long and flops in front of his face a lot. He has freckles on his nose and cheeks and his long eyelashes frame his eyes that are more green than gold like mine. He's at that point where he resembles a man more than a boy. His baby cheeks have thinned and his jaw line is more pronounced. He has prominent muscle from hard physical labor since he was old enough to swing a hammer. Dad had to show him how to shave last year because sporadic facial hair had grown in patches on his lower cheeks and on the outside of his upper lip. He'll make some Romani girl very happy.

"Want to tell me who you were out with all night last night?" he returns. We're playing this game again.

"I will if you will." I'm desperate for someone to talk to, and if we both have something to hide, my secret will be safe with him.

"O-okay." His stutter tells me he's unsure. "But you have to go first."

I sigh. Where do I even begin?

"I have been hanging out with a gorger. He kissed me and I like him a lot." Verbal diarrhea flies out of my mouth. Leander smacks a palm to his forehead as shock spreads across his face.

"Thea! What the fuck were you thinking?" he whisper shouts.

I throw myself flat onto my back and groan.

"I wasn't thinking. That's the problem." I drape an arm over my face.

"You have to break it off. If Mom and Dad, or hell, if Wen finds out you kissed a gorger, you could be exiled. That's forever, Thea. You can't come back from that." His tone is stern, and he is telling me things I already fucking know and it causes my temper to rise.

I sit up quickly and look him dead in the eyes. "You don't think I know that? I've already broken it off. A couple times actually."

"Who is he?" His curiosity is piqued.

"His name is Lawrence. He works at The Grand Royals Casino."

"How'd you meet?"

"Funny story. Remember the guy you stole the wheels off his car at the beach?" A soft smile plays at my lips.

"You're kidding!" Leander's eyebrows pop up.

"Nope," I say, popping my P.

Leander shakes his head in disapproval. "It better be over for real."

"Okay!" I snap.

"Okay!" he snaps back.

"So, what's your secret?" I arch a brow at him. He doesn't answer right away. He just stares at the lump of the book below him while his hands split blades of grass into hairline pieces before he tosses them back into the field.

"Well, you know how Freedom and I dropped out of school when we each hit eighth grade?" He squints over at me, the sun hitting his eyes. "I, uh, never really dropped out."

"What? How? Why?"

"I mean, I dropped out of the high school we were going to, but I enrolled in online high school instead." Leander pulls the text book from under the blanket. I read the letters on the book P-H-Y-S-I-C-S. It's a word I don't recognize. "I've been going to the library during the day if I can, or in the evenings, whenever I can get there."

"Wouldn't Mom and Dad have to sign you up for that?" We both know neither one of them would do that. They've always told us an education is a waste. The only reason they allow the boys to go is because they need to know how to read well and do basic math for the jobs they'll be doing.

"I kinda forged their signatures." Leander cringes. "I knew they wouldn't agree, but Thea, I'm good at school. Really good, actually." He sits up straight and turns his whole body to me, excitement filling his voice. "I get fantastic grades and my on-line advisors say I have a chance at getting into a good college."

I smile at my brother and rest a hand on his knee. "That's amazing, Leander. I'm proud of you." I pull my hand away and set it in my lap. "I just don't know how realistic it is for you to go to college. You know what Mom and Dad would say. This is uncharted territory for us. No one has ever gone to college."

He sighs. "I know, but I'm in my senior year and I need to tell them soon so I can start applying for colleges."

"What do you think they'll say?" I take the book from him and skim through the pages. It's all just a blur of letters and numbers. I don't understand any of it.

"I hope they'll want what's best for me, but realistically, it'll be a fight." He takes the book from my hands and hides it under the blanket again.

"Does Danior know about this?" Danior is his best friend and I'm curious if Leander has shared his secrets with him. The two of them have been especially close the last few years, camping away from the compound at night. I have my suspicions, but I would never vocalize them. None of my secrets would even compare to that one.

"No. I don't think he would understand." He runs a hand through his hair. "Apparently he's leaving to be married anyway." His legs draw up to his chest and he wraps his arms around them, resting his chin on his knees.

"Well, I'm here for you, brother. Whatever you need." I give him a soft smile.

"I know. I'm here for you too. I want to be, at least. But if you get caught with a gorger, Thea, I won't be able to help."

I nod at his words. I wouldn't expect him to stand up for me in that situation. Getting caught with a man who isn't my husband or fiancé and not one of us is one of the worst things I can do in my parents' eyes.

CHAPTER 12

Lawrence

MARK STOPPED BY MY OFFICE WHEN I SHOWED up to work late and hungover after my drunken night. He didn't even ask questions. He took one look at me, gave me a pat on my back, and walked right back out of my office.

That was weeks ago and since then, I've become obsessed with working. Again. The only thing I can get to make sense are the numbers. Everything my employees hand in to me, things I wouldn't normally question, are double and triple checked by me. When I go home, after everything has been organized and reorganized, I play with the stock market. I research companies I don't even plan on investing with, but at this point, I'm doing whatever I can to keep my mind busy.

This morning started out no different. Run, coffee, shower, fifteen minutes to work. Park my car and walk through the casino toward my office. Only now, instead of paying attention to how to cut operating costs, I look at every woman I encounter. Hoping to see one with wild hair, throwing around sass like confetti.

I see her in every young woman who passes. I don't understand how I found myself in this situation. Sure, I've seen attraction at this level. But those were just movies or TV shows. I've never seen a grown ass man pine after forbidden fruit in real life and if it weren't happening to me, I would be disgusted. Life is about getting ahead and challenging yourself, not going after a young girl who you have no business being with.

It's then I spot her. She's wearing cowboy boots and a white dress that billows around her as she moves through the casino. Her hair is down and I fixate on the way it bounces and swirls. Fifty feet, that's the entire distance separating us. I pick up my pace, desperate to get closer. She weaves in and around the crowds with purpose, but I gain on her. I get a whiff of incense and it makes me smile. When I'm finally close enough, I reach out and grab her upper arm, halting her forward momentum.

"Thea," I call over the noise of people and slot machines. She turns and instead of gold eyes, I'm met with boring brown ones. Instead of a cute button nose, this girl has a sharp pointed one. And instead of full, pink lips, this girl's mouth is a straight line. "I'm sorry. I thought you were someone—" I don't finish. I just turn and walk the other way, back to my office where there are numbers waiting for me. Formulas for me to write. Spreadsheets waiting for me to input numbers.

I have to get her out of my mind.

CHAPTER 13

Theodora

"INDIE, I BROUGHT YOU SOMETHING." I hold my hands behind my back.

Indie holds a single finger to her chin and closes one eye. "Hmmm, I pick this one." She reaches out and taps my right hand. I bring both of my hands out front and open them, the right revealing a new button.

"I love it! Thank you, Thea!" She grabs the button from my hand and inspects it. "*The Biggest Little City in the World*," she reads. She removes her jean jacket and searches for an empty space. When she finds a suitable place to put the button, she attaches it and then puts the jacket back on.

Indie collects buttons from all the different places we have been. Mom used to do the same thing, but Indie spent so much time going through Mom's buttons. She gave them to her and told her to continue the tradition.

She has forty-seven buttons, well, forty-eight now. They aren't the enamel pins you see people buying these days. The buttons she collects are the old-fashioned, steel pin-back type. Her jacket must weigh two pounds extra just in buttons, but she loves it.

"I didn't have one for Reno. I could never find the perfect one." She pulls the lapel of the jacket out and looks at the button again. "This one might be my favorite." She gives me a hug and meanders off, admiring the button as she goes. I smile, knowing I made her day.

I grab a few carrot sticks Mom was cutting up, accepting the hand slap she gave me before I could escape.

"Those are for dinner!" she scolds. I just smile while chomping. I grab a bottle of water and make my way to the picnic bench closest to our trailer. Sitting down, I eat my snack and watch the activity going on around me. I wonder what Law would think if he spent a day here. He would hate it. The chaos, the dirt, the inability to sterilize. I smile, but my heart hurts.

The first couple days after I left Law, standing there, a-fucking-gain, I spent playing my guitar and singing on each street corner closest to The Grand Royals Casino. Hoping to get a peek at Law.

It didn't happen.

What did happen was a sixty-five-dollar busking without a permit ticket, but lucky for me, I don't exist. I gave him a false name and went on my way. Poor Kristi Webster, she'll get that ticket and be so confused.

After that, I spent my days at the library with Leander and did some good old Internet stalking, but my boring, stable Law had no social media profiles anywhere. I stooped to reading his LinkedIn profile and finding his headshot on the casino's website.

Eventually I had to accept this is my life, and I went back to doing what I do best. Conning people. Only now it wasn't for the money, it was for the distraction. Dad took me to festivals. We did some old-fashioned pickpocketing and walked away with close to fifteen hundred dollars. It was nice to spend some bonding time with Dad. We hadn't done that in a long time.

That's where I got Indie's button. There was a vendor selling all sorts of Reno memorabilia to all the vacationers. It wasn't hard to pocket the small button. I also pocketed a Grand Royals Casino magnet, but that's for me. Just a little something to remember Law by.

"Thea!" someone calls my name, and it snaps me out of my fog. Wen is sitting in front of me. "I've said your name like five times."

"Sorry. Just thinking." I go back to munching on my carrots.

"Hopefully you're thinking about the wedding." His tone is reprimanding, and it grates on my nerves.

"I have time." This is what I say every time someone bothers me about wedding plans.

He slams his hands down on the table, causing me to jump. "You have four months. You've wasted two months already. How much longer are you going to wait?"

"Chill the fuck out, Wen. I don't see you doing anything to help plan." His moods are so hot and cold lately. I never know who I'll be talking to.

"I'll chill the fuck out when you start at least pretending to want this marriage." His voice is loud enough everyone who was milling about is now staring.

I lean over the table and whisper, "I'll start pretending to want this marriage when you turn into a decent fucking human being." I don't even sit back down before his hand is around my throat. He brings my face within inches of his.

"Have you ever taken a second to think maybe *you're* the fuckin' problem here, Thea?" Spittle hits my face. I clutch onto his hand, trying to pry it from my throat, but it's too tight and I'm not getting enough air.

"Hey, hey, hey!" Kezia's dad, Mr. Boswell, sets a hand on Wen's shoulder. The contact snaps Wen out of it. He releases me and steps back.

"This is your fuckin' fault." He points an accusatory finger at me, kicks the wooden table, and storms off.

"You all right, kid?" Mr. Boswell asks me.

I'm still trying to catch my breath, my hands gently holding my throat, and tears blur my vision. I give him a shaky nod. He gives me a sympathetic smile and walks away. When he's gone, Charity runs up to me, her tiny arms wrapping around my waist.

"I didn't know what to do." Her face is smooshed into my stomach, muffling her voice. It's not that Wen's behavior is all that unusual within our group. The men around here are treated like the kings of their castles and women are treated like, well, less than that. Occasionally, one of the daughters, or even a wife now and then, will do something that earns them a backhand, but not in my family. Dad has never laid a hand on any of us girls or Mom. Both of them are terrible at punishing us, and we have pulled some shit that probably was deserving of some punishment. Mom and Dad have always just found humor in our mistakes.

"It's okay, Char. You did the right thing by not getting involved." I pat her head soothingly.

I look around to see who else witnessed what just happened, and the rose-colored glasses I've been using get crushed to the ground. Everyone is going on like nothing happened. They peer at me through their periphery, but they all keep at what they're doing. Chasing kids, hanging laundry, cooking food, working on engines. They were all doing everything but coming to my rescue. That's when I see Mom. She's in the trailer's window behind the curtains. As soon as she knows I can see her, she disappears from view. It hurts worse than all the rest of this. Mom didn't step in. She didn't even try to comfort me afterward. A couple tears escape and I angrily wipe them away. I already look weak by being demeaned. I don't need to cry.

I pry Char's arms from around my waist and kneel down to her level. "Are you okay?"

"Yeah. Should I go kick his ass?" Her squeaky voice sounds as fierce as a mouse and her face is scrunched up in anger. She's so fucking cute, but I force away the smile threatening to break free and put on a matching stern face.

"That's nice of you to offer, but us Vanslow girls, we fight our own battles, right?" We both nod in agreement. "Okay, so you go run and play. I'll see you at dinner."

She assesses me one more time. I see her internal battle, so I stand up and give her a playful swat on the ass. She giggles and runs away.

Stepping into the trailer, I close my eyes, count to ten, and then take a few calming breaths, preparing for this confrontation. I find Mom cleaning the small kitchen. It rarely gets used, so it's never dirty.

"Mom." My voice is small and hesitant. I fucking hate it. This isn't me.

"Oh, Thea. Didn't hear you come in." Lies.

"Can we talk?" I sit on the couch, my bare thighs sticking to the plastic.

"Sure. What's up?" Mom sits next to me. Her tone is aloof, and her eyes dance around. Everywhere but at me.

"I know you saw. You were looking through the window." I pull my hair in between my fingers, twisting and twirling. I've done this since I was a child. The repetition soothes me.

"Saw what?" She plays dumb.

"Don't be daft. You saw. You saw what Wen did, and you did nothing about it!" My voice gets louder, almost hysterical.

"All I saw was my bratty ass daughter and her husband reminding her who was in charge." When she finally looks at me, her face is screwed up in a glower and it pisses me off.

"For one, he's not my husband—" I start.

"Yet," Mom interrupts, and I roll my eyes.

"Second, he has no right to put his hands on me like that." Each word comes out sharp and pointed. "Third, you should've tried to stop him. You're my mother!"

"Oh, Thea, you have so much to learn." She shakes her head and looks at the ceiling. "It's not my place to butt in on your fuckin' business with your future husband. Once he proposed, you became his. His to do with as he pleases. I know you know this."

"You want me to learn how to take abuse from my husband?" I ask incredulously.

"No, Thea. I want you to learn how to act right. How to know your place. How to be a good wife. Instead, you push and push the poor boy. It's not right." She crosses her legs and meets my eyes.

"You're kidding, right? Dad would never lay a hand on you. You don't know what it feels like to be treated that way!" I shout. Mom places a hand on my knee and she turns somber.

"Yes, Thea. He did. When we were first married, I was just like you. Headstrong and crazy. Where do you think you got it from?" She audibly blows out a breath. "There was an adjustment period. There always is for married couples, but for our people, it's particularly difficult. Most of the time, the girls are moving to a new area, a new family, a new everything. My marriage to your father was arranged, just like yours. Only I had to move from the East Coast to the West Coast. I was angry and sad. I acted out. It only took a few times before I realized my place. I had two choices. I could keep pissing off my husband and keep getting smacked around, or I could accept my life, start acting right, and try to be happy. I chose the latter and everything changed. I fell in love with your father. I was gifted you beautiful kids." She pats me on my hand twice. "Now it's your turn to make a choice." She stands up and walks out of the trailer, leaving me shocked and confused.

CHAPTER 14

Lawrence

"YOU'VE GOT TO GET BACK OUT THERE, BABY boy." Mark crosses his legs and flicks a stray hair off his brow.

"Did you break into my office just to lecture me?" I briefly look away from the spreadsheet I'm working on.

"I wouldn't call it 'breaking in' per se. More like bribing Monica to let me in despite your objections." He grabs my business card holder, reads my card, and then sets it down. Crooked. I reach over and straighten it. Putting it back where it was before.

"Whatever you did to get in here, I'm sure you can see yourself out." I wave to the door.

"I think you need to come out with me tonight." Mark ignores my request.

"That's actually the last thing I need to do. After last time, I've gone sober. No more alcohol for me, ever." Imagining the blue drink still turns my stomach.

"How will you meet someone new?" He holds his arms out in a questioning manner.

"That's easy." I save the spreadsheet and close my laptop. "I'm not. I'll download Tinder and stick to hookups when I need to like every other single man out there." I'm not there yet, because Thea still haunts my mind. I don't tell Mark that. He doesn't need more ammunition. "Don't you think if you spent more time on your own love life and less on mine, you might find someone of your own?"

"Me?" He clutches his chest with both hands and his eyebrows shoot up. "I'm already in a relationship."

"Oh, yeah?" News to me, since he never talks about anyone.

"Yep, I'm in a serious relationship with Chris O'Donnell. He's daddy as fuck." Mark fans himself.

"The actor?" I quirk an eyebrow.

"He just doesn't know it yet. One day I'll meet him and it'll be instalove. Until then, I have Ben and Jerry." He stands up and buttons his jacket. It's silky and fuchsia.

"Is he even gay?" I pack up my briefcase and look around to make sure everything is as it should be.

"What? I can't hear you," Mark says as he walks out the door, shutting it before I can question him further. I chuckle and flip the lights out, ready to head home for the day.

It's been a few weeks since Thea said goodbye and I'm finally coming out of the fog she left me in. Mark has been harassing me daily, and while he's annoying, it's also nice of him to check in on me.

Fifteen minutes later, I'm home. I pause in the doorway. Something's off. A few somethings, actually. There's a pair of beat-up leather sandals on the shoe rack, an empty glass on my kitchen island, and a small human-sized mass curled up on my couch, soft snores filling the room. I smile and shake my head. Just can't shake this girl. One of these days, I'll chain her to my bed and not let her pull any more disappearing acts. Preferably before she gets married.

I toe off my shoes, remove my suit coat, and loosen my tie before heading to the sleeping figure. I take a seat on the coffee table in front of her. She's lying on her stomach, one arm and one leg hanging off the side of the couch. Her long, flowy skirt has risen to mid-thigh on a leg that's draped over the edge and I have to fight the urge to drag a hand up her long, toned leg.

I scan a path up her body. I stop at where her cropped tank top exposes her bare back, paying attention to the two dimples above her ass I want to lick. Hair covers her shoulders and part of her face. I gently brush it to the side so I can see her face clearly. Her long lashes kiss the top of her cheeks and her full lips are slightly parted. She's stunning.

"Creeper." Her voice is more hoarse than usual, heavy with sleep.

"Only for you." I let out a small smile. Thea sits up and stretches her arms out, her face scrunching up. "Want to tell me how you got into my house?"

"You're an amateur. Sliding doors are notoriously easy to unlock from the outside," she explains. No shame in sight. I look to my back door and then back at Thea.

"I'll have to look into that."

"You don't want me to break in?" She peers up at me through those long lashes coyly.

"I don't want anyone to break in. If you want to be in my house, I'll give the code to the front door," I say honestly, and she blushes. "Why are you here, anyway?"

"I had a terrible night last night, and I needed to get away." She gathers her hair in one hand and brings it over her shoulder, making it easier for her to play with the long strands. Something dark catches my eye. Her skin is bruised around the base of her neck. I grasp her hand and pull it from her hair. I gather the long strands and lift them up, revealing a similar bruise on the other side.

"What the fuck is this?" She shies away from my touch

and pulls her hair from my clutch. I regret my tone instantly. "I just mean, what happened?" I ask gently this time.

"It's fine. I'm fine. I handled it." Her spine straightens and her face hardens.

"I don't care you're here, Thea. I'm just worried. You can't break into my house with bruises around your neck and expect me to not ask questions." I stand up and put some distance between us so my anger doesn't scare her further.

"I can go. It's okay. I was just up all night and I was so tired." She stands up too, picks up her purse from the chair, and throws it over her shoulder.

"No. Don't go." I approach her cautiously. I've never seen her so skittish. "Just sit down. Let's talk about it." I pull her purse from her shoulder and down her arm before setting it back onto the chair. Her eyes meet mine and what I see breaks my usually unemotional heart. She's crying.

She allows me to walk her back to the couch. I sit before tugging her to sit across my lap. My arms wrap around her waist tightly. Her head rests on my shoulder and she sniffles.

I give her a minute before I whisper into her ear, "What's wrong, Trouble?"

"I fucked everything up." She sounds so defeated and weary.

"How'd you do that?" I rub up and down her thigh to soothe her. She's always so fierce, seeing her like this puts me on edge. If she weren't on my lap, I would be cleaning. Starting with the dirty glass on the counter.

"Um, I got mouthy with Wen. I've gotten mouthy with Wen a lot lately. I think he finally had enough yesterday. He… well, he choked me."

I pull her from my shoulder by her arms and hold her out, needing to look her in the eyes.

"He did what?" My severe tone causes tears to pour from her eyes.

"I just misunderstood how things are," she sobs out cryptically.

"What things? I don't understand." Anger is bubbling up from within me, but I try to tamp it down. Thea's upset enough without me adding to it.

"In my mind, my dad was a gentle giant. I mean, he sometimes gets drunk and into fights, but with us, he's never. He would never." She shakes her head.

"Wait, we were talking about Wen." I can't keep up.

"After Wen did… what he did, I went to my mom. I thought she would cancel the wedding. I thought she would be upset, but it turns out my dad was the same way at first. I guess it's their way to put their women in their place. I just didn't know. I was so stupid." She nuzzles her face into my neck and drapes her arms around my shoulders.

"You're not stupid. It's abuse, Thea. I know you know it is, it's why you're so upset."

"I don't know. I'm so disappointed in my dad, in my mom, in fuckin' Wen. I'm so confused, Law." Sobs wrack through her body, and I let her get it all out while I rub her back. After a few minutes, her shuddering stops and she sits up. Her eyes are red and swollen, her cheeks damp with tears. I cup her face in my hands and wipe them away with my thumbs. "That's not all." She swallows hard.

"What else?" I ask through gritted teeth. The anger I had forced down comes roiling back up. I swear I'll kill the fucker.

"Later, Wen said he wanted to apologize, but I was just so mad. I couldn't even look at him. I started to walk away, but he grabbed my arm. I couldn't hold myself back. I kicked him in the balls and told him I wouldn't marry him." This makes me smile, but Thea jumps from my lap and starts pacing.

"That was good, love. I'm proud of you." I try to reassure her.

"No, it wasn't good, because he and his dad told me if I was backing out of the wedding, I had to leave the group." Her hand shoots to her hair, and she twirls the strands feverishly. "My parents… they did nothing. They just let me leave."

I stand up and walk to her. I pull her hand from her hair, wrap her arms around my waist, and cup her face in my hands so she's forced to look me in the eyes.

"It's going to be okay. We'll figure it out." I don't understand how it will be okay, but I don't tell her that. Her family is her entire world and unless she's allowed back, she'll be crushed. Destroyed. "Let's have some dinner. You can stay here tonight and tomorrow we can work on it. Things will look better after you get some sleep." I know it's all a lie, but she could use a reprieve from all the upset.

"Are you sure?" She trembles slightly. I'd do anything to bring back her spark. She may be trouble, but she's my trouble. How her family could condemn her is beyond me, but now that they have, I will make damn sure she has no reason to leave me again.

"Yeah, Trouble. I'm sure." My forehead meets hers and I look into her unusual orbs. We share a breath, then two. I trail the backs of my fingers down her arm, goose bumps forming under my touch. Her hand comes up to my cheek, and she brings my mouth down to hers. Tentatively, she kisses me gently and chastely. I allow her to explore at her own pace, letting her have control. Her pillowy lips feel so good against mine. When her tongue peeks out and sweeps over my lower lip, I open for her and she slides into my mouth, cautiously probing.

It doesn't take long for my need to overwhelm me. I take control of the kiss, picking up the pace. Our breaths are shared, our hands are all over, and the urge to make this girl mine is overwhelming. I crouch to grab the bottom of her long skirt, dragging it up her legs. I stop at the back of her thighs and hoist her up. Her legs lock around my waist and I back her against the wall and pin her there with my hips, her heat on mine.

We devour each other, teeth and tongues, sloppy and sexy. She grinds her sex into me and the friction makes me moan against her mouth. I grab her hands and pin them above her head with one hand while the other goes to her breast. Over her tank at first, but when I don't feel a bra, I can't help but pull her tank up. I pull away so I can inspect the perfect tits that have driven me crazy for so long. Barely a handful, but absolutely perfect. I lower my head and take one dark nipple into my mouth, sucking hard.

"Jesus Christ, Law," she breathes out. I flick her nipple with my tongue before releasing her, giving her peeked tip a chaste kiss before dragging my tongue up her chest and neck. She tastes spicy and sweet and completely intoxicating. I suck her earlobe into my mouth and drag my teeth down until it pops free.

"I need more, Trouble," I whisper into her ear. "Will you give it to me?"

Her cat eyes go from lust filled to unsure in one bat of her eyelashes. It halts all the desire coiling inside me. I let her legs fall to the ground, simultaneously letting go over her arms and pulling her top back down. I don't back away. Instead I place a hand on either side of her, boxing her in.

"What's going on in that head of yours?" I ask.

"Um." She stalls. I reach out and hold her chin between a thumb and forefinger.

"I need your words."

She opens her mouth and drops a bomb. "I feel like I should tell you I'm a virgin."

My jaw drops, along with any remainder of an erection I had. I release her chin and back up a step. I assumed she would say something about Wen and how she doesn't feel comfortable moving forward until she settles things with him, but a virgin? She's so comfortable with her body and her sexuality, I never would have guessed. This is a good reminder of just how young she is. Life has made her mature, so it's so easy for me to forget I'm fourteen years older than her. She's barely an adult.

"I don't have a contagious disease, Law. I just haven't had sex yet. I was hoping to change that." She crowds my space now, grabbing my loosened tie and pulling me into her. My hands stay at my sides. I open my mouth to speak, but all my words are stuck in the back of my throat. She rolls her eyes and releases me, followed by a little shove backward. I've offended her.

"If I had known you'd be so turned off, I wouldn't have told you." She walks to the kitchen and busies herself by filling up her glass with filtered water from the refrigerator. "I guess you probably don't want to hear you were my first kiss, too?"

She tips her head and guzzles the water down. I follow the swallowing motion of her long and slender neck. Dirty visions of her swallowing something else hit me hard, but I shake my head.

"I was your first kiss?" I ask, folding my arms across my chest. I'm battling my baser instincts to be her only everything and my brain who doesn't want her to go against her core beliefs. I'm not sure she's ready for the weight of these decisions.

She rolls her eyes again and sets the glass down. "Of course you are. Romani girls aren't allowed to have any contact with a man before marriage." She approaches me, a wicked gleam in her eyes. "What's wrong, Richie Rich? Afraid to deflower me?"

"Thea, this isn't a good idea." My words mean nothing to her. She just smirks and steps even closer.

"I'll need you to be gentle," she taunts. Her hands go to my chest where she unbuttons the top few buttons. I'm frozen in her trance. "Do you think you can do that?" She undoes the rest of the buttons and places her hands on my bare abs. I flex on instinct and she quirks a brow at me. She lifts on her tiptoes and leans into my ear to whisper, "Will you make it good for me, Law?" Her hands trail even lower, but I stop them before they get to my hardening cock. I swallow, hard.

"Thea, you have no idea how bad I want that right now." Fuck if that isn't the truth. I've wanted to dick this girl down since the second I saw her dancing by the bonfire. "But you've had a rough day. When we have sex for the first time, I want it to be when you're ready and not just searching for comfort after a horrific day."

Glancing at where her hands rest at the button to my pants, she freezes for a long while. When she finally looks up, I see anxiety and I know I've made the right choice. Her forehead rests on my chest. I put my arms around her and she snuggles into me willingly.

"Law?" I feel her voice against my chest more than I hear it.

"Yeah, Trouble?" I run my fingers through her hair, testing to see if I can bring her the same comfort she brings herself with the motion.

"I'm scared I've lost my family forever." Her voice quavers.

"I know. I can't say I understand, because I never really had much family to speak of, but I know they mean everything to you. I'll do anything I can to help." I press a kiss to her head.

"Law?" she asks again.

"Yeah?" My fingers still run through her hair.

"I'm starving. I haven't eaten since yesterday at lunch." Her stomach grumbles at the mere mention of food.

"Well, let's get you fed then." I separate from her and open the fridge. "I can make pasta or baked chicken."

"Pasta, please," she chirps and jumps onto a stool at the island.

I gather basil, tomatoes, garlic, and some fresh pasta. As I cook, Thea blabs away. Telling me stories of growing up gypsy. She makes me laugh at all the outrageous antics from her crazy family. As I'm draining the pasta, she tells me about the time she foraged wild mushrooms and put them in the casseroles she was making for dinner.

"I had just pulled the first batch from the oven when Dad and Leander walked through the door. They had spent the day on the Oregon timber lines and were starving, begging me to feed them before the rest of dinner was ready. I dished them up huge helpings. It didn't take long for me to realize they were psychedelic mushrooms." She laughs.

"You're kidding!" I stop what I'm doing to listen to the rest of the story.

"Nope. Dad came up to me and was touching my face, asking me when I started to sparkle. Leander was scooting around the ground on his ass, insisting there were aliens trying to probe him." Now we're both laughing hysterically. "Mom was so annoyed because when Dad saw her, he ran away screaming that a demon was trying to steal his soul. She couldn't understand why my skin sparkled to him, but his wife was the monster."

"What did you do with all the casseroles?" I ask, already knowing she didn't just throw them out.

"Mom made me throw them away." A mischievous smirk takes over her face. "But Wen and I snuck a plateful and ate it out in the woods. It was one of my favorite nights. We walked the forest for hours. Everything was so beautiful and so fucking funny. I've never laughed that hard in my life." She snickers and I laugh too, but after a minute, her face falls and she blinks back tears. "I miss my family."

I walk around the island and take her in my arms. "I know, but we'll fix this. Just wait and see."

"I trust you, Law. I know you'll help me make this better." She sniffles and I keep her close, praying I don't let her down.

CHAPTER 15

Theodora

AFTER A SOMBER DINNER, I CLEAR THE TABLE AND go to the kitchen to do the dishes. I'm so used to having to boil water to wash dishes, having running water and a dishwasher feels extravagant.

I've never used a dishwasher, so I scrape the plates and start shoving dishes wherever I can get them to fit. I'm very aware of Law's scrutiny of me as I lay plates across the bottom, stacking them in. I shrug. Looks good to me. I close the dishwasher.

"How do I start it?" I ask, pressing random buttons.

"It's okay, you don't need to start it. You probably want to shower before bed, and it'll use all the hot water." He stands up from the stool he was sitting on and takes my hand in his, stopping me from my button pushing on the dishwasher. "I'll get fresh towels out for you."

"That would be amazing. I have a gym membership just so I can use their showers, but all the old ladies ambling around butt ass naked creeps me out. I mean, more power to them. I hope I'm that confident when I'm ninety after water aerobics." I follow him into his bedroom. "But, it'll be nice to shower without getting an eyeful of wrinkled, saggy tits."

He opens a linen closet while peering back at me over his shoulder, his mouth gapes. "You don't have showers?"

"We don't have running water. Sometimes we'll stay in campgrounds for a night or two that have hookups. But we still can't use the showers, because we've all converted them to storage." I take a fluffy towel from Law that smells like a rainforest, not the cheap laundry detergent Mom and I make from Borax.

"Dare I ask about the toilet situation?" His eyebrows shoot up high in question.

"That's our one concession. Mostly all the boys piss outside, but they always allow the girls to use the shitter. The men take the RVs to a dump station when it's necessary."

Law walks me into the bathroom.

"I don't have girly shampoo or anything, so you'll smell like me until we can get you some." He opens the shower door and pulls out a bottle and hands it to me. I pop the top and take a whiff. It smells like cedar and citrus. I think I'll enjoy smelling like Law.

"It's great. Thank you." I put the shampoo back in and hug the towel to my chest.

"Oh, I know you didn't have clothes with you. I'll set some of my things on the bed for you. They'll be too big, but it'll do for tonight." He smiles at me and then turns and walks out, shutting the door on the way out.

I strip my clothes and get in the shower. I use the manly smelling shampoo and conditioner, knowing I'll be able to smell Law every time I play with my hair. I spot his razor and use it to shave my underarms, legs, and bikini area.

After my shower, I step into his room hesitantly, wondering if he's in there waiting for me. His bedroom is empty, and the door is shut too, so I let the towel fall to the ground. I sort through the clothes he set out for me. I hold up a pair of boxer briefs and blush. There's also sweatpants, and a T-shirt. I pull the underwear up my legs. They go all the way to my boobs, so I roll them down a few times. I throw on the T-shirt. It hangs to just above my knees. I know the sweatpants will be too big, so I toss them back on the bed.

Plates are banging outside the bedroom, so I follow the noise. One look into the kitchen tells me I was right about what Law would do about my dishwashing when I imagined it all those weeks ago. He has all the dishes I had put into the dishwasher stacked in the sink. He's scrubbing them with a brush and then reloading them into the dishwasher. I cover my smile with a hand, just watching him. I didn't think watching a man doing dishes could be sexy, but here we are. I sigh.

He must have changed while I was in the shower because he's in a pair of gray sweatpants and a black T-shirt, the same thing he laid out for me. The muscles in his arms flex and move as he scrubs, and I can see his ass tighten every time he bends to put a dish in the washer. He's so fuckin' sexy. After a few minutes he stops and looks toward his bedroom, catching me watching him.

"I can explain." He turns the water off and holds his hands up in defense.

I just wave him off, giggling. "It's fine. I kind of knew you would." He gives me a stiff nod and goes back to scrubbing. I walk up behind him and wrap my arms around his waist. "Why are you washing the dishes before you put them in the dishwasher?"

"The dishwasher doesn't have the ability to get all this dried on food off, so you just scrub it off and then the dishwasher can sanitize them." He leans over to put the plate in, but I don't let go. I just bend along with him.

We don't talk anymore as he washes the pots and pans and then loads them in the dishwasher. I note how he loads them. He doesn't just lay plates in like I did. He stands them up between the little dividers. I'll do that next time. If there is a next time.

When he's finished, he turns the water off, puts a packet in the dispenser, starts the dishwasher, and dries his hands on the towel he had draped over his shoulder. He turns me around in his arms and kisses my forehead.

"What are you wearing?" he asks, taking in my bare legs.

"The pants were so big and your shirt is like a dress, anyway. Actually, it covers more than any dress I own." I hold out the sides, showing the boxy shape.

"It turns me on seeing you in my clothes and smelling like me." He trails kisses along my neck. "You ready for bed, Trouble?"

The question forces a yawn out of me and I cover my mouth.

"I'll take that as a yes." He stoops down and throws me over his shoulder. I squeal and giggle all the way to his room.

He gives me a swat to the ass before he tosses me onto the bed and I scoot myself up to the headboard. When he looks around the room, his brows furrow. I follow the direction his eyes are trained and spot my wet towel on the ground. He picks it up and goes into the bathroom. I can see him through the mirror as he picks up the clothes I also left on the floor of the bathroom. My fingers go to my hair and I drag the strands in between them.

"I'm just going to put these in the wash real quick." He walks out the bedroom door. I'm a bit of a messy person, something Mom complains about all the time.

A minute later he returns. I expect him to be annoyed and lecture me about my bad habits, but instead he has a smirk on his face.

"What?" My fingers are twirling through my hair rapidly.

"I like you in my bed." He grabs the back of his shirt and pulls it over his head, exposing his chiseled chest dusted with brown hair. I scan down farther to the defined abs that have the same scattering of hair. He is all man and I feel wetness grow between my legs.

"Oh, really?" I scoot down the bed and lie on my side, holding myself up on an elbow. I pat the space next to me. "I'd look better in your bed with you next to me."

"I don't know if it's a good idea. I was just going to grab a blanket and pillow and sleep on the couch." He walks to his linen closet outside the bathroom and grabs a blanket.

"You don't have to sleep out there. I can keep my hands to myself." Lies. I want to run my hands up and down his torso. I want to lick every rung on the ladder of his abdomen.

"Maybe you can, but I don't trust myself being in a bed with you." He sits down on the edge of the bed. I tug his arm until he's lying down facing me, mimicking my position on his side.

"We can be good," I coax. The look on my face must betray me, because he shakes his head with a smirk playing on his lips.

"When I take you to bed for the first time, it won't be to sleep, Thea." He leans in and kisses me long and deep. "It'll be to kiss you from head to toe and to show you all the pleasure you've been missing out on."

He pulls away and stands up, grabbing the blanket and a pillow off his bed. I throw myself onto my back with a huff.

"Don't throw a tantrum like a brat. You and me?" He motions between us. "We're happening. Just not until we get everything else figured out." Then he leaves, switching the light off and closing the door behind him.

I lie in the dark, mentally replaying the events of the last twenty-four hours. Isn't it bizarre how quickly your life can change? Yesterday I woke up, still engaged, and wondering how I was going to get out of the marriage. I could feel the clock ticking away. Counting down until the moment I had to throw a lock and chain around my wild and free heart, throwing the key away forever.

I should be happy, I should be relieved, but the price I had to pay is unthinkable. I can't accept my family will just let me go. I'm dying inside from the sting of rejection. Do they think so little of me to dispose of me so easily? I don't understand how they could just let me walk away.

I toss and turn. This bed is like lying on a cloud, the most comfortable thing I've ever slept on, but my brain won't shut down. I give up on sleep and pad out of Law's room, set on getting myself a glass of water. The sound of deep breathing fills the quiet space. I tiptoe over to the couch and see Law on his back, one arm under his head and one across his bare abs, the blanket covering his legs.

I lift the blanket up and snuggle into his side before pulling it over the top of both of us. Law briefly tenses and lifts his head. As soon as he sees me, he sighs and wiggles his arm until it's underneath me. He draws me even closer to his side before relaxing, his breathing going back to deep and rhythmic.

I smile and put a hand on his solid abs, playing with the hair there. It doesn't take long for sleep to pull me under after that, Law's stiff couch and hard body being so much more comfortable than an empty bed.

CHAPTER 16

Lawrence

I WAKE UP ACHY FROM BEING PINNED UNDER THEA ALL night. My neck is kinked and my arm is dead asleep, pins and needles shooting up and down. I couldn't care less. I have the most beautiful girl in my arms and her soft snores filling my ears.

She groans and stretches before opening her eyes. They're sleepy and happy, her fingers dancing around on my abdomen.

"You snore." I grin down at her.

"I do not!" She defends, sitting up. Her tone defensive, but she's holding back a smile.

"You so do." I sit up next to her and stretch my limbs, the blood flowing back into my extremities. "But it's cute."

"Yeah, well, you fart in your sleep," she grumbles, making me laugh.

I stand up and walk through my bedroom and into the bathroom. After I do my business and brush my teeth, I re-member I forgot to lay a toothbrush out for Thea. I open the drawer and set it on the counter.

"Trouble!" I call out from the doorway to the bathroom. "I put a toothbrush on the counter for you."

She appears quickly. "Thank you. I didn't want to ask if you had an extra, so I just used yours last night."

I cringe and run my tongue along my freshly brushed teeth. She must see the motion because she looks away.

"It's fine. I'm fine. I'm just gonna—" I point inside the bathroom. "I'll be done in here in just a second." I go back inside and pull a second toothbrush out of the drawer. After tossing the old one, I brush my teeth again. Logically I know I've shared her spit every time we've kissed, but irrationally, imagining her use my toothbrush makes me recoil in disgust.

Thea is sitting on the bed when I come out of the bathroom. Her fingers are in her hair and she's staring at the ground. I drop to my knees in front of her and pull her hands into mine. I'm well aware of my issues, and when Chloe left me, I turned introspective. I realize my compulsive proclivities are probably responsible for most of the relationships in my life being strained. Thea is important to me, this relationship is important to me, and unless I want her to leave me too, I need to make more of an effort.

"I'm sorry. I shouldn't have assumed—" She trails off.

"No, it's okay." I tip her chin up to look at me. "I know I'm a… challenging person to get along with. It's my issues, not yours."

"Yeah, but this is your house and you've been so amazing to let me stay."

"Listen to me. I want you here." I peck her lips. "You just be you and I'll just be me… following you around and picking up after you." We both let out a little laugh and I stand up, pulling her up to her feet with me. "Go do what you need to do, then we can head out and do some shopping to make things more comfortable for you here. Your clothes are dry. I'll set them on the bed for when you're done."

She nods and goes to the bathroom, shutting the door behind her softly. I strip the bed sheets. She didn't sleep in here all night, but she still was in the bed, therefore, I need to wash the sheets. I put them in the washer and grab Thea's clothes from the dryer. I put new sheets on the bed and lay Thea's folded clothes on the comforter.

After a day of shopping, we return home. Thea heads to my bedroom to change into one of the comfy outfits we picked up today. She fought me the whole way, but I was able to purchase her a few outfits and some bath products she'll need while she stays with me. She insisted she could pay on her own, but I don't know how much money she has and whatever she has needs to last. Plus, I have a lot of money and rarely the opportunity to spend it on someone.

We didn't talk about what her plans are for the future or how we will try to get her back in the good graces of her family. I think Thea needed an emotional break and spending the day doing mundane tasks was just what she needed to forget.

I pull a few things out to make for dinner and start chopping vegetables. When the chicken is baking and vegetables are roasting, I hear the bedroom door open. I look up and see Thea. Her hair is damp and pulled over one of her shoulders. She has on a skimpy black tank top and matching sleep shorts. My jaw drops.

"You're beautiful," I say dumbly. She blushes but doesn't look away. She just walks toward me, her hips swaying, and a barely perceptible bounce in her breasts. I see it, though. I salivate over that movement.

Sex has always been a simple release for me. An itch to scratch. Don't get me wrong, I'm a giving lover and always make sure my partner gets off before I do. I just never felt a carnal need to possess until her. Until Thea. The need to consume her is overwhelming and holding out feels insurmountable. It doesn't help she's always teasing me, always pushing boundaries, always increasing my desire. She's trouble and for the first time in my life, I'm holding out my arms and saying, "Bring it on."

"It's comfy." She downplays, sitting down on a stool. I stalk over to her, pulling her legs open and moving into the space I created. She locks her ankles around my waist. My hands rub up and down the smooth skin of her naked thighs. I bring my nose to her neck and inhale. She no longer smells like me, but the amber and clove that has replaced it is much more suited to her personality. "Do I smell good?"

"You smell intoxicating." I place open-mouthed kisses on her neck, sucking on her skin lightly. Not enough to leave a mark, although the thought of seeing her dark skin marred with love bites does something to me. Her breath hitches and her hands move to my hips.

"That feels so good," she says breathily. I move my lips to hers and kiss her. Our tongues make love, the nerve endings sending sparks straight to my dick. My jeans get tight and uncomfortable. I'm so lost in this woman when the buzzer blares to tell me dinner is done, I almost ignore it and take Thea to bed and eat her instead, but I regain control and step away, breaking the kiss.

I turn my back to her and adjust myself. My dick hates me with all of this foreplay and no relief. Even taking care of myself in the shower this morning wasn't enough to satisfy me. Distraction is the name of this game, so I pull dinner from the oven while Thea sets my small dining table.

"Where's your family?" she asks over dinner.

"Dead," I tell her. She drops her fork to her plate.

"All of them?" She places her hand on mine. I know she's trying to soothe me, but it's unnecessary. I've come to terms with their deaths long ago.

"Yes." I take a bite of my dinner.

"How did they die?"

"My mom and dad had me when they were older. Mom was forty-eight and Dad was fifty when I was born. I wasn't a planned baby and I'm not so sure I was even a wanted baby. Both of my parents were university professors and heavily involved in their departments, so a series of nannies mostly raised me," I explain.

"That's so sad. I would hate not to have brothers and sisters or extended family. It must have been lonely." Her fingers are rubbing circles on my hand, but I pull it away. I don't need pity.

"I didn't know any different. I was enrolled in the best schools and was given a life of privilege. I didn't want for anything." I pick up my plate and take it to the kitchen, done with this conversation.

"But did you have friends? Cousins? Grandparents?" She turns around in her seat so she can see me.

"I had a few classmates I played lacrosse with through high school and again in college. I don't know if they were friends, but we were friendly. My grandparents on both sides died when I was young and they were all only children, so there is no one from my lineage left except me." I scrape my plate and begin washing dishes.

"What about girlfriends?" She brings her own plate to the kitchen and scrapes it into the trash.

"What is this about? Why all the questions?"

"I just started thinking. I know little about you. I want to know everything." She shrugs.

"I've had a few girlfriends. My last girlfriend I had proposed to. You probably remember me saying she left me the night I met you." I don't want to be talking about this. It's in the past.

"That's right. I remember. So you're probably still mourning the loss of that relationship." She grows quiet. I set the plate I was washing down and turn the water off, then face her.

"I'm not mourning anything, Thea. Chloe and I were more of an arrangement. I didn't want to spend my life alone, and she liked my money and status. It was as simple as that." I kiss her sweet lips, just once. She looks so sad and I can't take it. I don't know if I can help her understand what she has done for my life, but I try. "Before you came barreling into my life, I was pretty robotic. I lived with unemotional parents and was raised by people who were paid to spend time with me. The night I saw you, something in me changed. You were so full of life and so free and uninhibited. I've never met anyone like you. You may drive me a little crazy, but you pull me out of my comfort zone, and I needed that. I didn't know I needed it, but I did. You did all that, just by existing."

Her smile turns big, and she wraps her arms around my neck, pulling my face to hers. "I've never met anyone like you, either. I had just come to terms I would marry someone I don't love, but that night, you saw me. Not a woman who will cook and clean for you, have your babies. You saw the real me," she says against my mouth and then places a gentle kiss on my lips. "I admit, at first I just wanted to shock you because I could tell you were uptight—"

"I'm not uptight," I argue. Her eyebrows rise. "Okay, I'm a little uptight."

"You're a lot uptight." She smiles, just inches from my face. A warmth builds in my chest from the intimacy. "But it's okay, because even after I pulled my stunts, you were there for me. My family's love and acceptance have conditions, but you don't. I don't have to do what you say in order for you to care about me. I've never had that."

I bring my lips to hers and we kiss for a long moment before I pull away. "Why don't you go relax? I'll finish up the dishes and we can watch a movie or something."

"I can help." She picks up the scrub brush and turns to the sink. I grab her by the waist and turn her back to me.

"Yeah, that's not going to happen." I take the scrub brush from her hands. "Get out of here." I swat her ass on her way out, making her giggle.

CHAPTER 17

Theodora

I wake up Monday morning all alone. Spending the weekend with Law gave me the best two days I've ever had. More than once he asked if he should take me home to talk to my parents, but I denied him each time. Thinking about why I left in the first place fills me with so much anger and resentment, it's not smart for me to talk to them yet.

I sit up in Law's bed and stretch, smiling at the Law sized imprint in the sheets next to me. I finally convinced him to sleep in bed with me. I'd be lying if I said I didn't tempt him to take me, but he refused. I understand why he wants me to handle my shit with my family first, but being with him just feels so good, I want to wrap myself in that warmth and never let it go. Now he's at work and I'm left to my own devices.

I make the bed and decide to lie to Law and tell him I washed the sheets before making it. I'm learning more of his strange ways and most of the time I just let him do his thing, but sometimes his requests are so bizarre, I have to push back. Like washing the sheets every day. Who does that?

I shower and dress in one of the sundresses Law bought me. When I left my family, my purse was all I had with me. Five thousand dollars. That's all I have to my name. I'm not sure what I'll do, but I know it's enough money to get a small apartment and to live off of for a short time. I have no skills. I've never had a job. Hell, I don't even have an ID. All of this is just too daunting for me to figure out, so I push it away.

Law owns a three-bedroom ranch style home in a planned community, only I doubt any of the other houses around here have the upgrades he has. I enter the kitchen and look around. Marble floors throughout like it's a fuckin' casino, granite kitchen counters, black stainless steel appliances with computers in them, it's all too much for me. Everything sparkles and there is not a speck of dust to be found.

I've never seen the other rooms, so I go exploring. On the other side of the living room is a hallway I'm assuming will take me to the rest of the house. The first door I open is a home gym. The floor is covered in a black rubber material. A large weight station is in the center, a TV mounted in the corner, and the windows have black-out curtains on them, making the temperature in here much colder than the rest of the house. I close the door.

The next door is a bathroom. It has the same fixtures as the master bath. Much like the rest of the house, it's pristine and looks unused. I step out and close the door. I come across a hallway closet that's organized with rows and rows of cleaning supplies. He probably has enough in here to last the rest of his life. However, knowing Law, maybe only a few months.

The last door I open is a home office. There's a large L-shaped sit stand desk that's ultra-modern and sleek. A bookcase lines the back wall and it's full of books I can't even read the titles of. It makes me feel stupid and worthless. What is Law doing with someone like me who can't even read or write? I wonder if I'm just a pet project for him.

I turn to leave, but a small photo album catches my eye. I walk over to the small sitting area across from the bookshelf. There are two small leather chairs with a small round table in between. I sit down on one of the chairs and open the book. The first page is a picture of an older man and woman with what I'm assuming is baby Law. The man and woman stand proudly behind a high-back chair where the baby is sitting upright. None of them are smiling, not even the baby. He's dressed in a tiny, adorable suit with a bowtie, one finger in his mouth that pulls at his bottom lip, revealing two tiny teeth on the bottom. He's so cute with chubby cheeks and big brown eyes.

I turn the page and there's the exact same picture, but I'm assuming about a year later. Same pose. The man and woman, both with graying hair and wrinkles around their eyes and mouths. They're both dressed impeccably, not a wrinkle in their clothing, standing behind the same chair, baby Law sitting up straight. His hands are in his lap and his face is straight and serious.

Every page I turn is the same picture, but a year later. It's kind of creepy. His mom and dad have the same serious expression, but with every page I turn, I see them aging. By the time I get to the last page, Law is sitting on the chair with a cap and gown on. It's his college graduation picture. I can tell by the UNLV embossed sash. His parents are trying to stand up straight, but over the years they have grown old and frail. They don't wear the smile of parents who are proud of their son for all his accomplishments, they just have that same flat expression from page one.

I close the book and try to return it to the exact position it was in, knowing Law could tell if I moved it. It would help if there was a dust line from where it had been placed, but this is Law's house. There is no dust.

I leave the room and go back to the kitchen. I make a cup of coffee, loading it with cream and sugar before sitting at the island. My mind is hyper focused on those pictures I just saw. It's just so sad to me. I have photo albums too, but mine are full of my brothers and sisters all smiling and having fun. Poor Law has never known that kind of happiness.

I decide I'll do something nice for him. He's helped me so much the last few days, I should return the favor. Maybe I can make him a nice dinner since he's cooked for me every night I've been here.

Grabbing my purse and putting on my shoes, I head out to get ingredients. I'll make Mom's famous spaghetti pie. It's easy and delicious.

"Something smells good!" Law calls out, taking his shoes off.

"I cooked." I beam, taking the spaghetti pie out of the oven and setting it down on a hot pad. Law comes up behind me and places a kiss right below my ear, his arms wrapping around me. I lean back into him. The butterflies I've been missing all day have now returned.

"I see that. Can't wait to try it." He steps back, removes his suit coat, and untucks his button-down, giving me a peak of his defined abs. "Do I have time to change?"

"Sure, it should probably cool down a little, anyway." Law leans in and kisses me chastely before sauntering to the bedroom. I admire the view of his tight ass in his slacks until he disappears from view.

I reach down plates, gather silverware, and set the table. By the time I have water glasses filled and our dinner plated, Law has returned.

"What is this?" He holds a fork of spaghetti noodles and vegetables, taking a sniff.

"It's spaghetti pie. My mom makes it all the time, and it's a family favorite." I shovel a bite in my mouth. It tastes like home and makes me miss all my people.

Law hesitantly takes a bite, and his brows lift. "This is fantastic!" he compliments, and I thank him.

"Did I have all these ingredients to make this?" he asks over another large forkful.

"No, I went out today. I wanted to do something nice for you after all you've done for me." I straighten my spine.

"Thea," he says, putting his fork down. "I don't want you to feel you owe me anything. I wanted you in my life before you even broke into it."

I reach over and set my hand on his. "I know and I wanted that too. It's just if this had happened before I met you—"

"You would have figured it out." Law stops my destructive speculation. "If there's one thing I know about you, it's that you are resilient. You would've been okay, even without me."

"Maybe so, but it would've been a lot harder. Not just because you've given me somewhere to stay, but also because you've been here for me. Emotionally, I mean. Not having my family, my support system, it's hard, but you listen to me and encourage me." I lean toward Law and he meets me halfway for a kiss. When I break away, I place a hand on his slightly stubbly cheek. "I'm just thankful for you."

"Don't mention it, Trouble. I'm glad we found each other." He rests his forehead against mine for a second. When he pulls away, he gathers our plates and forks and takes them to the sink. "Where did you go shopping at, anyway? I hope you didn't have to walk far in this heat."

"I took the bus." I gather our water glasses and napkins. "I went to a few places. Not every store had what I needed."

"What did you need that a regular grocery store didn't have?" He stops washing dishes and looks at me. I've been avoiding this conversation, hoping it wouldn't come up. I know how he feels about my shopping habits and I'm sure he'll freak out.

I brace myself on the counter with both hands. "Well, I went to Whole Foods and found the pasta and some parsley. Then I went across the street to a restaurant, I forget what it's called—"

"La Fromage?" he suggests.

"Yeah, there. They had the ricotta and parmesan," I explain.

"You went to a restaurant for ingredients? Didn't Whole Foods have cheese? Does La Formage even sell ingredients like that?" His face pinches in question.

"Kind of," I say and quickly continue. "And you had the milk, bacon, frozen peas, and eggs already."

"I still don't understand why you just didn't get everything at the grocery store."

I look down, wondering how long it will take him to figure this out. I peek up at him through my lashes, and his expression changes. He shifts, looks up at the ceiling, shifts again, looks down at the leftover dinner, goes to the cupboard where the trash bin in, and pulls it out. "Where are the grocery bags?"

"I didn't have any," I whisper.

"Thea, where did this food come from?" He places his hands on his hips and bends over at the waist slightly, as if he'll be sick.

"I told you, Whole Foods and La—" I get cut off. Again.

"From inside the store? Like you went inside, got the things off the shelf, and paid for them?" He's little green and looks exasperated.

"I didn't have to. They had just thrown out—" I jump when he cuts me off this time.

"Please tell me you didn't get these things out of the trash. Please." His voice is louder now and I can't bear to make eye contact.

"The noodles were still in the box. They only expired a month ago. And after I washed the parsley—"

"Thea!" He booms, stalking toward me. I think he's going to stop in front of me, but he zooms right by and runs to his bathroom. I hear the toilet lid flip up and then retching. I follow him in and rub his back as he vomits the dinner I so carefully made for him.

"Are you okay?" I ask with a cringe. His forehead is resting on the arm he's draped over the toilet seat.

"Just peachy," he bites out.

"You're being silly, Law. The food was just fine." I try to soothe. He must not have liked this response because he bolts upright.

"Do I look fine to you? I'm literally draped over a toilet bowl. I am not fine." He stands up and goes to the sink, rinsing his mouth out before brushing his teeth. When he's done, he throws the toothbrush away and gets a sanitizing wipe out. He wipes the sink and toilet down and tosses it in. "I'm not *fine*, Thea." He storms out of the bathroom and I follow, hot on his heels.

"You're making a big deal out of nothing. If you hadn't known where it came from, you wouldn't have thrown up." I shrug.

"I can't even believe I'm having to argue with you about digging spoiled food out of dumpsters!" he hollers at me. He pours a fresh glass of water and drinks it all down then goes back to scrubbing dishes furiously. When he scrubs one of the dainty water glasses we used at dinner, it shatters in his hand. "Fuck!"

"Hold still. Let me help." I rush to his side and hold his hand under the water, trying to assess where the blood is coming from. There is a shard of glass in his palm. "I need to pull this out. It's shallow. You won't need stitches." I grab hold of the shard and pull. Law winces but says nothing. "Where's your first aid kit?"

"There's one underneath the bathroom sink." He's still holding his hand under the water. I run to the bathroom and grab the kit.

"Okay, let me fix you up." I pull his hand from the water

and dab the cuts on his fingers and palm. When they're dry, I put some antibiotic ointment on them and bandage them up. When I'm finished, I have wrapped his entire hand in gauze and first aid tape.

"This might be overkill," he says with a smirk, holding up his bound hand.

"There were a lot of cuts," I reason.

"Thank you," he murmurs softly.

"You're welcome," I huff, crossing my arms over my chest. Law stands in front of me, his hands resting on my shoulders. I look up and his forehead is creased in concern.

"I'm sorry I got so angry." He pulls me into his body and I go willingly, smashing my face into his neck and breathing in his manly scent.

"I'm sorry I made dinner." My words are muffled against his skin. He pulls me back again to look into my eyes.

"Don't be sorry you made dinner. I'm thankful you went to all the trouble." He takes a deep breath in and out. "Just next time take my credit card and purchase the food from inside the store, okay?"

"Yeah, okay," I agree, but cross my fingers behind my back. I just won't tell him next time.

"Trouble, I'm serious. I know it's something normal to you, but believe me. It's not normal to other people." He pulls my hand from around my back and uncrosses my fingers.

"Ugh. Okay. Fine. I'll waste your money and buy the same thing from inside the store I can get for free around back." I throw my hands up in defeat.

"Thank you."

"Yeah, yeah. Whatever." I look at his padded hand and re-alize something. "You can't finish the dishes with your hand like that." I point to the wrapped up hand. "Looks like I'll have to do them."

He looks up and mutters something I can't hear. Maybe a prayer?

"Fine, but I'm going to instruct you on how to do it." He compromises.

"Yay!" I squeal, not because he's letting me do the dishes. Fuck that, I hate doing chores, but having him watch me do dishes will drive him crazy and I live to make this man crazy. Judging by how this dinner went, I'm thoroughly succeeding.

CHAPTER 18

Lawrence

FTER FORTY-FIVE MINUTES OF EXHAUSTING arguments, the leftover dinner has been tossed in the trash and the dishes are loaded, the dishwasher on. I still can't believe Thea wanted to save the rest of the spaghetti casserole. A shiver runs down my spine just thinking about eating it again.

If I'm being honest with myself, it was good. It was rich and flavorful. But if I even think about the food being pulled from dumpsters, nausea roils in my gut. So I push it away and attempt to move on. I'll be damned if I let her shop or cook for me again. I don't trust she'll respect my wishes.

Thea jumps in the shower, while I strip the bed and put on fresh sheets. The little liar tried to tell me she washed them before making the bed up, but I saw a few strands of her long, wild hair still on her pillow. I gave her a swat on the ass for lying and she ran into the bathroom squealing and giggling. I smile as I tuck the corners in, military style.

I've just pulled off my shirt and pants when she leaves the bathroom wearing yet another cami and sleep short set. This one is purple and silky. My jaw hangs open at the sight of her pebbled nipples under the thin fabric. She walks past me to the clothes hamper and sets her clothes and towel in it, glancing at me over her shoulder with obvious pride in herself. I shake my head. Only Thea would want praise for putting her dirty clothes in the hamper. A sock falls on the ground and she bends over to retrieve it. Her bare ass cheeks peek out and my cock hardens. She makes her way back to me and her mouth falls open.

We've spent three nights together so far and except for the first night, they've all been in my bed. We've spent hours kissing and tasting each other, but have stopped at below the waist activities. Sometimes my troublemaker will let her hand drift to the waistband of my briefs, but I stop her, determined for her to figure her life out before taking that step.

My mind is at war with my dominance. Part of me wants to make her mine so she can't ever go back, but then reason sneaks in and I think if she decides she wants to go back to her family and the only way to do that is to marry that fuck-wit, Wen, I want her to still have her virginity intact so it's possible. Despite the anger thinking of that asshole, Wen, brings out in me. What she and I do together, she should never regret. Ever. Because I won't. Touching her, kissing her, exploring her with my lips, my tongue, my teeth. I will regret none of it. I care enough to ensure all of this is for the right reason.

"Is that for me?" She flirts and points to my erection.

"It's because of you," I stammer out, swallowing hard. "I should have paid more attention to what you purchased to sleep in." I run a finger down her arm, watching the goose bumps appear on her skin.

"You don't like it?" She looks down at herself. "It's comfy."

"It's sexy," I deadpan. She moves past and climbs onto the bed, crawling to her side, exposing her perfect peach-shaped ass as she goes. She lies on her side and pats the space next to her. I turn the lights out and climb in, pulling her body flush to mine.

"Law?" she whispers against my lips.

"Yeah, Trouble?" I whisper back.

"I want to feel you." Her hand drifts down my arm, along my side, and then finally reaches between us, settling on top of my aching dick.

"You do not understand how much I want that—"

"But?" She interrupts.

"But you know what has to happen first," I say. She flops onto her back and sighs.

"I'm not ready to face them." She covers her face with her arm, but I peel it away while climbing on top of her, spreading her legs and settling myself between them. She wraps her limbs around me and we come face-to-face.

"Then you're not ready for this." I thrust my hips against her and we both moan at the contact.

"What if we just touch each other?" I can hear the sexual tension in her voice. It's the same tension coursing throughout my body.

"You want me to make you feel good, baby?" I move to her neck and suck the skin into my mouth gently.

"Please, Law. I need you." Her fingers dig into my shoulders and the sting spurs me on.

"If you want me to stop at any point—"

"Yeah, yeah. I'll tell you. Now get to it!" Her heels dig into my ass, driving my hard length against her center.

"Bossy," I murmur against her throat. I bite down and she gasps.

I pull her tank over the top of her head and take an appreciative look at her breasts. I palm each one. My injured hand stings at the pressure, but I don't let go. I love the way they feel. I squeeze hard and let go, watching them bounce back to their resting position. Her nipples are somewhere between pink and brown and are the tiniest of mosquito bite in size. I take one between my teeth and pull. She squirms beneath me, trying to get friction between her legs. I'm not having it. Any pleasure she has will be because I gave it to her.

After a few more sucks, licks, and bites, I move down her body. I don't leave one inch of skin untouched as I make my way. I've never had the urge to eat someone whole until this girl. Everywhere my mouth lands is somewhere I want to explore, somewhere I want to devour.

I finally make it to the band of her sleep shorts. I trail a finger down the front and between her pussy lips. The fabric is soaked. I can't bring myself to take the time to pull them down, so I nuzzle my face to where she needs me most, inhaling deeply at the musky scent that is all her. I lick against the silky fabric and Thea moans loudly.

"Law! Oh my God!" Her hands go to my head. She rotates between tugging at the hair I keep long on top of my head and scraping her nails along the short stubble on the side.

"Does it feel good?" I ask, knowing full well it does.

"It would feel better if I didn't have my shorts on," she sasses. I ignore her and keep eating her through her shorts, still getting her taste on my tongue with the amount of juices that have soaked through the material. She squirms and writhes underneath me, begging for more.

I take pity on her and drag her shorts down her body. I sit up on my knees and her legs fall open. Her pretty pink pussy is wet and mostly bare. Only a short tuft of hair sits above her slit. I reach down and give it a little tug.

She blushes. "Law!"

She's embarrassed. It doesn't matter. This is all new to her, but soon there will be nothing I can do that will make her uncomfortable. *If she stays with you*, a voice whispers in my head. I shove it away and get back to devouring the most perfect pussy I've ever seen.

My tongue reaches her first, and the contact makes her hips buck up. I pin her down by weaving my arms under and around her thighs, bringing her legs to rest on my shoulders. I pull her lips open with the fingers of my injured hand and expose her clit. Wrapping my lips around it, I suck. Hard. One of her arms slams against the bed and a cacophony of curses leaves her mouth. I smile against her folds and drag my tongue up her slit.

"Law! It feels so good, something is happening. I don't know what... I think I'm... Law, please!" she calls out, her nonsense echoing in the room.

I insert a finger slowly in her channel. She's so tight. I haven't been with a virgin since I was one myself and the temptation to drive my straining cock into her is overwhelming. Instead, I hook my finger and find the place that will make her feel the best. With solid pressure there and my tongue flicking her clit, it doesn't take long for her walls to squeeze my finger. She's coming. Her raspy voice gets raspier as she calls out. To God, to me, to anyone who will listen.

Her hips thrust up and her thighs tighten around my head. I don't let up until her body relaxes and her harsh breaths slow. I bring her down gently, slowing my movements until I've stopped completely and removed my mouth. I look up her body to her face, but it's too dark to tell what's going on. I wipe my mouth on the inside of her thigh and crawl up her body. What I see is so beautiful. She's smiling, teeth showing and all.

"How do you feel?" I ask. Her eyes pop open and her smile gets impossibly bigger.

"I didn't know it would feel like that." She beams.

"Haven't you ever had an orgasm?" I mean, I know she's a virgin, and she hasn't so much as kissed anyone but me, but surely she's explored her own body.

"No." She laughs. "We're a family of seven living in a trailer. For another, they teach girls if we even touch ourselves we're impure and not worthy of marrying."

I freeze. My intention was to keep her pure in case she went back to her family, now I realize I still ruined her, I feel like shit.

She kisses my lips. "Don't worry. You did nothing I didn't want."

"But what if you go back?"

She groans and pushes me off her body. I flop onto my back, groaning too. My dick is still hard and when it loses its new favorite resting place between Thea's legs, I ache. She drags the sheets on top of herself, covering her breasts.

"You don't get it. I won't ever go back and become Wen's wife. Ever. There was nothing worth losing my family over until I discovered there actually was. I refuse to be physically punished for not being who Wen wants me to be." Her expression is more serious than I've ever seen. A smile breaks across my face. I can't contain it. "What? Why are you smiling?"

"I'm just so damn proud of you." I pull her into my chest and she rests her head on me. "Part of me wanted to lock you up in my house and never let you go back, but a bigger part of me knew you needed to make your own choices. I knew you would just run if I tried to make them for you." I rub up and down her still bare back.

"I would never go back, Law. I just wasn't ready to accept it until now. I'm most likely going to lose my family. I'm uneducated, unskilled, and undocumented. It was just a lot to come to terms with. Leaving Wen means everything changes. Everything. My sisters, my brothers, I won't get to watch them grow up. One day, probably soon, they'll all move on to the next place and I won't be there with them." Wetness hits my chest and I squeeze her tighter to me.

"You'll have me. I know I'm not any consolation to your family, but you'll still have me." I kiss her head. "Unless you make me another dumpster dinner. Then all bets are off."

She smacks my stomach and laughs.

CHAPTER 19

Theodora

THE NEXT MORNING, I WAKE UP AND DECIDE I need to get out of the house. I need to look for somewhere to live. I need to find a job. I need to do anything except sit here and think about losing my family.

I shower, dress, and head out, hopping on a bus going downtown. The library has free Internet, so I get off on the stop closest. Law gave me a smartphone yesterday, but I don't understand how to use it, so I threw it in my bag and there it's been ever since.

The library is low-key. Like always. It smells of dusty books and old people, a scent I find comforting. There are a few retirees sitting in the comfy chairs reading newspapers, a few people on the computers, and a circle of preschool kids getting a book read to them by a librarian. I find a computer and sit my ass down. I can read well enough to search for rentals, but trying to put together the words in the listings proves to be complicated. Tears sting as they form and I realize I can't do it. I need help. Frustrated, I log out and grab my bag to leave. Fuck this.

As I fly past the row of computers, I look over and spot Leander in the corner. I don't want him to see me upset, but I don't know when I'll get the chance to see him again, so I take a few calming breaths, dab my eyes, and make my way over to him.

He's concentrating on the computer screen. He has a binder next to him and he's furiously writing something down on paper.

"Leander?" I take the seat next to him. He bolts upright and looks at me for a few long seconds before saying anything.

"Thea, what are you doing here?" He knows I don't read well.

"I was just trying to find an apartment." My voice is hesitant and I wonder how much I should tell him and if he'll run and tell my parents.

"An apartment? What the fuck do you want an apartment for?" His voice creeps louder and I hush him.

"I need somewhere to live." My fingers go to my hair and start twirling.

"No. What you need to do is swallow your goddamn pride and come home. You know you will eventually, anyway."

Anger pulses through my veins at his words. If any of my siblings would have my back, I hoped it would be him.

"I'm not coming back. I'm not marrying Wen. Do you even know what he did to me?" I pray he says no so I won't want to punch him in the throat.

"Yeah, I heard and I get it. Wen has turned into a douchebag, but you have to come home and work things out. If not with Wen, then at least with Mom and Dad." He pleads with me.

"How are Mom and Dad? Freedom? The girls?" I'm dying for any news. Especially about my kid sisters. I miss them something fierce.

"They're well. They miss you. Mom and Dad won't talk about it, and everyone's been somber. The girls cry for you every day. Freedom acts like nothing is wrong, but it's just him trying to be tough." He looks down and I can see he's upset by all this too. I blink away tears.

"Maybe I'll come over during the day when the men are working and try to talk to Mom," I suggest.

"You should." He reaffirms.

"What about you? How are you? How's school?" I motion to the notebook he has laid out. A smile instantly spreads across his face.

"It's good. I'm graduating soon. My advisors wanted me to apply to some universities, but I need to work to help support the family. So, I applied to the community college and got in. I'll be starting in the fall." Pride radiates from him and I can't help but be proud of him too.

"That's amazing. Really, it is!" I lean over and give him a hug.

"Thanks." He pats my back in return.

"Have you told Mom and Dad?" I pull away from him. He shifts nervously in his seat and his smile falters.

"Not yet," he says with a sigh.

"You'll figure it out." I squeeze his hand and change the subject. "You turn eighteen next month. Have Mom and Dad spoken about a bride?" I waggle my eyebrows at him. I've never seen Leander with a girl. Granted, there aren't too many around his age. Kezia is the closest, and she's a few months older. For whatever reason, it makes a difference to the parents.

"They've been talking about bringing in a girl from the Midwest, but I'm not ready for that." Leander looks uncomfortable. Usually when a guy hits eighteen, he's demanding a wife. The Romani are proud men and want to prove their manhood by bringing in a wife and having kids.

"What about a girlfriend? Anyone you've met?" I tilt my head, just happy to be having any kind of conversation with my brother.

"No, Thea. Drop it!" He shuts his binder a little too hard, and it startles me. I don't know why it set him off.

"Fine. Fine." I hold my hands up in surrender. "I was just asking."

Leander sighs, looks down at his binder for a second, and then back up at me. "Have you ever just felt like you don't belong?" he asks.

I motion up and down my body.

"Um, have you met me? Have you noticed my current situation?"

"Yeah, sorry. I guess you do." He stands up and puts his binder and pencil in his backpack. "I gotta go."

"Already? You can't hang out with your sister for longer? Maybe go to lunch?" I ask hopefully.

"No, sorry. I'm supposed to be at work." He swings his backpack over his shoulder and looks down to where I'm still sitting. "Go talk to Mom, okay? And visit your sisters."

I give him a weak smile. He walks away and I'm left alone.

He's right. I need to go talk to Mom. I need to try to make this better without marrying Wen. I get up and leave the library, heading to the bus stop.

At the compound, all the little kids sit at tables while their moms serve lunch. Indiana munches on a sandwich, Charity pours drinks, and Mom serves alongside the other women.

The second Indiana sees me, she throws her sandwich down and jumps up, yelling my name. She doesn't even slow when she reaches me, knocking me clean on my ass.

"Hey, Indie. I missed you." I wrap my arms around her small body and squeeze as tight as I can.

"Thea! Guess what?" She pushes away from me so she can look me in the eyes.

"What, firecracker?" I give her my full attention. Really, this question could go either way. Either she'll tell me she farted on me or she'll say she gets to eat ice cream for breakfast now. Her enthusiasm doesn't have levels. Any news deserves sky-high excitement with this one.

"Mama said if you didn't come back, I get all your bras and undies!" she yells despite me being six inches from her face.

"Oh, really?" I scowl. "What do you need with my bras and undies?"

"Someday I'ma have boobies like you. I wanna be prepared," she says seriously. This kid has been wanting to be a teenager since the second she could talk. She's never been into dolls or kids' toys. She only wants to play with makeup and dress-up clothes. Skanky dress-up clothes, so I guess she fits right in.

"Oh yeah? Have you been staying out of my stuff?" I mock scold her. I know what her answer will be. She's always digging through my stuff in her quest to be like me. She completely ignores my question.

"I'll prolly have bigger boobs than you, so I don't even want 'em." She squeezes my boobs in her small hands and I knock her away, laughing.

"You're probably right. Better wait and get your own bras." I stand up and brush my dusty ass off.

"Did you come to 'pologize?" She looks up at me with her head tilted.

"I just came to talk to Mama." I look over at where Mom is watching our exchange.

"Mama said you can only come back if you 'pologize." Tears fill her eyes. "So 'pologize, Thea, okay? I want you to come back. I miss your ass."

I laugh at her words, half little kid, half grown adult.

"I'll try, okay?"

She nods and runs off, leaving me to take the walk of shame alone.

I catch Mom peeking at me through her periphery, but doing a damn good job at ignoring my presence.

"Mom. Can we talk?" I ask, placing a hand on her arm.

"You should come back later, when Wen is here." Her tone is cold.

"I didn't come to talk to Wen. I came to talk to you." I let my hand fall away from her. She drops the bowl of cut fruit she was holding and turns to me, arms crossed over her body.

"I don't know what you think I can do for you, Thea."

I try to swallow my tears because I wasn't expecting this level of hostility. I thought she would at least be happy to see me.

"I don't need you to do anything for me. I just missed you, missed my family, and wanted to come talk to you about how we can fix this." I look at the ground, knowing if I see the anger I'm hearing in her voice, I'll lose it.

"You know how to fix this. I can't help you. Braithe is so offended and Wen is, well, he's pissed the fuck off."

I throw my hands in the air, losing all self-control. "What about me, Mom? What about my pain? What about the way Wen treated me? You want me to just ignore it and take whatever punishment he sees fit for his strong-willed wife?"

"Yes, Thea! Yes. Better yet, I want you to just settle the fuck down. Stop being so headstrong. Accept your place in this family and live a nice, calm life." She's yelling now and everyone is watching the show.

"Excuse me." Nuri interrupts our shouting match. "I just wanted to ask for a minute with you, Thea."

I look at the quiet woman I had always assumed was just shy. Now realizing it's so much more than that.

"Sure," I say. We walk to the drainage ditch in silence until I can't take it anymore. I turn to her. "What's up?" I shouldn't be so clipped with her, but I'm still fuming from my fight with Mom.

"I need you to keep this between us." Her gaze is cast down.

"Okay, I can do that." Because honestly who am I going to tell at this point?

"Thea, I would have loved to have you for a daughter-in-law. You are funny, clever, smart, and so pretty." If this meek woman scolds me, I might lose my shit.

"But," I bite out.

"I would have loved to have you as a daughter-in-law, but my son doesn't deserve you. If you marry him, you will be marrying a younger version of my husband and I wouldn't wish it on anyone."

I freeze. "Nuri."

"I love my husband and I love my son, but I have spent so much of my life trying to make them happy and still never quite succeeding. I had to change who I was to fit into my husband's life and I don't want that for you. I want you to be the bold and brave woman I had the pleasure of watching grow up." Nuri holds both my hands in hers.

"I don't want to lose my family," I say through my own tears.

"I can't help you with that. Gypsies are a prideful people, you know that." She releases my hands and wipes her tears away. "I love you, Thea. No matter what you choose, I'll still love you."

I pull Nuri into a hug, more confused now than I was when I left Law's house this morning.

"Thank you, Nuri," I say into her hair.

"Are you staying somewhere safe?" she whispers.

"Yeah. I am." That's the only thing I know for certain right now. Law is my safe place to land.

I don't say goodbye to Mom, but I hug both of my sisters tight and promise to see them soon, even if it's a lie. Charity tells me she packed some of my stuff while I was talking to Nuri. I accept the duffle bag she gives me and take off again. This time it feels so much more permanent.

CHAPTER 20

Lawrence

THEA'S BEEN LIVING WITH ME FOR OVER A WEEK. She's slowly becoming more depressed and more introverted. When she came back from visiting her mom, she was a different girl. She isn't laughing, joking, or even smiling. I'm beside myself with worry for her.

I don't know what she does all day while I'm at work, but I know she's mostly been watching TV. She's discovered Netflix and has taken the term *Netflix and chill* to a very literal level.

Every day I come home to dishes stacked in the sink, clothes strewn across the floor, and trash on the counters. My anxiety is spiking so high from seeing my house this way. I spend hours every night cleaning. After everything is clean and in its original order, the maddening girl snuggles up to me, apologizes, and cries. She won't talk about it, just cries herself to sleep.

I'm losing my mind. Something has to give. Therefore, on my way home today, I stop by a music store. I know nothing about guitars, so I enlist the help of the clerk.

"This is a 1964 Gibson Dove. It's in practically new condition. It's what I would recommend if you're wanting high-end." Matt, the employee, pulls a beautiful acoustic guitar from behind a display case. "It has this trademark mother of pearl dove inlaid on the pickguard. The back and sides are maple and the top is spruce. It has such a sweet, bright sound to it."

I take the guitar and inspect it closely. There's a dove sitting on a branch with red flowers all around and I know this is the one. "I'll take it."

"Sir, this is a four-thousand-dollar guitar." He takes the guitar from me and puts it back in the display.

"I said I'll take it." I pull the black Amex from my wallet and set it down on the counter. The clerk takes one look and pulls the guitar back out.

"Well, all right." He smiles, happy about the sale.

After he sets it in a black leather case and talks me into a few accessories, I load the guitar in my car and head home.

When I walk in the door, I'm hit with a pleasant smell, but it's still a very foreign scent from the usual pine and lemon I'm used to. I look around and see pots on the stove have bubbled over the sides and onto the gas elements. Cutting boards line the counter with half chopped vegetables lying on them. The refrigerator door is open and a very fine, long skirt covered ass is sticking out from inside.

I tamp my anxiety down by taking a deep breath. At least she isn't curled into a ball on the couch. Cooking might be an improvement to her slow withdrawal from life. I walk up behind her and grab her hips, pulling her ass into my groin. She startles and bolts upright and I wrap my arms around her waist.

"Whatcha making, Trouble?" I whisper in her ear.

"A stew my grandma used to make." She looks at the giant bubbling pot and sighs. "I tried to half the recipe, but even that was too much." I turn her around and her arms go around my neck, my arms around her waist.

"Did you go shopping today?" I left a credit card on the

counter for her before I left for work, hoping she would venture outside.

She scowls. "Yes, Richie Rich. I took your credit card and went to the store. I even brought back receipts, so you'd eat dinner with me."

"Thank you," I murmur before planting my lips on hers. She tastes like rosemary and thyme. After getting my fill, I pull away. "It smells delicious."

"I hope you like it. I've been missing my family and hoped this would make me feel closer to them." She pulls away and stirs the pot.

"I think that was a good idea. I'll go change and then I can help." I hear clattering and a few muffled curses as I move away. I shake my head. I must be crazy for this girl to not be losing it over the disaster she's creating. I change and pick up the mess she's made in my room. I would get irritated at having to constantly pick up after her if it weren't for the tiny panties she leaves lying around. Any intimacy we had been working toward has died. If I'm lucky enough for her not to cry herself to sleep, then she's falling asleep while telling me stories about her family and explaining more about their history. I'm happy to get to know her better, but having her sexy ass prance around my house in barely there clothing is driving me and my dick insane.

After I inspect a receipt that showed all the ingredients for this dinner, we sit down to eat. It's very good and I'm once again impressed by her cooking skills.

"You could open up a restaurant with the way you cook," I compliment over a bite full of rich meat and potato.

"My people are very good at large portions, cheap ingredients, and full flavor." She beams. "There are so many things I love about being Romani. Our history, our family values, our music…" She trails off, losing herself in memories.

"Oh! That reminds me." I wipe my mouth with a napkin and go out to the garage to grab my gift out of the car. "I picked up something for you today." When she sees the case in my hand, she jumps from the table and runs over to me.

"You bought me a guitar!" she squeals, clapping and jumping up and down. I set the case on the sofa and she falls to her knees in front of it. She opens it up, and a gasp escapes her lips. "Law. This is too much. I can't accept this." She closes the case and I kneel next to her.

"It's not too much. It's just right. I've been dying to hear you play, and you know how much I love when you sing." I open the case once more and pull the guitar out, handing it to her.

She holds it out and inspects it closely. "My grandpa had one just like this. He's the one who taught me to play. He won his in a poker game he cheated on to win, but it was his pride and joy. Probably still is, though I haven't seen him in a few years."

"How come?" I sweep her hair off her shoulders and kiss the bare skin there.

"He and my grandma retired in Florida. He had a bad back and arthritis from all the years of manual labor and by the time we forced him to a doctor, he was told the damage was irreversible. They left and we haven't heard from them in a while." I stand and pull her up too before sitting her down on a chair and handing her the guitar.

"Maybe we can visit one day," I offer. "But for right now, I want to hear you play."

Her smile lights the room as she puts the guitar in position and starts getting to know it, playing a few chords here and there, adjusting as she goes. I sit on the couch and watch her. She looks every bit eighteen years old with a big guitar dwarfing her frame, her long, curly hair lying over her shoulder and her pink lips pursed in concentration. It should feel wrong for a man my age to crave such a young and wild girl, but fuck if it doesn't make me want her more.

The opening chords to "Blowin' in the Wind" by Bob Dylan fill the room. I'm struck by her musical ability, but when she opens her mouth and starts singing the lyrics? She strikes me deaf, dumb, and blind. Her eyes close as she sings with emotion. I lean forward to rest my arms on my legs and watch her, absolutely stunned at how gorgeous she is.

The song wraps up and I stand up in front of her, taking the guitar from her hands. I set it back in the case before pulling her up to me, needing to be close.

"That was beautiful," I tell her. "You're beautiful."

"Thank you. It was the first song I learned." She tips her head up and licks her lips. I don't make her wait long before I'm kissing her. Our lips move together rhythmically. This is a sensation I never want to end.

"You're making me fall for you, Trouble," I murmur in her ear before sucking the lobe into my mouth.

"You're not so bad yourself," she says, her breath picking up pace.

We kiss for minutes longer until the kitchen steals my attention and I'm reminded of the absolute disaster she made in there. Thea must sense my mood change because she pulls her lips from mine and looks over her shoulder, sighing.

"I'm just going to go get that cleaned up," I say, giving her one last kiss.

"You have some messed up priorities, Richie Rich," she jokes, but her eyes are on my lips and I almost give in. Almost.

CHAPTER 21

Theodora

I SIT ON THE COUCH AND PLAY WITH MY NEW GUITAR
while Law cleans up dinner, just thinking about the last
week. It's been a rough one. I'm bored, I miss my family,
and I know I'm driving Law crazy. I can see it in his demeanor
every day when he comes home and sees what a mess I've
made of his house. I want to be good for him. I want to clean
up after myself. I want to please him, but I just can't bring
myself to care.

Then he gave me this guitar. This expensive, beautiful guitar I never would have purchased for myself and it hits me
how hard he's trying. It makes me feel like a brat who's been
taking advantage of him. Here he is adjusting his life to my
brand of crazy, and all I'm doing is moping and being sorry for
myself.

I need to figure my shit out before I push him too far.
I look over into the kitchen, watching him wash dishes and
wipe down counters. He curses when he scrubs the burned
on food off the gas element of the stove. I set my guitar down
into the case and lock it. He shouldn't be cleaning up my disaster alone.

In the kitchen, I grab a sponge and start wiping down
counters with the bleach spray he uses, wiping every inch,

just the way he's shown me. I put the leftover vegetables in the fridge's crisper and put the spices back in the cupboard, lining the labels up perfectly. I close the door and turn around to find him with a hip resting against the counter, arms folded across his chest, watching me.

"Did I do it right?" I ask, hooking a finger at the cupboard. It's not that I can't do things the way he likes, it just all seems pointless to me. It's not pointless to him, though. I promise myself I'll try from now on. At least until I find my own place. Then all bets are off. Fuck the crisper. It can't possibly make a difference, right?

"Yeah, Trouble. You did it right." He grabs my hand and starts pulling me to the bedroom. I cover my smile with my other hand. Law has been incredibly patient with me, and I've just been a terror. Time to show him how thankful I am.

Once in the room, he grabs the hem of my tank and pulls it over my head, exposing my tits. A guttural moan comes from deep within his chest. He palms a breast with one hand and the other goes to the back of my head, bringing my lips to his. Before I had this, before I had kissed a man, I pictured it being awkward and uncoordinated. It never is with me and Law, though. It's like our lips had found their home in each other.

I drag his shirt over his head, loving my soft breasts on his hard chest and the tickle of his chest hair. He trails kisses down my neck, across my collarbone, and up the other side of my neck. I reach down and unbutton his pants while he does the same to me. By the time we hit the bed, we're in nothing but our underwear.

Ever since he put his mouth on my sex, I've been thinking about what it would be like to do the same for him. Had I been able to control my emotions the last few nights, I might have already had the opportunity, but I got trapped in my head. My emotions got the best of me and every time the tears spilled from my eyes, I got a little angrier with myself. I'm not a crier. That's not me. I'm a woman of action and tomorrow I'll take the first steps in regaining control over my life. But as for this moment, the only kind of action I want is in his boxers.

I pull away from our kiss and look into his muddy brown orbs that see more than a pretty face when they look at me. I trace the outline of his lips with my tongue, killing time while I build up the courage to do what I want to him. I slowly let my hand roam south until I'm resting a palm on his hard length. I've felt his hard cock lots of times. Against my stomach, against my palm, against my core, but always with clothing between us. I want to touch it bare.

"I see your wheels turning. What do you want?" He tucks my hair behind my ear.

"Well, you put your mouth on me. Now I want to put my mouth on you."

His eyebrows shoot up and I smile seductively at him. I place a single kiss on his lips, one on base of his throat, then stream single kisses down his chest and abdomen until I get to the band holding up his white boxer briefs. He has a defined V and a trail of hair that leads down. I want to see how far it goes, so I free his hard dick and watch with a hungry interest as it slaps against his stomach. I palm his balls and take a good look at his dick. Moisture glistens as pre-cum leaks from the tip. I have no idea what I'm doing, but I'm not about to ask for guidance. I mean, I get the gist. I just put the dick in my mouth. Right?

Pep talk over, I move my hand up from his balls and fist him at his base. It's so hard and velvety with a large mushroom head. I bring my lips to his tip, placing a gentle kiss there. His pre-cum coats my lower lip and I lick it off. The taste isn't horrible, and it encourages me to do more. I wrap my lips around the head, licking up the slit. Law hisses and my gaze shoots up his body. His breaths come faster.

Thankful I have done nothing wrong, I pull off of him with a pop before going down again, farther this time. Hollowing out my cheeks, I suck him all the way down before coming back up and swirling my tongue around his tip, tasting more pre-cum.

"You're making it so hard not to come," he moans out.

I look back up to him and his pupils are blown. I keep my attention fixed on him while I suck and lick, taking in as much of him as I can. When he hits the back of my throat, I swallow to fight my gag reflex. This was the right thing to do because his hips thrust up. I reach a hand up his body and drag my nails down his chest and abdomen. He grabs my hand and moves it to his balls, showing me the way he likes to be massaged. After only seconds of my ministrations, he warns me he's going to come. But if he thinks I'll pull away, he's mistaken. Mama didn't raise no quitter.

"Fuck. Fuck! Thea. So fucking good!"

I take him deep again and again, swallowing each time. Before I know what's happening, his dick pulses and hot, thick ejaculate fills my mouth. I can't swallow fast enough, causing some to spill from my mouth and down his shaft. I use it as lube to pump the section of his cock I can't fit in my mouth until he softens. I release him and wipe the spilled semen from my lips, then I lick it off.

"You are the sexiest woman I've ever known," he pants out and I just grin up at him. I pull his boxer briefs back up and cover his dick, placing one last kiss over the top of the fabric. Law pulls me up until my body is flush with his. His hands slips into my underwear and a finger presses against my clit. "Open your legs for me," he whispers.

I drop onto my back and let my knees fall open, giving him room. One finger gets inserted inside me. It goes in easily because I'm dripping wet. He pumps in and out of me slowly. His lips go to my neck, biting, sucking, and licking. Each movement turning me on more.

"You're so wet for me." Law pulls his finger out and rubs the moisture all over my sex. He alternates between rubbing my clit and pumping inside me. The switching techniques keep my orgasm at bay and after a few minutes, I'm desperate for the release.

"Make me come," I beg.

"My naughty girl wants a second orgasm?" he teases.

"Please, Law," I beg again. He inserts a second finger inside me and as they move in and out, his palm grinds against my clit. The dual sensations are exactly what I need, and within a few seconds, an overwhelming pleasure is shooting all over my body. My toes tingle and I see stars under my closed lids. Every muscle in my body tenses and I whimper aloud. I never want it to end, but after only a minute, my body relaxes and I'm able to open my eyes again. Law's gaze is fixed on me and I blush.

"I love watching you," he admits. He pulls his fingers free from inside me and his hand out of my panties and rests it on my sex possessively.

"Creeper," I tease.

"I've loved watching you since the moment I first saw you." His voice is filled with sincerity. I'm taken aback and my instinct is to throw out a joke to lighten the mood. Despite what's been going on lately, I'm not a serious person and I run from talking about feelings.

"You have?" I ask instead.

"You know I have." His lips give me a gentle kiss and then he pulls away. "There's a light within you that shines in everything you do. You've lived more in your eighteen—"

"Almost nineteen," I correct and he nods.

"Almost nineteen years than I have in all my thirty-two years. You find fun in everything you do." He's quiet for a moment, just staring at the wall. Then he sighs. "I'm a serious person—"

"You don't say," I cut in and he presses his lips together.

"Having you around is teaching me to lighten up a bit. You're just so different from any relationship I've had." He brushes strands of hair off my forehead and brings his hand to cup my cheek. "I'm not a man who can read emotions, I'm not even a man who feels emotions often, and it seems like every other woman held her opinions of me in until they grew so big she'd explode. I don't have to worry about that with you." His thumb caresses my check gently and I relish in the loving gesture. "You are what you are and it makes things a lot easier for me."

"So, I'm easy," I say with a smirk.

"That's not what I meant, and you know it."

"Yeah. I know what you mean. Not everyone appreciates me wearing my heart on my sleeve." I turn serious.

"That's their problem, not yours." He reassures me and it feels so good to have someone tell me they like me just the way I am. I was always encouraged to be myself, but it seemed to change when it was time for me to get married. Self-doubt crept in and I've been struggling with my confidence. Lawrence came into my life the second I needed him most. Even if I didn't know it.

"Thank you. That doesn't seem a strong enough way to tell you how I feel, but until I can find the right words? Thank you." We hold each other's gaze for a long moment and I'm filled with so much emotion. So much love. I push it away. It's too soon. Law finally breaks the eye contact and gets off the bed, holding a hand out to me.

"Let's take a shower and go to bed." I take his hand and he leads me to the bathroom. Before we can get there, his phone rings from where he left it in the kitchen. "I'll check that. You start without me." He releases my hand and walks out of the bathroom.

I start the water and let it warm up for a moment. I step under the spray and let the water pour over my head while I think about how I got to this place. My nomadic soul has adjusted to being settled so easily. When I think about staying in Reno, staying with Law, I don't feel panic. I just feel excited. I want to see where this goes and if it weren't for my family issues, everything would be as close to perfect as my life has ever been.

I hear the bathroom door open, and I poke my head out from the glass enclosure. Law is standing facing the shower. "You gonna come join me? I'm awfully lonely in here." I flirt.

"Thea." The tensing of his facial muscles tells me something is very wrong.

"What's going on?" I smile with false hope he'll return it. He doesn't.

"Baby, come on out." He grabs the towel I had hung up before I got in and holds it wide-open for me. I turn the water off and step into it. He wraps it tight around me, turns me around in his arms, and looks down into my eyes.

"What's wrong? Just tell me." Anxiety courses throughout me. He just looks at me, not fuckin' talking. "Law. Tell me."

He swallows a lump in his throat and his mouth opens. What comes out makes little sense to me. My mind goes fuzzy and I feel faint.

"Thea!" I distantly hear him shout. "It's okay. It'll be okay." He lifts me up and carries me to his bed where he sits me on the edge. "We need to go to the hospital."

"The hospital?" Nothing is making sense. Why do we need to go to the hospital?

"Your family is there waiting for you. You need to go say goodbye." He grabs another towel from the linen closet and dries my hair. He's being so gentle.

"Who do I need to say goodbye to?" I look at him in confusion.

"Didn't you hear me?" His thumbs brush my cheeks. So gentle.

"What did you say?" I've never been this light-headed before. Maybe the water was too hot.

"Thea. Your mom. She, uh, she passed." His words hit me like a ton of bricks. My heart throbs in pain and I briefly wonder if I'm having a heart attack. Tears I didn't even know I was crying drip onto my bare thighs. "We need to get you dressed to go to the hospital."

"What? I don't understand. You must be wrong. She's only thirty-six. She's so young." I'm not sure he understands me through my sobs.

"I'm sure. Your brother called. He said you told him about me and he wasn't sure you'd be with me, but he had no other ideas on how to find you." Leander called Law? Everything is so confusing, like my mind is stuck in the slow lane and the information is speeding so fast, I can't keep up.

I don't fight him as he pulls a shirt over my head. I don't help him as he pulls underwear and a skirt up my legs. I can't even hold my head still as he runs a brush through my tangled hair. I do, however, go to him when he yanks me onto my feet and pulls me out to the garage door, sitting me in the passenger seat and reaching over my body to buckle my seat belt. I notice he's dressed now too. When did that happen?

He walks around to the driver's side and sits himself down, buckling in. He opens the garage door and starts the engine, but he doesn't move.

"I need some guidance from you on this. I don't think it's

a good time for me to meet your family, but I'm struggling with leaving you there." His hand rests on my knee and I grasp it with my own.

"Please don't leave me. Not right now. I need you." I am too scared to walk into the hospital alone, and I'm not even certain I fully understand what's going on quite yet.

"Okay, I'll stay with you." He kisses my tear-soaked cheek.

He throws the car in reverse and takes off in the hospital's direction. We speak no more words, just hold each other's hand with a bruising intensity. All too soon, we pull up to the hospital and Law finds a parking space near the emergency room entrance. I don't move. It's too soon. I didn't have time to process, to think things through, to come to terms with what happened. I just need more time.

"Baby, we need to go in. Leander said they're waiting for you." He soothes.

"Waiting for me for what? She's already dead." More tears stream down my cheeks and I wipe them away roughly.

"They need to take the body away," he mumbles. "But they wanted you to say goodbye."

"No. I don't want to say goodbye. I don't want to be without a mom!"

Law pushes a button and his seat goes backward, then he's pulling me over the console and into his lap, his arms squeezing tightly against my middle. I nuzzle my face into his neck and cry like I've never cried before.

"Shh… shh… I'm so sorry, Thea. I'm so, so sorry." He tries to soothe. We stay there for some time before Law places his hands on my shoulders and holds me away from him, demanding my eyes. "It's time to go in now, okay? I promise I'll be right by your side. We'll do this together."

I nod and climb back over to my side and exit the car. Before I can even close the door, Law is right by my side, enveloping my hand in his. This is the very last way I ever imagined introducing my family to him, but I don't have time to worry about that now, so I push it away and refocus on my mom. My mom who died.

We walk through the automatic doors to the E.R. and my family bombards us. Law lets go of my hand and mouths, "I'll be right here." I nod and take Charity into my arms, hugging her tight. I feel the small hands of Indie wrapped around my waist and Freedom sets a hand on my shoulder. Leander stands next to Law, his head down. After long minutes of crying and sniffling, my siblings peel themselves off me. They part and I see Dad, hands in his pockets, forehead furrowed, and desperately sad eyes. I release any animosity I had been harboring and run into his arms. The big bear of a man catches me and my feet leave the ground.

"Daddy," I whisper into his neck. "What happened?"

He sets me down, but doesn't let go. "I don't know. She was just fine. She made dinner. We were all just sitting down to unwind. I don't understand. One second she was right fuckin' there next to me. The next second, she was on the ground, not breathing. Braithe called nine-one-one. I don't know what fuckin' happened." He sounds just as confused as I feel.

"What did the doctors say?" I pull out of his arms and look up into his devastated eyes. I'm not sure I've ever seen an emotion outside of pissed, happy, and indifferent out of Dad before.

"They aren't sure. We have to wait for an autopsy, but they think…" His shoulders begin to shake. I rub a hand up and down his arm. "They think she had undiagnosed heart disease. They were asking me all these questions. About all these symptoms." He drags a hand roughly through his hair. "Thea, I didn't know. I didn't know what it meant. She told me she was tired. She told me her heart was racing a couple of times. I guessed she was just aging. I mean, fuck, I'm tired all the time too."

"It's not your fault, Dad." I rub circles on his back, trying to comfort him when my world has fallen apart too.

Leander walks up to us, his sad green eyes brimming with tears. "They got her on all kinds of machines. There's no chance of her waking up and even if she did, she'd be brain dead. Her heart stopped beating and she wasn't breathing for over a half hour."

I hug him to me and his tears soak my shirt. "I'm so sorry I wasn't there. I'm so sorry."

He pulls away from me and grabs my hand. "You need to come say goodbye." He leads me through the hall, but I stop and look at the spot I left Law. He's still standing there, his strong arms crossed over his chest and his head down.

"Just a second," I say to Leander. I go to Law and place a hand on his arm. He looks up at me, lines of worry around his eyes. "Please come with me?"

"Whatever you need." And I can see he means it. This man would give me anything I asked for.

We walk down the cold and sterile hallway, into the ICU. The nurses show us to her room. We stop right outside, none of us wanting to see our new reality.

"I'm gonna go back and help Dad with the girls." Leander squeezes my shoulder, tips a chin at Law, and walks away.

"I'm here for you." Law wraps an arm around my shoulder and we walk in.

Mom is lying on the hospital bed, wires and tubes criss-crossing all over her body. There is a breathing tube down her throat and her chest rises and falls in a jerky way that's not natural. I approach slowly, a hand covering my mouth and tears pouring down my cheeks.

"Mama," I croak out and pick her hand up in mine. I bring it to my lips and place a kiss there. "Mama, what happened? This wasn't supposed to happen. We were still in a fight. I didn't have the chance to say I'm sorry." Law places his hands on my shoulders and he gently massages. It reminds me he's here, that Mom never even met him. I pull one of his hands off my shoulder and bring him around to my side. I clear my throat before introducing Law to Mom.

"This is Law. Lawrence. He's... well, he's my person. I met him all the way back when the boys stole the tires off a car at the beach, remember? You tried to punish them, but you were no good at that." I smile at the memory. "Anyway, he's a good man. He's been taking care of me all these weeks. All these weeks we didn't have to be fighting. We shouldn't have been fighting." I turn my head into Law's chest and sob.

"Shh... shh... it's okay. I've got you." Law soothes.

I turn back to Mom and carefully lean over her and kiss her on the forehead and then murmur softly, "I'm so sorry, Mama. I promise I'll take care of the kids. I'll make sure Charity showers and wears clean underwear. I'll make sure Indiana gets pins from all over the country. I'll make sure Freedom doesn't get arrested, and Leander? Well, I already know that boy will be okay. He doesn't need me, but if he does, I promise I'll be there for him." I take another look at her and add, "I'll make sure Dad's okay too, all right?"

Not being able to look at her anymore, I turn to Law and crash into his chest, sobbing. His arms wrap tightly around me and he holds me there for what seems like hours. A light knock on the door separates us.

Dad steps into the room. He looks Law up and down, clear disapproval on his face, but he shakes his head and turns his attention to me. "Do you need more time?" I shake my head and he disappears momentarily. When he comes back in, my sisters and brothers are with him. Each with their own look of sadness and despair covering their faces. Charity rushes to me and I scoop her up into my arms. She's getting too big to be held, but I won't deny her this comfort. Not today.

My siblings each take a turn kissing Mom on the head and cheek, whispering their own goodbyes to the matriarch of our family. When it's Charity's turn, I carry her to Mom's bedside.

"You have anything you wanna tell her?" I ask softly.

"I love you, Mama. You were the best Mama ever. I love you." She bursts into tears and digs her face into the crook of my neck. I rub circles on her back, trying to soothe her, but knowing there's no comfort to be found for any of us today.

Dad nods to the nurse I didn't notice was standing in the doorway. She makes her way over to the machines and flips them off. The sound of air being pumped into Mom stops first, then the beeping. The alarms sound, alerting us to Mom's heart not continuing to beat on its own, and the nurse turns it off too. It's suddenly deathly quiet, save for the sniffling of the sad little girl in my arms. We all stay in our own grief for a long while before I notice Charity has cried herself to sleep.

I turn to face Dad. "She's asleep. I'll take her home." A disapproving look crosses his face as his gaze goes from me to Law.

"My home," he scolds. I roll my swollen eyes.

"Jesus. Yes. Your home," I snap. I make eye contact with Law and he follows me out of the hospital room. My heart breaks when I realize this was the last time I will ever see Mom.

CHAPTER 22

Lawrence

W E PULL UP TO THE COMMUNE AND FIFTY OR more people are standing around. A cluster of women are hugging each other and crying, a bunch of kids are playing cards quietly, and the men look to be keeping themselves busy with menial tasks. I cut the engine and look back at the sleeping form in my backseat.

"I can carry her… if you want?" I undo my seat belt.

"Thank you. Not just for that, but for being here for me. I know it must be awkward."

She's right. It has been awkward. Not only with this being the first time I'm meeting her family, but also because, while I understand emotions, I don't feel them the same way other people do. I didn't cry when my parents died. I didn't say goodbye and fuss around their bodies. No one called me and told me to come to the hospital. It wasn't expected of me and I wouldn't have gone even if it had been. They were my parents, they died, now I don't have parents. The end.

Thea's family, though. Their emotions run high. They all cried in agony and whispered their love to a mother who was not even there anymore. It made little sense, but I knew enough to stand stoic and be respectful. Thea's dad didn't look all too excited to see me with his daughter, but the rest of the family didn't even seem to take note of me.

"It's fine. Really. Don't worry about me. Let's go tuck your sister in." I step out of the car and scoop the tiny girl from the seat. I follow Thea, but she gets stopped with every step forward she takes. The women hugging her and crying, telling her how sorry they are. The men patting her on the back and side eyeing me. One particular young man wrapped Thea in a hug and kissed her head. Had I not had my arms full with a child, I would have pulled her from his arms and shown him Thea was mine. I know who that guy is. He's the one who put his hands on my girl.

Eventually, we make our way up the few steps and into a travel trailer. I've never been inside one, never had any desire, and stepping into this one, I don't think I want to again.

The incense scent, woody and smoky, hits my nose, and it reminds me of when Thea and I first met. It's a fond memory and I make a mental note to Google where I can find incense. I'd like for my home to smell like hers. Maybe it would help me convince her to stay.

I look around, taking the nomadic home in. It's a long and narrow, open space. How a family of seven lives here is beyond me.

Directly to my left is a bathroom. The pocket door is open and I can see toothbrushes litter the counter, laundry fills the small tub, and bins filled with God knows what are stacked on either side of the toilet. Straight in front of me is a kitchen that doesn't appear to be used often. On the counters sit small bins stacked to the ceiling with what appears to be pantry foods. To my immediate right is a mustard-colored sofa with a flower print on it. The cushions are each wrapped in a plastic cover. Do they leave them on all the time? To the far end, on the left, is a big bed with curtains drawn open. It strikes me how painful this must be for Thea. Her mom will never sleep in that bed again. Not for the first time tonight, my heart aches for her. Above the bed is a loft, with aluminum stairs leading up. I hope I'm not to get this little one up there.

"She sleeps up there." Thea points to the loft. I sigh and Thea smiles ever so slightly. "But I think we can lay her in my parents'—" She stops herself and takes a deep breath, letting it out slowly. "My dad's bed. I doubt he'll sleep tonight, anyway."

I lay the child down and Thea covers her with a thin blanket. The air is thick and hot inside their home, so I doubt she'll even need the thin covering, but I don't say anything. Thea places her hands on her hips, standing on the other side of the bed from me.

"I think I'll stay here tonight. My family needs me right now." Her golden orbs don't meet mine, like she's nervous to tell me she isn't coming home with me. She shouldn't be. I think her family will need her too.

"I understand. Will you call me or come see me tomorrow?" I ask. I've spent every day with Thea for a long time now. I don't want to change that. I've grown quite fond of our time.

"Yeah. I will." We both walk to the front of the bed and meet in the middle. Her arms lock around my neck, mine go around her waist, and I bury my face in her hair.

"I'm sorry about your mom. Should you need anything, just call me. I'll keep my phone close." I pull away and look into her sad, gilded eyes.

"I know. I will." She promises.

I walk out of the trailer with Thea right behind me. Once outside, I turn to her and lean in to give her a kiss. She turns her head and my kiss lands on her cheek. I look at her in question, but her gaze is trained to whatever is behind me.

"Is this who you've been shacking up with?" an angry

voice accuses. I turn to see the guy who had his lips on Thea's head earlier. An involuntary growl rumbles through my chest.

"Not now, Wen." Thea's voice is icy. "Don't start with me. Not today."

"I'm not starting shit." Wen throws his hands in the air. "I'm just curious who my fiancée has become a dirty whore for."

Anger surges through my body. I pivot, my fists balled and ready to get in this guy's face. Thea grabs my arm and stops my forward motion.

"You know as well as I do I'm not your fiancée." Thea's face screws up in disgust.

"Maybe you've forgotten the bride price was paid?" The prick inches closer, his eyes darting me to Thea. "You think your daddy will be able to give that money back now that he has a funeral to pay for?"

I feel Thea sag. Her grip on my arm tightens like I'm the only thing holding her up right now.

"She isn't fucking yours. If it's about money, I'll gladly relieve them of the debt so she doesn't have to marry an inconsequential asshole like you." I seethe.

"It doesn't work like that. We've made commitments. This is what her mom would have wanted for her." Wen then steps to the side to direct his next words to her. "You gonna go against your mom's dying wishes, Thea? You're that selfish?"

Thea's breath stutters and I know she's crying. This girl has had enough to cry about today. This guy doesn't get to toy with her emotions like this. Fucking pathetic using guilt to keep hold of something that doesn't belong to him.

Wen steps close to my face and I can smell booze and sweat emanating from his body. I don't back down. He's inches shorter and I use my height to my advantage, glaring down at him under my nose.

"She isn't a possession. She's a fucking human being, and you'd do best to remember that," I say through gritted teeth.

"That may be true where you're from, but around here, she's a possession. My possession." That's all it takes for me to lose my temper. I shove him in the chest, causing Thea's hand to drop from my arm. She gasps. He stumbles back a few feet, but is back in my face in seconds, grabbing hold of my shirt with one hand, the other pulling a fist back and ready to punch. I don't give him the chance to land it. I place my hands on the top of his shoulders and bring his body forward, my knee connecting with his nose. A sickening *crunch* sounds through the quiet of the crowd that has gathered around us. "Motherfucker!" he yells out, his hands clutching his nose that is gushing blood.

I stalk over to him. Taking advantage of his position, I shove him over and he lands on his ass, his hands still covering his likely broken nose, blood dripping between the fingers. I tower over him, and loud enough for everyone to hear, so there will be no mistaking, I seethe, "If you *ever* lay a hand on that woman again, I will kill you." I grab his shirt, pull him up, and point to Thea. "She means everything to me. Everything. So you'll keep your distance and leave her alone."

I don't wait for him to answer. I just shove him away from me and walk back to Thea. Her fingers are twirling frantically through her hair. I stop their fretting and bring her hand to my mouth, place a quick kiss there, and whisper, "If he bothers you again, call me." Thea's blinking rapidly, most likely to ward off any tears, but she nods. "I'll talk to you tomorrow." I palm the back of her head and bring her lips to mine, placing a possessive kiss there for everyone to see.

As if my car is a beacon, I focus on it and ignore the whispers and judging stares of the people who have gathered to watch the drama. I'm damn lucky none of them stepped in to help the pathetic bastard or things would've ended differently. Not that it would have stopped me from standing up for Thea. Nothing would have stopped that. I needed to make sure those people know she's worth more than a bride price. More than an arrangement. She's worth every damn thing, and it's about time they started treating her that way.

I drive home wondering how this became my life. All it took was a chance meeting and I'm no longer the man who is detached and emotionless. I didn't even dip my toes in before I left behind my world of systematic calm and jumped head first into her anarchic waters.

It's been a week since Thea's mom died and I've only seen her once in that time. She came by the next evening to collect her purse and what meager belongings she had left at my house.

While I understand why she's taking this time with her family, I miss her. More than anyone has ever missed someone, I'm sure of it. When Chloe left, I was sad to be alone again, but I didn't miss her specifically. Thea is different. I feel lost and tormented without her wreaking havoc on my head and heart.

While I still have been going into work, not even the numbers have been able to keep my mind off Thea. I can't shake the niggle that something is off. Rationally I know it's the disconnect that has me twisted in this way, but my mind obsesses over all the things that could go wrong without me even knowing.

It's in the middle of one of my neurotic moments that a knock sounds on my office door. Mark doesn't wait to be called in before he's barging his way in and calling out to Monica that he has a pass to come in whenever he wants.

"There's my favorite sad sack." Mark's lower lip juts out as he sinks into a chair in front of me. "How's it going, dollface?"

"It's going just fine, but I have a meeting in ten." I lean back in my chair and cross my arms over my chest. "A meeting you aren't invited to."

"Don't be touchy," he drawls. "I just wanted to see if you've heard from our girl yet?"

"She's *my* girl, and yes. I've heard from her. She's coming over tonight." Thea finally used the phone I gave her and figured out how to text. It's the only way we have communicated the last week. I've asked if I can come to her, spend time with her and get to know her family, but she has denied me each time. I ask about Wen and she assures me he is keeping his distance, so that's one thing, I guess. Late at night, my imagination runs wild and I picture that dick manipulating his way into Thea's grieving heart. I want to be the one there for her. I want to be the one comforting her. I want to be the one to mend her broken heart.

"Oh, goodie!" Mark claps his hands rapidly. "Maybe you can get in and stop being such a grump."

I cross my arms. "I'm not talking to you about sex." *Or our lack of sex.*

"Fine, fine." He stands up and buttons his deep purple sport coat. It's covering a button-down that has an eggplant print, if I'm not mistaken. Do we even have a HR department in this company? "I expect that frown to turn upside down when I see you tomorrow morning, Mr." He wags a finger at me and walks out.

I shake my head and get back to work. I've fallen behind and it's only causing my anxiety to worsen. I've always been a dependable employee, never allowing my personal life to interfere with my work. I guess I've never had a personal life worth interfering with my work before.

The hours drag on, but I make a dent in my list of catch-up work. No doubt only being able to focus because I know I'll see Thea tonight. When I pull into my driveway, I spot her sitting on the swing, rocking back and forth slowly. I park in the garage and walk around front to join her.

She looks gorgeous, but distraught. She seems to be in a trance and doesn't notice my proximity. I take a moment to drink her in with my eyes. She's wearing one of her many long and flowy patterned skirts and a long-sleeved ruched crop top made from a gauzy fabric. Her hair is braided over her shoulder, but a few wisps hang down and it's those strands she's twirling through her fingers. Her face is lax, but her lips are pursed, the only indication that whatever she's mulling over isn't pleasant.

I take a seat next to her and she snaps out of it. A soft smile breaks through her stoic stare and she willingly allows me to pull her onto my lap. My arms wrap around her middle and she rests her cheek on mine. I breathe in her smoky cedar and teak scent for a moment before bringing her lips to mine. There's no tongue or desperation, just our lips melding into each other, getting reacquainted after such a long break.

"I've missed you," she whispers as she pulls away. I rub a hand over her shoulders, kneading the tight tension of the muscles there.

"I've missed you too," I say honestly. "Let's go inside. I want to make you dinner."

"I'd love that. I miss your cooking." Her admittance makes me smile. I hold a hand out to her and she takes it. No arguments about not needing help. No scolding about chivalry. I would think it was a nice change, but I can't shake this ominous feeling I've had since she asked to see me tonight. I hope I'm wrong.

CHAPTER 23

Theadora

ENTERING LAW'S HOUSE, THE SMELL OF BLEACH stings my nostrils. I immediately feel remorseful, knowing not having contact with me in so long probably caused many late night cleaning sessions. Everything looks exactly the same, but I wouldn't expect any different.

"I'm just going to change. I'll be right back." He disappears into the bedroom and I sit down on his hard and uncomfortable sofa I love so much because I spent my first night with Law curled into his side on it.

I lean back into it and think about the last week. The pain and heartache at having to put Mom to rest still curls around my heart. We cremated her body and released her ashes into the Nevada desert, freeing her to roam the earth, even in death.

That wasn't the hardest part of first few days after her death, though. Trying to be the strong big sister my siblings needed me to be, while also grieving myself, was almost enough to break me. Indie and Charity have cried themselves to sleep in my arms every night, while Leander and Freedom retreated into themselves, becoming shells of the rough and tumble young men they once were.

Dad has been a whole different story. He turned to

alcohol, getting drunk and starting fights with the other men every single night. He even tried to get into it with me one night, lashing out about me not being around during Mom's last days. I stood up from the green plastic chair I was sitting in next to him and stormed off. He got up to follow me, not done spewing his venom, but he was too drunk. He tripped and fell into the dirt. I didn't even bother helping him up. I just left him there to yell out hurtful comments from the ground.

It hasn't been until the last day or two things have calmed down. Dad put the fuckin' bottle down and started to come up with plans, started being a dad to my siblings, and apologized to me for his behavior. That was when I finally felt comfortable enough to come see Law.

I take in every inch of his space, storing it in my memory to recreate later when I need somewhere happy to escape to in my mind. It's then I notice the framed pictures on the mantle. The one of his parents is still there, but the gold, shiny frame that housed the picture of him and Chloe isn't there. In its place is a distressed wood frame. I walk over to the gas fireplace and take a closer look. It's a picture of me and Law. We're snuggled up on the couch, about to watch a movie. We both have on such big, stupid grins. I pick up the photo, inspecting it closer. His hand is draped around me and holding me close. I smile at the memory.

"I love that picture."

I look up and see Law. He's standing with a hip resting on the island and his arms crossed over his chest.

"I love it too. Can you send me a copy on my phone?" I place the frame back and walk over to him.

"I'm glad you're finally coming around to the twenty-first century." He smirks. I uncross his arms and wrap them around my waist. I lock my wrists behind his neck.

"What can I say? I'm a Gen Z." I smirk back at him and he rolls his eyes.

"Ugh. Don't remind me, youngster."

My lips touch his gently for the briefest of moments before he takes control. His head tilts to the side, eliminating any remaining distance between us. His warm palms cup my cheeks as he devours my mouth, plunging his tongue in my mouth where it reacquaints itself. I drag my nails down his back and then under his shirt. His muscles flex with every movement.

He takes my lower lip between his teeth and pulls gently, opening the floodgates between my legs. Soft kisses make their way across my cheek and stop when he sucks my earlobe into his mouth and flicks it with his tongue. My thighs squeeze together to ease some of the ache that's building, but knowing it won't be enough until he's filling me, taking my virginity.

As he's making his way back to my mouth, I yank his shirt up and over his head. His chiseled abs and that damn V has me shaking my head in disbelief. His pecks jump one at a time. He winks at me. Cocky asshole.

He takes my hand in his and pulls me into his bedroom. I'm not surprised when I see the tightly made bed and not even one sock on the ground. He sits on the edge of his bed and brings me to stand between his legs. I sigh in pleasure as his mouth licks and sucks at my covered breasts, dampening the fabric. Law hooks fingers into the band of my skirt. He pulls it down over my hips and it falls to the ground on its own. He reaches around me and squeezes the globes of my ass. I dip my head down and meet him for another searing kiss.

"These skirts are my favorites," he murmurs against my lips.

"Why's that?" I breathe out.

"Easy access," he says with a smile I feel instead of see.

I shut him up with a kiss I take control of. My tongue plunges into his mouth, my teeth skimming along his lips.

"This shirt has to go, Trouble." His voice, deep and breathy. I take a small step back and peel the tight fabric off, draping an arm over my breasts. "Have I told you how much I love that you don't wear bras?"

"You might have mentioned it once or twice." I've never been shy with my body, but I've never been naked in front of a man before Law either. Every time I'm exposed to him, it feels special because he's the only one.

He pulls my arm away, revealing myself to him. "These breasts…" He sucks one into his mouth. They're small enough the whole thing fits between his lips. He releases it with a pop. "They're a perfect mouthful." My head lulls back on my neck and I moan at the sensation. "And these tiny nipples…" He bites down gently on one and tugs before releasing it and placing a kiss on the tip. "I could suck on them for days." He takes the other into his mouth and rapidly flicks the tight bud with his tongue, causing me to writhe, desperately needing some attention between my legs. "What's wrong? You're squirming." He quirks an eyebrow up at me.

"I just need…" I don't finish, hoping he'll fill in the blanks.

"What do you need, baby?" His hands move up and down my side from tits to hips.

"You, Law. I need you," I whine. He grabs my arms and pulls me down onto the bed next to him. Then, he's on top of me, his sweats covered legs between mine. I feel his hardness immediately and he thrusts up against me, sending shock waves up and down my body. "Yesssss," I drag out. He slides his cock up and down my slit a few more times before he stops everything. I want to throw a two-year-old tantrum, kicking and screaming, but instead I breathe out, "Why'd you stop?"

"What do you want, Thea? I need to know exactly what you want."

His pupils are blown and his lids are heavy, making them appear black and predatory.

"I want it all. I want all of it. With you." I've never meant anything more in my whole life. I need this moment. I need him to be my first everything. There are no more consequences, no more downsides. Just him and me crushing every barrier that used to stand between us.

"Are you sure? You won't be able to take it back." His hand cups my breast and he flicks my nipple with his thumb, making me forget that I'm supposed to answer. "Thea?" I shake my head and place a hand over his to stop the movement. I need to focus for a second longer, then all bets are off.

"I want your dick inside me, Law. I want you to thrust hard and deep. I want you to make me scream your name. I want you to fill me up with your cum." His jaw drops at my brazen demands. "Is that clear enough for you?"

The corner of his lip curls up in humor. "Crystal." He stands up and pulls my thong down my legs. He slingshots it across the room. I laugh in shock. "I'll pick that up later." There's my obsessive-compulsive man. Next, he pulls down his sweats, freeing his cock I'm sure is bigger than the last time I saw it. I sit up and take it in my hand, using my thumb to rub the pre-cum all over the head. A rumble comes from deep in his chest. "As good as that feels, now that I have the green light, I can't wait another minute to bury myself inside you."

"Me neither."

He climbs on top of my body, forcing me to lie back

down. "Drop your knees to the side so you're open wide for me, okay?" I do what he says. He sits on his haunches and takes himself in hand, intently fixed on my bare pussy. He reaches down and strums my clit with his thumb while pumping his cock up and down. "You're so small. I'm worried I'll hurt you."

"I've seen women give birth. Trust me, it'll fit."

He smirks at my sass. Growing impatient, I dig my heels into his butt and force him closer. He lifts my pelvis up and pulls me to him so my ass is resting on his thighs. He drags his swollen head down my pussy lips and stops at my rear entrance, smearing my juices all over before sliding back up to my clit. He does this again and again.

"Law! Please!"

"Patience. I need to take this slow." Every time his cock makes contact with my clit, tingles shoot through my body, causing tension to build deep within my core. With his next pass, he stops at my entrance and pushes in ever so slightly. "Look at your pussy, trying to suck me in." He's entranced, watching the erotic show we're making together. "Touch your breasts. Pinch your nipples." I do as he asks. I've never touched myself in this way and I didn't expect it to feel good. But when I pinch my nipple, my core clenches around the head of Law's dick. He sucks in a sharp breath. "Fuck." He grinds out.

He pulls out again and rubs his hard length against my clit once, twice, three times and it's too much.

I'm coming. "Law!" I shout out.

He takes that moment to push himself all the way in. I have no time to focus on the slight pinch because the orgasm rippling through my body is too intense. He lies over me and thrusts gently, over and over. My nails dig into his shoulder, probably drawing blood, but at this point, I don't give a shit.

I come down from the high and a giggle escapes my lips. I try to bite my tongue, but it's no use. I open my eyes that have been pinched closed through my orgasm and meet Law's that are wrinkled up at the edges in amusement.

"Are you all right?" he asks.

"I'm amazing. Keep going." His thrusts pick up pace and I watch as Law's skin glistens with exertion. I lock my ankles around his waist and lift my hips with each of his downward motions. He holds himself up on an elbow, his other hand gripping onto my outer thigh, caressing me lovingly.

His breathing gets jerky and his movements lose rhythm. I squeeze my inner walls and he roars out his release. His cock jolts out hot jets of cum, coating my insides. He collapses on top of me, our overheated and sweaty bodies sticking together.

We lie together silently, only the sound of our slowing breaths filling the air. He finds my lips again and kisses me long and slow. When the unavoidable time comes, he pulls out and groans, falling to his side next to me. His seed spills onto the sheets. I smile when I think about Law trying to sleep on these sheets tonight.

His hand cups my cheek and brings me to look at him. "How are you?" His forehead is pinched in the center and I can tell he's worried.

"I'm perfect. I told you. I wanted this for us." I reassure him.

"I was so worried I wouldn't see you again. You've been avoiding me." His thumb draws slow circles on my cheek and I bask in the tenderness.

"I had a lot to take care of. My brothers and sisters weren't okay. My dad was drinking. Everyone momentarily fell apart," I explain.

"How's everything now?"

"It's getting better. I know it'll take time for everyone to find a new normal, but we're on our way." I bring his lips to mine for a single, innocent kiss and then release him.

"I'm glad. I want to hear more. I want to know everything. Let's shower and I'll make you that dinner I promised you." Law gets up before pulling me to stand. We take a long shower, getting dirty again before we get clean. The ache growing between my legs will be the best of reminders for me. I dread thinking about how I'll feel when that ache disappears, like he hadn't been inside me at all.

Law makes me a dinner of saffron lamb kebobs that put The Green Olive's to shame. I make him laugh when I reenact his reaction to our first lunch together. The one in which we dine and dashed. In a lot of ways, he's much different from the man I knew that day. But then he scrubs the dishes and counters for over an hour and I'm reminded he's still Law. Just a slightly more relaxed version.

We go to bed that night and make love one more time. He pulls me so I'm on top and while I grind myself on him, he strums my clit. It doesn't take but a minute for me to spasm on top of him and his release to be pumped into me. And because he's Law, we take another shower and change the sheets before collapsing, naked and exhausted, in bed.

I drape a leg across his body, my head on his shoulder. My fingers twirl in the short hair on his chest and it's quiet. So quiet I thought Law has fallen asleep, so I whisper, "I love you, Richie Rich." His quick intake of breath startles me. He wasn't asleep. I lift my head up so I can see his face. What I see causes worry to course through me. His expression is soft and a warm smile plays on his lips.

"I love you too, Trouble."

Tears blur my vision and I try to will them away, but they fall anyway.

"Hey, hey, hey." He turns on his side and draws me close. "Why the tears?"

"I didn't think you felt that way about me too." I sniffle.

"Thea, you have completely turned my life upside down in the most maddening and amazing ways possible. You've shown me how much I was missing by not allowing people in. You showed me how to have fun for maybe the first time in my life. You're beautiful and smart, resilient and strong. How could I not love you?"

"It's just that you're you, and I'm me. We're so different and you're so much better than—"

He cuts me off. "I'm not better than anyone. How could you think that when I've been going through my life without color? When we met, it was the first time I didn't feel burdened by life. You're everything to me." We kiss for a long moment before resuming our previous positions.

The next time his breaths go deep and rhythmic, I slowly and gently peel myself from his bed. I stare at him for one more minute, trying to memorize his every feature. I gather my clothes, tiptoe from the room, and leave the man I love. Only this time, for good.

CHAPTER 24

Lawrence

I WAKE UP WITH A SMILE ON MY FACE. LAST NIGHT WAS amazing. More than amazing. It was everything. I'm excited to begin the day until I reach out and the only thing I feel are cold and empty sheets. I jolt upright and scan the room. My clothes are on the floor where I left them, but Thea's are gone. Grabbing my phone off my nightstand, I see it's 5:00 a.m. She isn't an early riser. A knot forms in my stomach. My brain is being logical, saying she's in the kitchen making breakfast, but my heart knows. Thea is a runaway. She doesn't do goodbyes and when things get tough, she runs.

I jump out of bed and open my bedroom door, searching the kitchen and dining room. She's not here. I go to the other side of the house and look in my home gym and office. Not there either.

That girl told me she loved me. She gave me her virginity and her heart. She's not running this time. I'll find her. I'll bring her back to my house and lock her up if I have to. There will be no more running from me.

I drag a hand through my sleep mussed hair. I scroll through my contacts until I see her name. I connect the call. The phone rings once before announcing the number has been disconnected. How can it be disconnected? The damn number is on my account. I connect a call to my provider while I pull on a pair of boxers.

"Wireless Central, Steven speaking. How may I connect your call?" a young man answers.

"Yes, I need to talk to someone about one of my lines being disconnected," I explain.

"I can help you with that. I just need some information from you." The kid sounds barely old enough to have a job, let alone be able to figure out why Thea's number was canceled. I give him the information he needs to verify my identity, and he puts me on hold. A minute and a half later, he comes back on the line. "Mr. Packwood?"

"Yeah, I'm here. What did you find out?" I impatiently demand.

"It shows that your wife called early this morning and canceled the line. She said it was no longer needed. After I pulled up your account, I remembered I was the one who took the call." He sounds ready to defend his fuck up.

"Well, Steven, that would be hard for my wife to do given I don't have a wife," I bite out.

"I'm sorry, Mr. Packwood. She answered all the qualifying answers to access your account. Are you sure you don't have a wife?" This kid. He's lucky he's not in front of me.

"I'm very certain I would remember if I had a wife." I disconnect the call and can barely stop myself from hurling the damn phone across the room.

I throw on my sweats and T-shirt, stumbling as I pull on socks too. I grab my keys and pocket my cell. Shoes are barely on my feet as I climb into my car. The five-minute drive seems to take forever, but I finally screech to a halt in the cul-de-sac I know so well. My car door flies open and I jump out, taking off in a sprint down the dirt path. I can already see what I'm running to, but I keep running anyway. When I reach the land that has been housing the girl I love, I crouch down and bow my head.

I don't want to look up. I don't want to accept what lies before me. I want to go back to my bed, back to the happiness I woke up with. I finally stand upright. There's nothing but an empty lot in front of me. The pad of land that once had trailers perched on it now sits empty. The smell of campfire permeates the air. A hole that's been dug into the dirt is still smoking. The sun shines bright and twinkles off the dew that's collected on the weeds and brush around the perimeter of the vacant land. I can see the fresh tire marks that lead back to the road, telling me they had to have left recently.

I walk around the space, picking up and inspecting a few pieces of trash left behind, but nothing gives me a clue where they've gone.

I pound on my chest with a fist, a sharp, stabbing pain is shooting through my heart. If I didn't know any better, I would think I was having a heart attack. However, this is not the first panic attack I've had in my life. I would recognize the symptoms anywhere.

I suffered these attacks when I was a boy. I would wake up in the night to an empty house. The help had gone to their quarters in a separate small house out back, my parents would be away at speaking engagements or wherever they would fuck off to, avoiding being parents, and I was alone. The first time it happened, the nanny found me curled on the floor under my father's desk. She took me to the hospital. That's when I was diagnosed with an anxiety disorder. My parents scoffed at this and told me I was weak and sent me to therapists. Through the years, they have taught me coping mechanisms and I can almost always talk myself out of the attack. Not right now, though. Right now, my breaths are shallow and painful, there's a ringing through my ears, and the hairs along my arms are standing up pin straight.

I clasp my hands together on top of my head and close

my eyes. I force steady breaths through my lungs and will my hands to stop shaking. I need to get it together so I can find her. Find her and make her come back to me. I've seen what my life can be, and it was so magical, I can't imagine going back to how I was. Who I was.

Kicking rocks and clumps of dirt, I make my way back to my car. I take one last look at the barren land and duck back into my car. I don't know how I'll find her, but I will. She, at the very least, owes me an explanation.

Needing to talk this through, I call the only person I consider a friend. After over a minute of ringing, a scratchy and sleepy voice answers.

"Somebody better be dead," Mark says in greeting.

"No one's dead." I reassure him.

"Then why are you calling me at... what the hell time is it, anyway?" I hear a rustling and his voice becomes faint, like he's pulling the phone away from his ear. "Five fucking thirty? Bitch, there better be a fire." There's more rustling and his voice is clear again when he says, "Is there? A fire, I mean?"

"There's no fire, and no one is dead. But something is wrong," I breathe.

"What is it? Did your gypsy girl steal all your shit? I knew that was going to happen. I mean, what did you expect? She's—"

"Don't call her a gypsy and she didn't steal anything." I exhale loudly. "She's gone. I woke up, and she's gone."

"She's probably out thieving her way into some coffee and donuts. I don't get why you're so worried." Mark yawns and I can hear him settling back into his pillow.

"You don't get it. Last night, we... well, we had a really good night. I woke up this morning, and she's gone. I went to where she stays and she's not there. None of them are. All of their RVs are just gone," I explain.

"Oh man. What're you going to do? I mean, if she didn't tell you she was going, maybe it's time to just let her go." He placates.

"I can't. I can't let her go. She's the first person I've ever loved, and not just the first woman I've ever loved. She's the *only* person in my life I have ever loved. My childhood, well, let's just say I had a unique situation growing up." I feel like a pussy admitting this to another man, but Mark is a pair of heels and lipstick away from being a woman, so I feel a little better about it.

"Fuck me, muffin. I'm so sorry. I guess all you can do is try to find her. Hold on a sec." I hear buttons on his phone being pushed and then a text message chimes on my phone. "There. I sent you the information on a guy I know. He's not cheap, but he's good. There was this guy I was seeing one time. He stayed over one night. He did this amazing thing where he stuck his tongue—"

"Mark!" I shout. He snaps out of his introspection.

"Oh right. Anyway, he took off with my vintage couture 1970s Chanel Boucle jacket. That thing was worth thirty-five hundred dollars. So, I found this investigator. Give him a call."

"Yeah, okay." I run a hand down my scruffy face.

"I've got to go. I have an hour before hot yoga and mommy needs her beauty sleep." Mark yawns loudly and ends the call.

I open the text message and see the contact for the P.I. I mull it over in my mind for a few minutes. Debating on whether to just let Thea go. She didn't want to tell me where she was going or even include me in her plans. Then I think about that asshole Wen and I picture the two of them getting married and my blood boils. He would never do right by her. Thea needs someone who will give her wings, not shackles to their cage.

The only thing I can do is try to find her. Make her talk to me and maybe there's a way for us to work things out. She just has to give me the chance.

I drive back home and go for a run in an attempt to clear my head. When that doesn't work, I go to my weight room, abusing my body until I'm exhausted. After cleaning up and showering, I make the call.

"David speaking," a deep voice scratchy from years of smoking answers.

"Hello, my name is Lawrence. I'm calling because I have a job for you," I explain.

"I'll decide if you have a job for me. Before we go any further, let me give you my fee. That usually ends most of the phone calls I get. I charge fifteen hundred dollars upfront. If there is any travelling, or the job goes longer than a week, I charge more." His voice is disinterested and robotic, like he says the same thing ten times a day. Maybe he does.

"Whatever. I can pay that." He could have said double that and I would pay it to find Thea.

"Well, all right. Let's meet at the diner on South Virginia and West Douglas." He perks up. "In an hour."

"I'll see you then." I disconnect the call. I think about all the information I have to give David and it's not much. I doubt he'll be able to find her. She doesn't even have an ID, she won't get a job wherever she goes, and even her family uses false identities.

I spend forty-five minutes scrubbing my bathroom with bleach. My hands crack and bleed from the constant chemical use. My need to disinfect and clean was bigger than I could handle. When work wasn't even taking my mind off things, I did the only thing that could make me feel better. Clean.

I jump in my car and head to the diner. The silence in the car leaves me with only my contemplation and when that becomes too much, I click on the radio. It's still on the pop station Thea had turned it to so long ago. A catchy tune is playing, so I leave it on. Focusing on the lyrics and not on my missing girl.

The diner is a dive. My hand can feel the germs seeping through the front entrance door. A bottle of sanitizer sits by the register, so I squirt a healthy dose on while I look for who might be the P.I. A large, black man sits by himself, a cigarette twirling through his fingers while he reads the paper. He has a fedora perched on his head and he's wearing a red and black flannel button-down. I walk up to him. "David?"

His head tilts ever so slightly to look at me, giving me a view of his face. He has deep set wrinkles through his fore-head and around his eyes, wrinkles that are most likely caused by a perpetual scowl. Like the one he's giving me now. He nods, almost imperceptibly, and I sit across from him.

"So, what you got?" he rumbles.

I explain the situation and the only information I have on her. He stays silent, but his eyebrows shoot up when I explain that she's never been assigned a social security number or even a birth certificate, that she's never had a job or a permanent residence. When I'm finished, he folds his paper and tucks it under his arm.

"You got the cash?" he asks. I pull the envelope from the breast pocket of my jacket and hand it to him. "I'll be in touch." He stands up and walks out with the unlit cigarette dangling from his lips. He tips his hat at the hostess as he walks out.

I get up too. I haven't had coffee or breakfast, but fuck if I'll do that here. I leave a couple dollars on the table even though neither of us ordered anything. I walk out and get into my car. I guess now I wait.

I waited for a week when David called and said he needed more money. The job was extending beyond a week. He assured me he would find her, so I gladly handed over another thousand dollars. Then I waited another week.

I'm in my office, spreadsheets pulled up on my laptop screen, when my phone flashes with an incoming call. David.

"Hello," I answer.

"I found your girl. Where are you? I'll send over the envelope," his slow and almost bored voice says. He found her. He really found her.

"How did you find her? Is she okay?" I ask.

"Do you want to chitchat about specifics, or do you want to know where your girl is?" Annoyance fills the line.

"I work at The Grand Royals Casino. I'm the CFO." The line goes dead and I set my phone down. Man of few words, that David.

Within twenty minutes, Monica brings me a large manila envelope.

"This bike messenger just dropped this off. I don't know what it is." She sets it on my desk. "You need anything, Mr. Packwood?" Monica has been hovering the last few weeks. We don't discuss our personal lives, but I can tell she knows something is up.

"No, thank you. I'm fine." I dismiss her, but she lingers by the door. "Is there something else?"

"I just wanted to say, I've been your employee for almost ten years. We aren't the type of co-workers to discuss our lives, but I just wanted you to know I'm a good listener. If you ever need anyone, that is. I care about you and want to see you settled and happy." She pauses, her hands wringing together. "It seemed like you were happy there for a bit. I hope you can be happy again. Just let me know if I can help." She doesn't give me a chance to respond and I don't know if I could have, anyway. She quietly closes the door behind her.

Monica has been my assistant since I started this job. She was the previous CFO's assistant, and she came with the position. She's an elderly woman, still sharp as a tack and adapted to my personality quickly. My heart warms that she would care about me enough to say all of that to me. I didn't know she cared about me one way or the other.

My focus goes back to the envelope. I pull out a stack of papers, including an invoice for travel expenses totaling eight hundred dollars. I shake my head. It'll all be worth it if he really found her.

The first few sheets are pictures. My eyes widen at the sight of Thea. She's on a beach in a bikini top and her trademark long skirt. Her arms are wrapped around herself and she's staring into the ocean. Her hair is blowing in the breeze and she looks breathtaking.

I flip to the next picture and it's her sitting in a chair outside her trailer. It's a wide angle and I can see that it must be an RV park. There are RVs on either side of her and fake grass under her feet. Her legs are pulled up to her chest and her chin rests on her knees. She looks distraught and it pangs my heart to not see her wide smile.

I briefly scan the next couple pictures. Thea in a grocery store with her little sisters. Thea going into a tiny home, being hugged by an elderly couple. This must mean she's in Florida. Those must be her grandparents. I pause on the next photo and shake my head, taking in the image. Thea is pulling out the wallet of an unsuspecting tourist. They're on a boardwalk where the poor schmuck is focused on a vendor's table. If you didn't know what to look for, you'd just see a woman brushing by the man. I know her better than that. The wallet is in her lithe fingertips, just barely out of his back pocket. *Still up to tricks, huh, Trouble?*

I flip to the papers behind the photos where I find the final report from David. I scan over it. She's in Florida. Bradenton, Florida. It mentions her grandparents live nearby. Apparently, only three of the families in the band went to Florida. They're all staying in an RV park. A few of the men have picked up seasonal fruit picking jobs. There was no mention of what the other families did.

I call Mark to my office and he gladly prances in. He's wearing a tangerine-colored suit. His suit coat is short-sleeved. I didn't even know such a thing exists. His tie is lime green. The only thing tame on him is the plain white button-down underneath the suit coat. I wouldn't even know where to find such an outfit, not that I would ever want to.

I lay out all the information for Mark and explain her ties to Florida. He takes it all in, being more serious than I have ever seen him. When I show him the pictures, the Mark I know comes back to the surface.

"Christ on a goddamn cracker. She's a sexy bitch, isn't she?" A growl erupts from my chest. "Calm down, tiger. You know my heat-seeking missile doesn't seek her kind of equipment." He flips to another picture. His head tilts. "Is she?" He tilts his head in the other direction. "She is! Your little clepto has been on the prowl."

"Yeah, I saw that." It makes me nervous she's up to her tricks. One wrong move and she could be in a whole world of trouble. *And I wouldn't be there to save her.* When Mark's done studying the pictures and has been caught up on all the information, he sets it all back down on my desk and looks up at me.

"So, Casanova, what're you gonna do?" He sits back in the chair and crosses his legs delicately.

"I don't know." I sigh. "I want to go to Florida and drag her back up here. Make her stay in one fucking place with me. Stop her from running again."

"She's a real-life nomadic gypsy. What if she doesn't want

to settle down?" Mark gets his phone out of his pocket, turns on the forward-facing camera, and starts messing with his eyebrows.

"I told you, don't call her that. It's derogatory, and I don't know what I'll do. I have a job. I have a house. I really don't want to live in an RV. I have a master's degree, for Crissake. I can't do manual labor like her dad." I rub at my temples. This is all giving me a headache.

"Well, mon frère, it sounds like you have a decision to make. But if I were you, I would think hard about what's the most important. Having a stable life and a stable job and a stable girlfriend you don't respect?" He stands up and walks to the door. "Or the love of your life at your side, no matter where you live or what you live in?"

He shuts the door behind him. Once again, I'm left wondering how this became my life. I think back to my parents' relationship. What little I knew and saw. I never witnessed affection. The only time I saw them spend time with each other was during meals and they were so cold, nothing more than cordial. If I go back to the relationships I had before Thea, I know my future will look exactly how my parents' did. I know I would never bring a child into that. I didn't deserve to grow up the way I did, and I wouldn't condemn my own child to that.

Then I think about my life with Thea. While I can't envision where we would live, I can imagine a little girl with wild and curly hair, golden eyes, and a smile where all of her teeth would show. And maybe a serious little boy whom we will pull out of his own head and show from an early age that there's more to life than school and studies. Most of all, I can picture the love we will show them. Between Thea and me, and between both of us with them. This vision of the future is exactly what I want.

I know what I have to do.

CHAPTER 25

Theodora

I KNEW I WAS LEAVING WHEN I WENT TO LAW'S HOUSE. I knew I would break his heart. I also knew I couldn't leave without seeing him. I couldn't leave without making love to him. I couldn't leave without telling him how I felt.

So, I put my heartache aside and spent one last amazing night with Law. Afterward, I cried my way home where we had packed up and were ready to leave. I took the shit Wen flung at me when I showed up with sex mussed hair and swollen eyes. I climbed into the front seat of the van, where my mom would normally sit, and I rode silently on our trip across the country.

There were too many memories for my dad in Reno. He was ready for a change, and he felt like he needed the help of my grandparents. I told him I could handle it, I could take care of the kids, but he said he didn't want to tie me down to his family when I should start my own. There was no talking him out of it, so the kids and I packed up all our belongings alongside most of the other families. Wen's family came with us, Braithe and Nuri still holding onto hope that I would come to my senses and marry Wen.

Kezia's family stayed behind with two others. They joined a larger band that stays on land outside of Reno. They wanted to stick with the housing boom because of the good money they were making. We all hugged and whispered promises to see each other again soon. I hope they find happiness with the larger group.

Bradenton is right outside of Sarasota and only thirty miles outside of Tampa. It sits on the Manatee River and I have to admit, it's a pretty area to live in. There's fruit picking work to be done this time of the year and the men had no problems getting hired on immediately. There's also a decent amount of tourism, so I've been able to pad my pockets easily.

Being around my grandparents has been nice too. They're settled and happy. It's good to see Romani finding peace even if they have resigned to stay in one place long term.

I've just woken up for the day when I hear a knock on our trailer. I climb down from the loft and peek out the window. Wen.

"Hey, Thea," he greets when I open the door.

"Um, hi. It's early," I deadpan. He travels the length of my body and I remember I'm wearing a sports bra and short shorts. Florida is hot and humid. My eyebrows lift and I pin him with a glare.

He looks nervously away and to his watch. "It's noon."

"Well, it's early for me. What's up? Shouldn't you be at work?" My hands go to my hips and I stare him down, giving him all the attitude I can muster before I've had coffee.

"I didn't go in today. I was hoping we could have a beach day. Explore the area more?" he begs. Ever since the day he put his hands on me, I've kept as much distance as I could considering we live side by side. He hasn't been taking the hint. He's doing everything he can to make me forgive him. Bringing me flowers, doing chores for me, and trying to enlist the help of my sisters. It will not work. It never would to begin with.

"I have the girls." My toe taps on the ground.

"Bring them! It'll be fun. Sun, sand, water, it'll be awesome." His hands go to the prayer position in front of him. Fuckin' pathetic.

"Fine. We'll go. Let me get them up and dig through to find their swimsuits." I go to shut the door, but Wen's hand swings out and stops it, making a slapping noise, and I jump.

Wen sighs. "I didn't mean to scare you. I've never meant to scare you. I'm sorry. I just wanted to say thank you. For coming with me today." His head bows and his attention is on the ground. The part of me that spent my childhood running crazy with this guy softens a bit.

"It's fine. You're welcome." I shut the door, without interference this time. Lord help me, but I feel bad for him now.

I look around the disaster in front of me. Without Mom here to organize us, things have gotten a little out of hand. Clothes are strewn about and dishes are piled in the sink. Now that we're staying in an RV park, we're using our kitchen and bathroom. This means more mess inside our trailer, but more importantly, running water. I feel like a princess. Almost as spoiled as I was living with Law. My heart twinges in my chest and I reach up and place a hand on the place it hurts. I didn't think heartbreak was a physical thing, but the spot that houses that blood pumping organ has been aching ever since the day we left.

"Up and at 'em," I shout, clapping my hands loudly to rouse the girls. "We're going to the beach!"

Hours later, we're perched on our own very small parcel of sand. It's an overcrowded beach and everyone is so busy. Kids building castles, wading through the surf, and crying over sandwiches that ended up being more sand than wich. But the view is amazing and the smell of warm, salty air invigorates me.

"Thea! Can we get in the water?" Indie asks excitedly. I

shade the sun with my hand, trying to find an empty spot of water where I can monitor them.

"Yeah," I say. "See that spot right in front of us?"

The girls look to where I'm pointing. "Yeah," they reply in unison.

"Just stay right there. Don't go out above your whoo-has. You don't know how to swim." A mom next to me shoots me a mean glare and I glare right back and snap. "I could have said pussy, but I didn't. I was being respectful." The mom gasps and covers her little boy's ears. I just roll my eyes and focus on my two little ragtags.

Wen plops down beside me, cooler in hand. "I could barely find you. It's so busy."

"You finally found parking?" I ask.

"Yep, like a mile away. When we're ready to leave, I'll go get the car so you don't have to trek out there." His shoulder brushes with mine when he leans back on his hands.

"We can walk. We aren't some princesses." My knee-jerk reaction lately is to throw out attitude with Wen. Deserving or not.

"I know you're not." He rotates his body to face me. "I've been wanting to talk to you."

I briefly look away from the girls and flash them over to Wen. He's wearing red swim trunks and his shirt is off. He's naturally dark-skinned from our heritage and at some point, between the last time I saw him without a shirt, he's become built. Not as chiseled as Law, but still, the boy looks good. His eyebrows rise at my obvious perusal.

"Don't get your panties in a bunch. Just haven't seen you without a shirt in a while. You've grown up." I spot the girls again.

"You have too." He hooks a finger in my bikini top and snaps it against my skin. I ignore the flirtation. "I really did want to talk to you."

"What's up?" The girls are splashing each other, which is in turn, splashing everyone in a five-foot radius. People pick up their toddlers and move them away and old people whisper to each other about their hair getting wet and shoot my girls dirty looks. I don't care. They're having fun and those girls need to have some fun.

"I wanted to apologize, you know, for that day." He takes my hand in his, but I keep my focus on the girls. "You hadn't been around much at that time, so you weren't there every time my dad, your dad, hell, all the men, gave me shit about my wayward woman. Every night, they poked and prodded, asking what kind of man I was letting my woman run around town. I got so fuckin' sick of hearing it. It's not an excuse—"

"No, it's not."

"It's just an explanation. I realize now, you aren't like Kezia or my mom. It wasn't fair for me to try to put you in that box." His thumb rubs circles on my hand and the sweet gesture softens my heart for him.

"I get it. I'm different. I wish I were more like them. It would make my life easier. I'm just not and to be happy, I have to be me. Especially now, after seeing my mom die so young and with no warning, I refuse to not be happy." I briefly meet his gaze and resignation is painted all over his face. Maybe he's finally getting it.

"I want you to be happy. I think I could make you happy." I pull my hand from his. "No, no. Don't get the wrong idea. I'm very much aware of how you feel about that. Just don't count me out. I might surprise you."

I don't understand what that means, but I also don't want to continue this conversation, so I stand up and go to my sisters. I spend the rest of the afternoon splashing and playing with Indie and Charity. Wen even joins us. The only thing that would have made it better is for the Law-shaped hole in my heart to be filled.

The drive home was full of heavy traffic and by the time we pull into the RV park, we're all on each other's nerves. Wen tells the girls to pipe down a minute when we make the last turn into where our trailers are.

"What the hell?" Wen grips the steering wheel tightly.

"What the hell?" I repeat, leaning forward to take in what is sitting in front of our homes. I don't wait for the car to stop. I open the door and jump out. I run over to where I see Dad talking to someone. I can only see his back, and maybe it's my broken heart talking, but he looks like—

Just then, he turns around and I get a good look at a tall man with dark brown hair that's short on the side and longer up top. He's wearing a cotton, short-sleeved button-down and a pair of tan shorts. His feet have… are those sandals? Oh my God. Lawrence Packwood stands in front of me in actual beachwear. I take off running until I reach his arms. He scoops me up and my toes leave the ground. He spins me around a couple times before planting a kiss on my lips. I put my hands to his chest and push away, just enough to see his gorgeous face.

"What are you doing here?" I ask incredulously.

"It's a long story. Want to come inside and talk?" He motions to the thing that first caught my attention. It's a motorhome. Not just a motorhome, but the biggest monstrosity of a motorhome I've ever seen. It's so big, I think a family of four could live in it and not even run into each other. And if I'm not mistaken, there's a garage in the undercarriage.

I look around. Dad and Wen are pacing the perimeter and discussing all the features of Law's beast, the girls are running around and cheering, "Thea's boyfriend is rich!", and Law is just standing there. In Florida. Eyebrows raised and a new sun-kissed glow to his skin.

"Um, yeah. Sure."

Law grabs my hand and pulls me up the stairs and into

the motorhome. I'm immediately hit with lavishness. There is an enormous kitchen with an island to my left. A sofa and two recliners down past the kitchen. To my right are stairs. A freaking staircase that must lead up to a bedroom. Maybe two? My jaw hangs slack.

"Is that a dishwasher?" I point to the wall above the sink.

"Yes, it is. Is that wrong? Should I have had them take it out?" He panics and opens the cubby where the dishwasher is.

"No. I just. I mean. This is a lot," I stammer. I think I'm in shock. Nothing makes sense, let alone the words coming from my mouth.

"I knew nothing about RVs when I picked it out. I just remembered you had complained about doing dishes by hand. There's also a washing machine in there, so you won't have to go to a laundromat." He points up the stairs.

"I'm sorry. Did you say me? *I* won't have to wash dishes by hand? *I* won't have to do laundry?" I'm having a hard time keeping up.

"I was generalizing. Not saying *you* had to do those things, specifically. I just solved the problems you mentioned about living in this type of dwelling." He pats the counter like it's a dog. "Obviously I'll be doing the dishes and laundry. You're amazing at some things, but domestic chores? Not so much." His hands find purchase in his pockets. He shrugs his shoulders and tilts his head.

"Why do you keep making it sound like I'm the one going to be living here?" I walk to the sofa and slump down in it. Law follows and sits next to me, taking my hands in his.

"It's what I'm hoping for." His brown orbs plead with me.

"How did you even know I was here?" I shake my head, trying to clear the blissful fog that's clouding my perception of reality. Law may be here in front of me, but it doesn't necessarily change our circumstances. Does it?

"My coworker, Mark. He knows a guy. I gave him a call. He found you and now I'm here." That's a simple explanation, right? I mean there were very few words, yet I'm still having a hard time.

"Mark?" I ask.

"Yeah. My coworker." His eyes dart back and forth between mine. Probably wondering if I'm having a stroke because it's taking me so long to grasp the words coming out of his mouth.

"I see. So, you found me and bought a motorhome and drove to Florida?" My heart picks up its pace, everything finally coming into focus.

"I did. When I woke up, and you weren't there after our night together? I panicked. I literally had a panic attack. I went to where you had been parked, but you weren't there. I looked for you everywhere." He leans in, his soft and gentle lips melting into mine. I've missed those lips.

"I didn't know how to say goodbye. My dad wanted to leave and there was no convincing him otherwise."

Law picks me up and pulls me to straddle him. His hands lock together right above my ass.

"It doesn't matter. What matters is I've come to ask you if you'll move in with me?"

I look over each shoulder, taking in the luxurious space.

"Move into here?"

"Yes. I mean, whatever you want. You want to live here? I'll buy ten more pairs of cargo shorts and invest in sunscreen. You want to move to Hawaii? I'll buy us leis and floppy hats. Wherever you want to go, we will go there. I just want you to be happy, and I'm hoping you can be happy living with me."

I squeal as happiness floods my veins. I can't believe he did all of this for me.

"Yes! I mean, of course I'll move in with you."

His hand goes to the back of my head and he brings our lips together, firm and deep this time. That is, until a voice sounds at the door.

"Knock knock."

I mouth the word "Dad" to Law and slide to the side of him. Our family are no prudes, I've walked in to find my parents bumping uglies more than I ever want to think about, but something about this budding relationship with Law has me wanting to protect it. From everyone.

Dad steps in and gawks as he looks around.

"This is, uh, fancy," he stammers out with a hand tugging on the back of his neck.

Law jumps up and clasps his hands in front of him. He rocks slowly back and forth on his heels. "I may have gone overboard."

"Yeah, kid. I think you did." Dad comes deeper into the motorhome and raises a brow as he looks us over. "Mind telling me what's going on?"

"Dad," I start, but Law jumps in.

"Mr. Vanslow, I'm sorry to show up like this. You all don't have cell phones and I had no other way of getting in touch with Thea." Law holds his hands out, palms up.

"No other way than by showing up in a three-hundred-thousand-dollar RV?" Dad asks and my jaw drops for the tenth time in the last ten minutes.

"This thing was three hundred thousand dollars?" I smack Law's arm.

"That wasn't the point. The point is, I love your daughter, sir, and I needed to let her know I was ready to live however or wherever she wanted." He straightens his spine and drops his hands to his sides.

"I don't know if Thea has told you, but our people only marry within our culture. It's been that way for generations."

Dad rests a hip on the counter and folds his arms in front of his big barrel chest.

"She did tell me, and with all due respect, I think in order for a relationship like that to work, you have to have willing partners." Law just mimics Dad's stance and folds his arms over his chest as well. "Thea isn't a willing partner."

I gasp. Dad and I have never discussed this. He has never left room for argument with any rule he has given us. I assumed it would be a waste of time.

"It doesn't really matter what you think of it, with all due respect," Dad mocks and I can see this is headed in a bad direction, so I shoot off the couch and step between them, but face Dad.

"Dad! Stop it." I close my eyes, take a deep breath, and expel it loudly. The brief calm gives me the strength to continue. I open my eyes. Here goes nothing. "I'm in love with Law."

He scans my face, but his cold glare made from stone doesn't falter.

"You're not in love with him. You don't even know him." His lips move, but his face remains pinched together.

"I know him. I've spent months with him. I even lived with him when you and Mom kicked me out." I flinch when his face slackens in shock. There's been no talk of where I was before Mom passed away. It was a *don't ask, don't tell* situation.

"You were living with him?" Dad roars and points to Law.

"Yes." My voice is quiet, but resolute. "We met a while ago and despite what either of us wanted, we just kept ending up together. We didn't mean for it to happen."

"I don't even know who you are right now, Thea." Dad turns and storms out, slamming the door.

I cover my face with my hands and fall into Law's chest. His arms wrap around me and he whispers soothing words that don't even register. This was exactly what I knew would happen when he found out about our relationship. Law brings me back to the couch and we sit down. A comforting hand rubs up and down my back for many long minutes until I get control of my emotions. I pull back from Law and see the worry etched into his features.

"Do you want me to leave? I didn't come to tear up your family." He wipes the tears from my cheeks with his thumbs.

"No. I tried to live without you the last few weeks. I tried to do the right thing. But I missed you. I would have ended up at your doorstep anyway." I sniffle.

"I'm glad you didn't. I don't have a doorstep anymore." A small smile cracks the corner of Law's lips.

"You sold your house?" I grip his arm tightly.

"Yes. I didn't think I would need it anymore. Not if this is to be my new home?" He motions around us.

"I don't want to live in a trailer, or a motorhome, or any home that's mobile."

"You don't?" Shock laces his voice. "Where do you want to live?"

"In Reno. With you." I admit. He pulls me into his arms and holds me tightly, wrapping me up in a hug so tight, my anxiety calms and my nerves settle.

"Of course you do." He kisses my hair. "You wouldn't be you without causing some trouble, would you?" He releases me and I instantly miss his body next to mine. "I better call and ask for my job back."

Not for the first time since he showed up, I gasp. "You quit your job?"

"I couldn't manage finances if I wasn't at the casino." He's so calm about it, but this is huge. Law lives for his work. I dive back into his arms.

"I love you." He brushes the hair from my face and kisses my nose.

"Love you too."

CHAPTER 26

Lawrence

I RENT A SPACE TO PARK THIS GIGANTIC, RIDICULOUS vehicle and move it. Thankfully, there's a good bit of distance between us and her family. When I first pulled up, Thea's dad had been nice. He didn't remember me from that day at the hospital, but was happy to talk to me about all the bells and whistles I was still discovering on my new home. It was deceptive of me, but I wanted him to like me before he knew I was there to be with his daughter.

All bets were off when Thea came home and ran into my arms. I scooped her up and breathed in her woody, incense smell. I fucking missed her so much.

Things fell off the rail after that, but my girl still chose me. I wish I could feel better about it, but I know what her family means to her. I saw what happened the last time she was disconnected from them. It wasn't pretty.

I can only hope we find a way for all of us to meet in the middle. Not for my sake, or Thea's sake for that matter, but for her siblings and for our future family too. Make no mistake about it, I'm putting babies in that wild one. Lots of them.

"Are you going to stay with me tonight?" I look over to my copilot after deploying the slides and hitting the automatic stabilizers. Her fingers are frantically twirling her hair.

"I think so. I'll go back over and settle my sisters, get my brothers up to speed." She opens the passenger door and jumps down. "But I'll be back in an hour or so."

I nod and watch her ass as she walks away. She was wearing nothing but a bikini top and cutoff jean shorts when she barreled out of Wen's car and she hasn't changed. Wen. He's a whole other issue. I saw him shooting daggers at me while Thea was in my arms. I don't trust the fucker.

I get out of the captain's chair and make my way back into the belly of the beast. I can't believe I sold my home, bought this thing, learned how to work it, drove cross-country, and all to drive back home and get my job back. I shake my head in disbelief.

When I approached the CEO about quitting, he insisted I call it a sabbatical. He told me I'd be back. I cringe at admitting to the annoying man he was right. Part of me is relieved, however. My muscles are made in a gym, not by doing hard labor. I'm not cut out for that type of work.

An hour later, Thea knocks on the door and comes in. Her eyes are puffy, but she has a gorgeous smile on her face. The one I love. The one that shows me all her straight, white teeth. The one that means she's truly happy.

"So, are we really going to do this?" I ask.

"Hell ya, we are!" She jumps onto my lap and I let out an *oof* as the air is forced from my lungs. She curls her legs into her chest and I wrap my arms around the whole of her.

"How'd things go out there?"

She sighs. "As good as can be expected. The girls are sad and want to come with me. The boys are stoic. And my dad? He's just pouting. He gave me a hug and told me to be safe. I gave him your cell phone number, and he promised he would pick up one of those prepaid phones. So I could talk to the girls. He was clear about that." She leans her head on my shoulder.

"He's going to miss you." I kiss her forehead.

"Maybe if he misses me enough, he'll forgive me for not marrying Wen." She huffs out.

"About Wen."

She lifts her head and looks at me. "What about him?"

"You were with him today." I'm hoping she lets me off the hook and doesn't make me admit how insanely jealous I am.

"We took the girls to the beach. We talked. He explained what was going on with him when, well, you know. I kind of get it." Her shoulders shrug, but my eyebrows lift to damn near my hairline. "The way we were raised, with women taught to be so submissive and meek. I'm not like that, and it messed with his manhood. All the guys were giving him a hard time while I was off gallivanting with you. I get it. He apologized. That was that."

I mull this over in my brain. I don't get it, but we were raised much differently. As long as he's apologized, he's not trying to steal my girl, and he never lays even a finger on her again, I can be okay. I smile just thinking about driving Thea thousands of miles away from him. Looks like I won.

"What are you smiling at?" Thea pokes a finger into my cheek.

"Nothing. Just happy you're finally back in my arms." Her lips land on mine and move in a way that makes my cock jump.

"I haven't seen the bedroom." Thea uncurls herself from my lap and holds a hand out to me.

"I'm not a very good host, am I?" I let her pull me up and we walk to the massive bedroom. There's a king-sized bed in here. Along with a full closet and dresser. A huge TV is mounted on the wall and there is a nightstand on either side of the bed. "Come here." I pull her into me and collapse us both on the bed, making her giggle.

"This bed is comfy." She sits up and scoots herself back to the headboard. I scoot back next to her.

"It is. I've spent a few nights in it now." I trace her lips with the pad of my finger. I lean in and take her mouth. She climbs on top of me and straddles my hips. She immediately starts grinding on my hardening cock. "I love you," I say in between kisses. She doesn't reply, but she doesn't have to. I can feel her answer in the way she kisses me, in the way she returns my touches, and in the heated way her eyes meet mine.

I pull the set of strings dangling down her back, then the set on the back of her neck. The bikini falls away and my hands go right to her bare breasts. Her nipples pebble against my palm. I trap the tiny buds between two of my fingers and squeeze them shut again. I swallow the gasp she lets out and plunge my tongue into her mouth. Warmth spreads throughout my body as my hard length gets worked over by her jean clad pussy.

I reluctantly remove my hands from her breasts to move them lower and unbutton her shorts. She rises and pulls them off, along with her bikini bottoms, exposing her bare pussy. She sits back down and her hands first shoot to my shirt, where she pulls it over my head, then those nimble fingers are unbuttoning my shorts. I lift my ass up so I can pull them down, but she pants out. "I can't wait." She frees my cock and with no preamble, takes me in to the hilt. We let out a collective moan of pleasure.

"Bend back, baby. I want to play with your clit." She arches her back and I can't help but suck a nipple into my mouth. I roll it with my tongue and Thea lets out a breathy whimper. I release it and drag my hand down her torso before settling my thumb on her clit. It's swollen and wet. I wish I could fuck her and lick her pussy at the same time, but I digress. I'll figure that out later.

"I need more," she says between thrusts.

"Can't have that, now can we?" I grip her hips and stop her bouncing. "Lie back." I move with her so I don't have to leave the silky wet sheath of her pussy. When I'm finally on top, I thrust into her. Hard. "Is that better?"

"Yes. Law. So good."

I continue to deliver hard, solid thrusts when my balls begin to tingle, alerting me to my orgasm.

I grab her hand that has been clawing its way through the skin of my shoulder. Licking her fingers, I then bring it between our bodies. "Play with your clit," I demand. She listens and within seconds she's writhing underneath me, her breaths coming out short and shallow.

"I'm coming. Oh my God!" she shouts and I quickly cover her mouth with my hand. We have been given the illusion of privacy, but I'm not sure how soundproof this thing is. Her next shouts are muffled and the vice-like grip of pussy, followed by the spasms clenching down on my dick, tell me she's coming. I lose any last semblance of self-control I possessed. I orgasm. I orgasm so hard I see black spots in my vision. After a few last, slower thrusts, I fall on top of Thea. She laughs and pats my back soothingly.

"I think you broke me." My words are muffled against her hair.

"I think you are breaking me right now." I realize she can hardly breathe with my body weight on top of her. I push myself to lie at her side, freeing my cock.

"Sorry," I grit out. She traces a finger along my hairline, no doubt stopping the beads of sweat from worming their way down my face. She looks pensive as she follows the path of her fingers with her eyes. "What's going on in that head of yours?"

"I'm just wondering if you have an extra set of sheets

because your semen is spilling out of me as we speak." She giggles, as if she's happy to be dirtying up my bed.

"I'll have you know I have four extra sets of sheets." I tickle her sides and she rolls around, laughing.

"I'd expect nothing else."

The following morning, Thea and I wake early. She goes back to her family so she can pack up and I get everything organized with the motorhome so we can start our journey when she gets back.

"Get out here, asshole!" a man's voice shouts from outside the screen door. I walk over to the door and find a pretty pissed off Wen.

"Wen," I cautiously greet as I step outside.

"I'm not letting you take her from me." He is pacing back and forth, his eyes trained on the ground.

I cross my arms in front of my chest and widen my stance, hoping it doesn't come to a fight, but prepared if it does.

"I'm not *taking* her anywhere, but we are leaving together. She can make her own decisions." I watch him pace.

"No. She can't. She was given to me. She belongs to me." He stops his pacing two feet in front of me. He fists clenched at his sides and wholly focused on me.

"I don't know what I have to do to get it through your head. Women are not property, no matter your culture or traditions." I keep my tone calm, but give no room for argument.

I see his fist coming before it lands and am able to sidestep it. Unfortunately for Wen, I was standing inches in front of my behemoth motorhome, so his fist slams into the fiberglass and aluminum.

"Fuck!" he shouts, holding his fist. He whips around

quickly, ready to throw another punch, but I hold my hands up like I'm trying to calm a wild animal.

"Listen, we can keep doing this. You can keep trying to kick my ass, and maybe I deserve it because Thea probably would be marrying you still if she and I hadn't met. But trust me, she would always resent you. She would wake up every morning and look out the window, imagining what her life could've been had she been able to make her own decisions. You could never own her heart. You could never possess her spirit. She would be yours in body only. Is that what you want?" I throw my arms out to my sides in frustration. Getting through to him is like trying to demolish generations of beliefs. It's impossible.

"You know she and I were in diapers together?" He lowers his voice, but his brow is heavy and bunched together in anger.

"She told me." I take a step back and lower my defensive stance, confused if his emotion is growing or tapering. Honestly, he is such a wild card.

"Our future was written the day we were born. You're ruining that. You think she would resent me for keeping her, but she'll resent you for taking her away from her family." Every word is bit out in anger, every period punctuated with a gnash of his teeth.

"She can come back whenever she wants. This whole freedom thing seems to be a difficult concept for you to grasp but listen when I say this. She isn't owned by me. Every choice she makes, every place she goes, will be of her own free will. Accept it." I walk past him on my way back into the RV, but pause before I close the door. "Or don't. Honestly, I don't care. I need to get back to this."

"Whatever," he mutters as he walks away with his head down. Poor schmuck. My girl leaves broken hearts wherever she goes.

Moments later the door is opening and I hear Thea huffing up the stairs.

"You will fit, you fuckin' piece of—"

I watch her struggle with a duffle bag, trying to make it fit through the doorway.

"You need help?" I ask. She drops the bag and looks up at me with strings of hair dangling across her face.

"Please!" she says as she brushes her hair off her face with the back of her hand. I sneak past her and grab her bag, twisting it until it fits.

"Is this all you're bringing?" There's a large duffel and her guitar, but it can't be all she wants to take to her new life.

She pats me on the chest. "Yeah, Richie Rich. I travel light. Unlike you." She motions to my giant vehicle.

I put her bag in the closet and then pull her into my arms, searching her face for any signs of distress or uncertainty. "You okay?"

"Yeah, I'm good. I'm sad, but we'll keep in touch and maybe we can come visit often." Her hands snake around my neck.

"Whatever you want, Trouble."

She beams at my answer.

I kiss her briefly, but then pull away. "If we don't stop, we'll never make it out of here."

"You're right. Besides, road head sounds fun." She shrugs a shoulder and moves to the passenger seat up front. I shake my head and follow her to the captain's chair.

When we're buckled, and the engine is running, I put the beast in drive. But my foot doesn't leave the brake. Standing in front of us is Leander, a duffel bag of his own on the ground next to him.

"What the hell?" Thea is jumping out of the RV in an instant and heading to Leander. They talk for a bit, Thea drawing him in for an embrace and patting his back. Leander with his head lowered and rubbing his nose. Thea looks in my direction, thinking for a moment. They both make their way to the driver's side and I jump down from the cab.

"What's going on?" I ask.

"Leander had just started college courses when we left. He was hoping he could come with us so he can get back to school." Thea pleads with me, but there's no question in my mind.

"Of course. I think that's a great idea." I turn to Leander. "Your dad know?"

"Um, he doesn't know I started up at the community college. Hell, he doesn't know I graduated high school. He thinks I want to go back to work and marry some girl he arranged for me. He's cool with it." Leander's dark hair hangs over his forehead and he flips his head to move it to the side.

"Okay. Let's get going then." I climb back up to the driver's seat and buckle in. Thea settles Leander in the back and then comes back to the cab. She leans over and kisses me full on the mouth, her tongue dancing lightly with mine. My hand sneaks up to the back of head and I hold there, taking her in to all of my senses. I taste citrus on her tongue, I see long lashes brushing the tops of her cheeks, I hear the slightest moan only loud enough for me to hear, I feel her wild and curly locks between my fingers, and I smell the incense that permeates her pores. For the rest of my life, this is all I want and need.

I pull away, but only barely. My lips still brushing hers.

"Marry me, Trouble," I whisper.

She giggles and I feel the small puffs of air against my lips. "You wanna marry me? The bohemian girl?"

"Please?" My serious eyes are trained on hers, who dance with mirth.

"I'll marry you, Law."

I draw her in for another kiss I feel down to my toes.

She pulls away and bounces onto the passenger seat. "I guess I'll have to get legal."

EPILOGUE

Lawrence

"THERE THEY ARE!" I CALL OUT. "THE NEWEST legal U.S. citizens!"

Thea and Leander make their way toward Mark and me where we have been waiting. We're all having dinner to celebrate finally getting them both social security numbers and birth certificates. It's taken over a year, an expensive lawyer, and so many hoops, but they've finally got the papers in hand.

Thea waves the small, blue card and a sheet of paper that will make it possible for her to get a driver's license, a job if she wants, but most importantly, now we can get married.

I stand up and bring her in for a hug and kiss. Leander stands to the side awkwardly. His documentation was a little more difficult and required me to pay a few fines. He used a false identification to enroll in school and seeing as that's a crime, he's lucky he didn't go to jail. My lawyer is just as good as she is pricey, so he got away with only a few hefty fines.

I pull away from my fiancée. "Leander! You remember Mark?"

Mark stands and shakes Leander's hand.

"I do. How are you?" The boy has grown into a man this last year. Gone is the shaggy hair and teenage attitude. What's left is a confident man who is in his second year of college. Thea is so proud of him and never wastes a chance to brag at how smart he is.

"My lawd, you've really grown up since I last saw you," Mark drawls, holding Leander's hand too long and peeping him up and down. I elbow him in the gut and his hand drops. To Leander's credit, he just chuckles and takes a seat.

Thea looks around. "You couldn't get us a table by the window?"

"There will be none of that," I scold. "Not today." When Thea suggested having this celebration at The Green Olive, I put my foot down. I had no intention of ever returning. She convinced me, though. Well, she convinced my dick. Asking me important questions while she's sucking me off is her preferred method of getting what she wants.

"I wasn't suggesting anything. I just wanted to be at our old table. Relive our first real date." She removes the napkin from atop her plate and settles it in her lap.

"What happened on your first date?" Leander asks. A mischievous smile creeps up Thea's lips and lights her eyes.

"It was nothing," I say at the same time Thea says, "We dine and dashed."

"Whaaaaaat?" Mark dramatically holds a hand to his chest. "The Chief Financial Officer of the biggest and best casino in Reno dine and dashed? I don't believe it."

"I, unknowingly, was the getaway car." I defend and Leander snickers.

"You guys should have seen him when he finally realized what I'd done." Thea jumps from the table and starts pacing with her head in her hands. Her performance is drawing the attention of the other diners and I lean over the table, my hands covering my face. "He was all, 'I think they got my license plate. I'm going to jail. No wait. Is it a felony? Maybe I'm going to prison.'"

I yank Thea's arm and pull her into my lap, having enough of her antics. "It's not funny," I say with my arms wrapped tightly around her waist, but the entire table is cracking up. I release my future bride and she settles in her own chair again.

We all order saffron lamb kebobs and mint lemonades. The dinner is full of laughter and talk of future plans. Leander is getting his engineering degree in renewable resources. It's the perfect job for someone who has spent his whole life living outside of the box. He's managed to delay his arranged marriage so far, despite their dad's growing impatience.

Thea has been taking some online adult literacy courses. Next, she'll be taking classes at the community college for adults who dropped out of high school, or like Thea, have hardly any education at all. My girl is like a sponge and to her surprise, she loves learning. At night, after I've gotten her naked and under me, she'll read me chapters from books she has been reading. I love seeing her confidence grow. She amazes me.

I look over and see Mark and Leander have their own quiet conversation, so I get down to business with Thea. I put my hand over hers and give it a squeeze. She beams up at me.

"When are you going to marry me?" I ask with an eyebrow quirked. "We have a home. Your dad finally approves of me. Now you have your documents. There's nothing left to do." When we returned from Florida, we lived out of the motorhome for about a month. Just until we found a house on the outskirts of Reno on some land. Thea has room to roam and the wild horses live in our backyard. It's gorgeous. Even her dad approves. It took him a few months of conversations over the phone before he agreed to visit. He still calls me a gorger and he's still not ready to move back, but he's been here twice. He loves the land we own. At some point, I'd like to build a home for him, the girls, and Freedom. Our own little commune.

"I'll marry you after I get my GED." It's the same answer every time, but I'm growing impatient. I want my ring weighing down her finger so she can never forget she's mine.

"I'm just going to put a baby in you then." I smirk and she rolls her eyes.

"No babies. Yet."

"You guys are having a baby?" Mark shrieks and the restaurant looks over at us. The women swoon and the men smile a smile that says 'your life is ending.'

"No!" Thea whisper shouts at the same time I say, "Yes!" Her angry stare is like a slap to the face, but it just makes my dick harden. I don't think that look delivered the desired effect.

"Not yet." I clarify.

Mark dismisses me with a wave of his hand. He and Leander go back to their conversation.

"I'm ready to get out of here," I say, bringing Thea's hand to my dick. Her eyebrows shoot up in surprise. She grips my length and leans toward me.

"Let's dash," she says, full of playfulness. She stands up and takes a few slow steps from the table. I discreetly adjust myself and then jump up and follow her.

"Where are you two lovebirds going?" Mark calls out. But we don't answer. I grab Thea's hand. We run outside and straight to the car, laughing the whole way.

When we settle in the car, Thea's out of breath and the smile I love so much is being prominently displayed.

"I think we just did the adult version of dining and dashing." Her hand cups my cheek and she drags her nails over my scruff.

"Was it still fun?" I ask. Thea has given up her life of crime for the sake of my sanity. I know she misses the thrill. She loves to brag about different cons she has gotten away with.

"It was still fun." She assures me. We drive away to the sound of both of our phones chirping, no doubt Mark and Leander wondering what hell has gotten into us. But that's love, I guess. Two people with different life experiences coming together, giving and taking until you create a combined existence full of everything good from the both of you. It's difficult, and sometimes it's not pretty, but when you get to where the two prongs of the fork meld into one road, the result is fantastic.

EPILOGUE

Theadora

I WATCH AS MY TODDLING LITTLE BOY CREEPS UP TO MY husband. He can barely walk, but Hanzi, or Hanz as we call him, is stealthy. His big brown eyes look at me for reassurance and I shoo him on with a wave of my hand. I'm sitting on a blanket in the park at Law's company picnic. He's been playing boss all day and Hanz is bored. So, we decided to work on his skills.

His pudgy little fingers get ahold of Law's wallet and he pulls it out. He's almost gone undetected until Law catches him in his periphery. He scoops up the tiny brown-haired boy and tosses him in the air. Law holds him in his arms, talking quietly in his ear. The little traitor points over to me. Law follows the direction of his finger and spots me. I fall over and roll to my side, laughing.

My two men make their way over to me, Hanzi giggling and playing with Law's wallet, pulling out the cash and sticking it down his shirt. *Good boy*, I think to myself.

"Did you really teach our two-year-old son how to pickpocket?" he scolds, setting our baby next to me. Hanz pulls the cash from his shirt.

"Here, Mama." He places the bills in my hand.

"It's a reputable skill." I argue.

"No, Trouble, it's not." Law sits with his back up against a tree and then pulls me between his legs. He brushes my long hair over my shoulder and pulls me back against him. His nose goes to my neck and he breathes in deep, sending goose bumps prickling along my skin. "And you'll regret teaching him that when his teachers' wallets go missing and they find them in our kid's desk," he whispers into my ear. I ignore him and focus on the chills his breath against my ear sends down my spine and straight between my legs. I run my hands up and down his thighs, squeezing once when I get to the top of his legs. "Mrs. Packwood, you don't want to get me hard at a company picnic. It's an HR nightmare."

Every time he calls me Mrs. Packwood, I'm taken back to our wedding. I made my wedding dress. I found the exact pattern I loved when Mom was preparing to make a dress for my wedding with Wen. It was simple and understated, two things I'll never be, but it made for a gorgeous dress. Besides, my family and I are outrageous enough without adding the crazy clothes. We were married in our backyard. My whole family attended, including all the families I grew up with. Including Wen. But that's another story.

I turn my head and offer my lips to him. He takes them, kissing me sweetly. I sigh and pull away, pivoting to see where Hanz has gone. I spot him a few feet away, sneaking up on Mark, who is talking to Leander. They're standing close and look very comfortable around each other. He's gone through his own trials the last few years when he told Dad he wouldn't take on an arranged marriage. Dad blamed me, but after some time, he forgave us both. I know he feels like he's failing Mom, but I know she's in heaven and is proud of her kids. Even if we do our own thing.

"I'll get him." Law moves from behind me.

"Wait. No." I set a hand on his arm, stopping him. "Just watch."

Hanz gets Mark's wallet out of his back pocket, but when he turns to run away, he squeals with laughter, grabbing Mark's attention. When Mark turns and sees him running as fast as a toddler can run, he smiles. Then he notices the bright orange wallet in his meaty paws.

"Hanz! Hanz! That is a Bottega Veneta. Give it back to Unky Mark." He speed walks after Hanz, but the baby just squeals more and picks up speed. He reaches us before Mark can get him. "Thea. Really. He's a baby, and you taught him to steal wallets?"

"He's got a knack for it. What can I say?" I shrug.

"You are a terribly irresponsible parent." Mark snags Hanz and the wallet. "Come with Unky Mark. I'm going to teach you how to flirt. It'll get you far in life and not break any laws." The two of them go back to where Leander is. Law and I laugh.

"I'm glad my brother came today." I mention and grab my guitar case. Taking it out, I lightly strum chords and hum along.

"Yeah. It's good to see him getting out. He's been working hard ever since he got that job."

I set the guitar down and twist around, sitting up on my knees in front of Law. My fingers go to my hair without me knowing. They twist and twirl in tiny sections of the long locks.

"I've got some news," I announce.

"Oh, yeah?" Law snags my hand from my hair and kisses my palm, keeping hold of it.

"Yeah. I was gonna wait until later. Leander agreed to babysit so we could go have dinner, but I'm too excited." I reach into the diaper bag and snag a onesie, giving it to him.

"*Trouble is coming.*" He reads and looks up at me. My hands are clapping silently and I'm smiling big. "Really?"

"Yep! Took ten tests this morning just to be sure!"

Law's been bugging me for another baby the second Hanz stopping wanting to snuggle all the time. Our child's only desire right now is to play hard until he passes out. Building blocks up high and crashing through them, scribbling with crayons so hard they break, and climbing… everything. Law misses coming home from work and holding a calm baby to his chest. With the anxiety that grips hold of him from all the messes Hanz makes, I agree a baby might help. Besides, we both want a big family. Might as well keep going while I'm still young enough to keep up.

Law pulls me into his arms and kisses my forehead. "Just when I think I'm the happiest man in the world, you tell me something that makes me even happier."

I wrap my arms around his middle, enjoying this small break without a child.

"Think we can sneak off for a minute?" I ask.

"What did you have in mind?"

"There's a maintenance building out by the pond. I was thinking we should inspect it."

I raise an eyebrow at him. "Let's do it."

He stands up and holds a hand to me. I think about ignoring the gesture, but if I've learned anything by being with Law, it's that I can let my walls down with him. For so long, I worried any weakness I showed a man would be used to exploit me later. If I accepted help up or a door being opened, the man would automatically put me into an inferior category. I hated feeling less than. Law is different. His kindness comes from his heart and he has no ill intentions. So, I accept his hand and we sneak off to find some privacy.

We make it undetected. Law's lips go right to my neck, trailing kisses across my throat. My hands go under his shirt and weave through the spattering of hair. Law picks me up and sets me onto some kind of wooden shop table. He lifts my skirt up and reaches up to my panties, dragging them down my legs.

"Have I ever told you how much I fucking love your skirts?" He pockets my panties.

"Once or twice," I pant out. This man can get me wet with just a look, but throw in pregnancy hormones, and I'm a mess of desire for him.

He unbuttons his pants and pulls out his dick. Finally, he's pulling my ass to the edge of the table and driving home. I moan and he puts a hand over my mouth. It only makes me moan more.

"Fuck me," I say, but it's muffled.

"What?" he whispers out and removes his hand.

"I said fuck me." It comes out too loudly. He covers my mouth with his own, forcing my silence with the stroke of his tongue against mine. He thrusts and fast and hard, causing an orgasm to start within minutes. I lock my ankles on top of his ass and pull him into me harder and faster. He grips onto the edge of the table, and the second my orgasm wanes, I feel his cock pulse inside of me. He grunts through gritted teeth and spills his seed inside my body.

When he's finally spent, he leans his forehead against mine. We share breaths and heartbeats. Our gazes lock and our souls entwine. There isn't a moment I spend with this man I would ever give up. I'm trouble, reckless, and bohemian. He's order, calm, and law-abiding. Together we make a bohemian law and this is our story.

ACKNOWLEDGMENTS

Kristi Webster, you make me proud every single day. No one works as hard as you do while also making it look as easy as you do. Every time I sit down at my laptop you are there cheering me on and telling me I can do it. Everyone needs a Kristi in their lives.

Ty-bot, thank you for reading Conversion, but maybe skip this one. Too much lovey-dovey feelings in this one for you. Thank you for supporting this dream of mine.

Genevieve, my sister from another mister, thank you for re-minding me daily that I'm awesome. You may think they are just words, but those words are the backbone of my confi-dence. I love you!

Sasha, Ariadna, Cindy, Amy, and Elizabeth, thank you for your courage to pick through my words and make them better. I love you all for using your precious time to help me on my journey. Also, Ariadna, thank you for all the amazing, pretty graphics you make me. I seriously can't thank you enough.

Emily A. Lawrence, I still make you work hard for your money, but how about me finally (mostly) conquering that/

who? I'm patting myself on the back. Thank you for not only fixing my words, but also for helping me along the way. You're the best.

Stacey Blake, without me even telling you what the book is about, you format and decorate my books so perfectly.

Mom, I wish everyone had a mom like you. You support me blindly and make me feel like I am the very best writer in the world. I'm so glad I have you in my corner.

To my readers & my Thirsties, thank you the most! You guys rock my world and motivate me to keep writing. I love nothing more than to get your messages and read your reviews. It's a great big book world, but you choose to pick mine up and that means everything.

AUTHOR LINKS

Sign up for my newsletter for updates on my books and alerts whenever I have something new for you!

authormistywalker.com/newsletter/

Signed paperbacks are available from my website:
www.authormistywalker.com

Come stalk me in all the places, I like it:

Instagram: www.instagram.com/authormistywalker/

Facebook: www.facebook.com/authormistywalker

Bookbub: www.bookbub.com/profile/misty-walker

Amazon: amzn.to/2NnrWhJ

Twitter: @mistywalkerbook

ABOUT THE AUTHOR

Misty Walker, born with the name of a stripper, horse or cat, but gifted with the ability to tell stories. She's fueled by coffee and motivated by the forceful voices in her head screaming to tell their story. If she's not reading or writing, she's spending time with her daughters, husband, and two dogs. But mostly she's reading or writing.

Made in the USA
Lexington, KY
20 December 2019